SUMMER BLUE

SUMMER BLUE

A NOVEL BY

Floyd Skloot

STORY LINE PRESS

1994

Published by Story Line Press, Inc., Three Oaks Farm,
Brownsville, OR 97327

This publication was made possible thanks in part to the generous
support of the Andrew W. Mellon Foundation, the National
Endowment for the Arts, the Oregon Institute of Literary Arts,
and our individual contributors.

Book design by Chiquita Babb

Library of Congress Cataloging-in-Publication Data

For My Daughter Rebecca

Blue poured into summer blue,
A hawk broke from his cloudless tower,
The roof of the silo blazed, and I knew
That part of my life was over.

—from "The End of Summer"
by Stanley Kunitz

SUMMER BLUE

PART ONE

Illinois

1

TIMOTHY PACKARD was happily married for six years. Then he was unhappily married for six years. Now he'd been widowed for six years.

At 41, he still felt young and expectant. It was just that the trend seemed bad.

In his work as a realtor, Timothy believed in cycles. When interest rates were high, he supposed they would swing back down. When the dollar fell, he trusted it would climb again. He read *The Wall Street Journal*, watched housing starts and the Dow, took note of industrial production. He felt the trick was guessing where the ceilings and floors were.

He thought the same principle should hold for his personal life. But Timothy worried that this wasn't the bottom yet. Things might not be ready to cycle up.

All that was left tangible from his dozen years with Charlene was their daughter Jill. The split-level was sold, the cabin near Lake Huron long gone, bric-a-brac from their annual travels boxed in his mother-in-law's attic in Fresno. He'd traded the maroon Mercury and was driving a Toyota. The Great Eradication of 1980.

Jill was fourteen now. She had three holes pierced in each earlobe and went to school with her eye sockets blackened like a raccoon. Timothy expected that she would appear one evening with her hair shaved off, except for a fiery scalping tuft like Chingachgook.

She went to sleep with Pink Floyd blasting, got dressed dancing into her jeans while Steppenwolf jolted her like caffeine, sang Jethro Tull songs waiting for the bus. She did her homework, when she did her homework, rolling her shoulders to the beat of Led Zeppelin.

Jill was rooted firmly in the bedrock of her father's worst time. And from her straight red hair to her long narrow feet she looked just like her late mother.

When the call came from Jill's principal, Timothy wasn't surprised.

He shut his office door and sat on the desk. The walls were so thin, agents could hear each other swallow coffee. He'd shut the door for peace, not privacy.

"Mr. Packard, from day one Jill has simply not been ready for high school. Day one."

"We've been over this before, Mr. Unger. You know my feelings about who's ready for who there."

"Ready for whom, you mean."

Timothy let it pass. Fucker can't help himself.

He picked up the book of residential properties listed for sale and laid it in his lap, open at random. Greengate, seventy four nine. It's got your three bedrooms, bath and a half, new central air.

"So why the call?" Timothy asked.

"Your daughter's missing classes again. Every day, and missing more than she attends."

"I'll talk to her."

"Doesn't hand in assignments, either."

"Ok. I said I'll talk to her."

"You realize she can't participate in sports if she cuts classes?"

"Jill doesn't want to participate in sports."

"Jill doesn't seem to want to participate in anything, Mr. Packard."

"Look, I appreciate your concern. Do you need something from me, a note or what?"

"Only that you know what's going on. In case we have to go to step four."

"Step four?"

"That's correct, Mr. Packard. Step one: detention. Two: a note to parent from Vice Principal. Three: verbal contact by Principal. And four: suspension."

"Now I know."

"We sent a pamphlet home in September."

After Timothy hung up, he stared down at the photograph of the house for sale in Greengate. There was a long snowy lawn and a slash of shoveled walkway. Thick icicles hung from the roof gutters.

It's May, Timothy thought. It's tornado season. And this house has been on the market since before the first snow.

He liked reading the reasons people gave for selling their homes. They were rarely true and seldom gave the buyer an edge, but the reasons resonated: need larger house, need smaller house, transferred, must relocate to warmer climate.

The real estate business was down these days, with money tight and what little industry there was in town leaving. But even though houses were hard to move, Timothy had had a fair year. It was a bad market for buyers and sellers both.

A good time to hold onto your house.

2

"TURN THE burner down."

"But it's never going to thicken, Dad. I'm tired of standing here."

"And keep stirring or it'll get lumpy." Timothy was tearing romaine, his back to Jill.

He didn't see her eyes roll toward the ceiling. She swirled the spoon in an S through the sauce and a little sloshed onto the burner.

"I'm also tired of the menu. Raw vegetable salad and for a little variety we've got steamed vegetables on the side. And let's not forget this cheese sauce, which looks like we bought it in a gag store. But get this, tonight only: a plop of brown rice for real excitement."

"We had chicken on Thursday."

Jill always tried to make him feel off balance on the days he'd heard from school. She knew Unger called him at work. So she greeted him complaining of cramps. The cramps always worked.

"If you set the table," Timothy said, "I'll dish everything out and light a candle."

"Too much trouble for a weeknight."

They ate in the kitchen, on stools drawn up to the cutting block. Jill tore a square of khaki paper towel for the placemat, folded another into a triangle for the napkin. But their plates were the hand-thrown stoneware he'd bought from a Sangamon County potter they knew and the silverware all matched.

Jill's tape player blared sixties hits. He would have preferred talking with her at dinner, but couldn't stop himself from getting caught up in memories.

They listened and smiled, Timothy's lips moving in sync with the lyrics. Jill was pleased because she knew how to master her father's moods. She tapped and rattled to the music.

In her left ear, she wore one each of the earrings Timothy had given her for Christmas, Valentine's Day, and her birthday. The right ear had just her birthstone, a small pearl. On her wrists and up her forearms, about a dozen braided bracelets made for her by friends. There was myrrh in a leather pouch hanging between her breasts, which were already as full as her mother's had been.

Timothy looked away. He heard Jill chomping salad in the silence between songs.

"I've got a deal for you," he said as the new song began.

"That's the Beatles, of course. Who else?"

He leaned over and stopped the tape. "No, I said I've got a deal for you."

"Oh." She lifted a swoosh of hair from in front of her eyes. "Or should I say uh-oh?"

"You told me you wanted to get away for the summer. Remember? A summer on the beach. This was all you talked about last quarter."

"That was the wintertime, Dad. We had a month straight of snow."

"Don't you still want to?"

"Sure." She picked up a chunk of carrot, dipped it in her puddled sauce, and popped it in her mouth. "Of course," she probably said.

"Then here it is: I get no more calls from school for the next month, till it's over. And you get no Fs. Then we go to the beach."

"Which beach?"

6

"You pick it. We could go to the east coast and spend some time with my mother. We could go up to Michigan again. Or we could go to the west coast, stay at Aunt Natalie's house in Oregon."

"For how long?"

"Eight, nine weeks. I haven't worked out all the details yet."

"Come off it," she laughed. "You wouldn't take any two months off."

He stood, began moving their dishes to the sink. She watched him closely.

"It's your turn to do the dishes," he said.

"How could you take two months off?"

"Jilly, you do the changin' and I'll do the arrangin'."

She rolled her eyes. "Very bad."

3

LATER THAT evening, Jill came downstairs for a Diet Coke. She strolled into the living room and curled next to Timothy on the sofa.

"So Unger hit step three today, huh?"

He read to the end of a paragraph, then put down his book. "What ever happened to step two?" he asked. "I don't remember seeing any note."

"That's part of what I was going to tell you."

She filled her mouth with soda and swirled it around, eyes shutting, head tilted back. Timothy remembered her doing the same thing the first time she'd tasted it, when she was spellbound by the carbonation. He remembered when her attempts to drink from a cup without spilling were an adventure for the entire family. And he remembered Charlene, even then, trying to reform Jill's manners.

In his old running tights ripped at the knees, wearing a Led

7

Zeppelin tee shirt, with a scarf holding back her hair, Jill sat touching his leg with hers. She looked twenty.

Then she swallowed and smiled, her mouthful of braces and simple, open face making him see how young she really was. So many changes. Timothy smiled back at her.

"Tell me all."

"Er and um," she said, enunciating like a talking computer. "I found this note up in my room when I was looking for my Cat Stevens tape."

He took it from her and put it on the coffee table unread.

"And I found this note, from my counselor, when I was trying to decide what to wear tomorrow."

She laid the second note on the first.

"Then I found this note from my science teacher in my backpack."

"Any more?"

"That would about do it."

"So what's going on?"

"Now we've got a clean slate, right Dad?"

"Jill, would you mind telling me what you're telling me?"

"Actually, the reason I came down was to say I like your deal. Two months away from here. Is there a reason we couldn't go to all three beaches?"

"Well, I thought we might drive. That would be a lot of driving and you always puke on long car trips."

"I just worked it out with the road atlas. From central Illinois to Grandmother to Michigan to Aunt Nat and back is almost a perfect triangle. My Humanities teacher calls triangles Deltas. He says Delta is the symbol for change."

Jill stopped suddenly. Timothy could see there were tears in her eyes.

The thick black smudges softened, starting to smear. He reached for her.

4

TIMOTHY WENT into real estate after Charlene's second affair. Or after the second affair that he knew about. She had been away from home often again, been out of town and out of touch.

The long, intense classes took his mind off his wife. He studied in the old dining room, spreading the texts beside his daughter's coloring books on the round oak table they'd gotten from his mother.

On weekends, Timothy and Jill drove around the city attending open houses, looking at exteriors from across the street, observing neighborhoods. Buckled into her car seat, Jill would point out chimneys while Timothy made detailed notes about roofs or landscaping. He became expert on school district boundaries, distances from parks and grocery stores, traffic patterns.

He figured real estate was going to provide his back-up money, something to augment his salary as an engineer for the power company. It was going to be filler for his lonely evenings and weekends.

Charlene thought he was trying to meet new women.

Then leukemia changed the priorities. At first, when Charlene got pale and tired, she thought she'd been working too hard. She thought she could take some time off in two or three months.

Timothy thought she was just peaked from her affair. They'd made her lose weight before, too.

The fever wouldn't go away. Charlene assumed she had some new strain of infection, something that wouldn't respond to the traditional antibiotics. But it was simply the wrong time for a lobbyist to take sick leave, so she never stopped.

She was dead within ten months. Acute cancer of the white cells that engulf bacteria, the doctors explained. What killed her as she lay in the hospital bed was actually a stroke caused by clumps of these white cells in her arteries. By then she was already a ghost.

Timothy left the power company after Charlene's death. He said he was tired of the formulas and specifications, bored with repetitions of resistance and flow.

Besides, his colleagues knew too much about his life. They understood his grief too well. He wanted to get away from their gentle smiles, their pauses in his doorway, the dinner invitations.

A Friday at the end of March was his last day as an engineer. He started selling houses full-time the next Monday. Charlene's life insurance money gave him leeway to take the risk. That would have made her laugh the laugh he liked to remember.

Timothy estimated that they played Monopoly two hundred and eleven times the first year they were married. Their favorite time for a game was after a light supper.

At first, they played on the dining room table with the stack of dirty dishes sitting to the side like an umpire. Later in the year, they played upstairs on their bed, usually naked.

Theirs was the Short Game, with Timothy as the banker dealing two deed cards to start them off. After a while, they altered the rules and he dealt a half dozen cards to speed things up. Before the first roll, they allowed a one-minute trading session, but dropped that when it was clear they could never make a deal.

Timothy was always the wheelbarrow. Charlene wavered between the race car and the Scottie, occasionally being the thimble when she felt domestic.

She loved the strategy. They were getting undressed one night before a game when she told him he played too recklessly.

"You leave too much to chance. I'm always three moves ahead of you."

"It's not chance. That's where you're wrong. I play by my instincts, my gut."

She smiled at him while unhooking her bra. "That too. You get all sentimental over Boardwalk because you grew up near the beach."

"You do the same thing. You like Illinois Avenue because we live in Illinois."

"Bullshit. I like it because of probability. It's the most frequently landed-on square."

They stood naked on opposite sides of the bed with the game board open between them. Usually Timothy could not concentrate on anything else when he could see Charlene nude. Even in the morning rush to get ready for work, he'd stop shaving to watch her in the mirror when she emerged from the shower. But now he looked only at the board.

"Listen," Charlene said. "With one or two houses, the dark blue properties are the most desirable. But after the third house, orange offers a better return. And green's value goes down the more you develop it. Ok?"

By the middle of that first year, they'd changed the rules so often that they wrote out a new set and kept it in the box. When you're in jail, you become a non-citizen: you get no rent payments, can't buy or sell or trade anything, can't mortgage your property. No Free Parking jackpot. Bumping lets you send the opponent to any square you choose.

Their final game was in early summer. Bodies glistening with sweat in the sultry air, they negotiated a rent-immunity deal as part of Timothy's trading Tennessee for two railroads and two hundred dollars. In the tense next circuit of the board, sure enough, Timothy landed on St. James Place.

He didn't have enough cash to cover the rent, since Charlene had erected hotels. She smiled at him and wiped a rill of perspiration from between her breasts.

"That's all right," she said. "You don't have to pay me this time, lucky."

"Fuck you, all right? I never should have made that trade, you suckered me."

He threw his wad of fake money at her and left the room.

The worst time was between her two affairs. First, Timothy stopped being able to use machines.

At work, he wrote memos on sheets of graph paper instead of the word processor at his desk. He computed estimates without a calculator, filling scratch pads with long division and complex multiplication problems. It made everything slow down for him. He used the stairs instead of the elevator, arriving at his desk on the twelfth floor in a sweat every morning and noon. He stopped using the telephone.

Then he quit driving after backing through the shut door of their garage one morning. He overloaded the dishwasher with soap and gouged such deep holes with the mower at the edges of their lawn that he decided to hire a kid down the block to keep it trimmed all summer.

Since Charlene seldom was home for dinner, Timothy was the family's cook. Trying to split an acorn squash with his cleaver, he slipped and sliced a six-stitch cut in his hand. He dropped the metal blade of the food processor and caught it in midair, laying open his thumb. All he could manage during this time were salads, sandwiches with prepared meats and cheese, cold cereal, meals that didn't require cooking.

It was Jill that snapped him out of it. She was eight and worried about being pudgy. To lose weight, she heard, all a person had to do was drink health food drinks instead of eating solid meals.

"Can you make this for me?" she asked one evening, handing Timothy a recipe torn from a magazine.

He read it quickly. "Sure. Get out the blender."

Jill burrowed into the cabinet under the sink to find the old machine. She backed out and handed it to him.

"Ok," he said, "now get out the ingredients. You need a banana, whatever berries we've got in the refrigerator, the yogurt, some wheat germ."

"Wait. Aren't you going to do it? Mom doesn't like me to use the blender."

"I can't."

Jill glared at him, holding the mixing bowl in both hands with all the ingredients piled inside. "Yes you can, I've seen you making those green drinks."

"That was before. I can't now."

"You just want me to be fat all my life!" she yelled, thrusting the bowl at Timothy. She stomped out of the kitchen. "You won't be happy till I look like Grandma."

It wasn't just machines. During this time, Timothy got sick almost every week, attracting viruses like a lodestone. He seemed immune to nothing, although he was never so ill that he couldn't work.

He grew a full beard and moustache, but was troubled by the strange image whenever he caught sight of himself in a mirror during the work day. So he shaved off the moustache. Then he shaved off the part between his sideburns and chin, leaving just a goatee. Gradually, he trimmed the goatee back until all that remained was a tuft of hair under his lower lip.

He watched Charlene drift away again like daylight on a late summer evening. It wasn't until she was clearly involved with someone else that Timothy took charge of his life again.

5

TIMOTHY WAS showing a house in the older part of the city, near Gardner Park. Houses there were easy to sell, despite their limed up water pipes or the evidence of water in the basements, because of the park. The neighborhood took care of selling the house. It had, he would say, the only hills between the Mississippi and the Wabash.

He figured Gardner Park could mean three grand in commission, the summer's airfare and more. It would be such a quick deal that he'd have time left over for a drink with Lauren Hazeltine.

Lauren worked for Prairie Savings and Loan. The wooing had been simple. She'd said yes to his clients on a mortgage one afternoon, yes to dinner that night, and yes to almost everything he'd asked in the months since.

She was short and thin, a runner with slim hips, bantam buttocks, and phantom breasts. Collarbone to anklebone, she was all point. They'd met at a 10 K road race.

With only shorts and a thin singlet on, Lauren's shocking strength became apparent—the woman's muscles were long, taut. She did weight-work at the health club three times a week. But in a business suit, she looked underfed and gauzy.

Until she spoke. Her deep, throaty voice was like a quarterback's barking signals at the line.

Timothy nudged Lauren from his thoughts as he drove through Gardner Park. City workers had mowed all morning and now the air smelled of wild onion. Late spring was putting on a good show for his clients, a professional couple that wanted more space and a formal dining room.

Archie Coe sat beside Timothy. But he twisted around so he could see and touch his wife in the back seat. He reeked of Old Spice in the humid afternoon.

"You could run in the park after work, Arch," she said. "No more changing downtown, coming home after seven. Just like the old days."

"Exactly how far would it be, Packard? One trip around this place." Coe asked.

"It's marked on the pavement." Timothy pulled off the road into a small lot overlooking the duck pond. "There's a three mile loop if you throw in that little hill behind the carillon. And the police even patrol for speeders to protect the joggers."

"I don't jog, I run."

They drove slowly out of the park and up the short block to the house. Timothy knew the effect that stopping by the duck pond had.

"Run to the park from your new home, even on a thick day like this, and you hardly work up a sweat. We're talking very close."

When they opened the front door, a blast of central air conditioning made Bess Coe gasp. Timothy made a note to suggest keeping the thermostat up a few degrees if the house didn't sell to the Coes. You don't want to call attention to the mechanical systems in an old house.

After the tour, they stood on the porch looking down the quaint brick street. Timothy sat on the railing, not mentioning that the bricks meant the city wouldn't plow it after winter storms.

"So what's the real reason these people are selling?" Coe asked.

"It says in the book they need a smaller place."

"But why do they need a smaller place?" He sat beside his wife on the porch swing. "That's what I want to know."

"I can't really say. Maybe the kids grew up."

"You saw the rooms. No kids have lived here for years."

"That's probably why. Too much house."

"I don't think so. Not in a market like this. I think a divorce." Coe smiled at his wife. "That's what I think, Packard. There's beds—active beds, beds that've been slept in—in both the master and that little room with the ugly lilac paper. This is a couple splitting up. I think they need to sell."

"I haven't heard that," Timothy said.

"Please." Coe reached for his wife's hand.

"I love this house," she said.

"Of course you do. I say we low-ball it."

By 3:00, Timothy was back in his office with a check for the earnest money. Coe had been right about a divorce. The sellers accepted his offer on the spot. Timothy figured it cost him about $500 in commission.

He dialed Lauren Hazeltine's private number, the one that rang on her desk. She picked it up on the first ring.

"Yes?"

"That's pretty gruff. No hello?"

"I'm in a meeting. Can I call you back?"

"At the office. I thought bank officers didn't have meetings."

"We're not a bank, we're a savings and loan." Then there were muffled words, as if she'd covered the mouthpiece with her hand.

"Hello?" he said.

"Hang around for a half hour, ok?"

"Time's money, Lauren. You know that."

"Then its value increases if you hoard it. I'll call you soon."

Timothy wasn't good at hanging around, but he agreed. There was a letter to the Zoning Board he could write.

He decided the letter could wait another week. Timothy sat on the office steps, drinking coffee and watching the street.

A couple trotted across to Wendy's, pushing twins in a two-seat stroller. God, he thought, suppose Jill had been twins.

Timothy had been in the delivery room with Charlene when Jill was born. He remembered it was the first cool night that June, the first night that both temperature and humidity had been under seventy.

When Charlene's water broke, he ran to the kitchen and grabbed an old jelly jar from the drainer. It still smelled of the evening's Claret.

Charlene was sitting up in bed, knees flexed, nightgown pulled up above her thighs. She grinned at him and nodded.

Timothy held the jar between her legs and the sheet to catch the fluid, which came in gentle spurts and filled the glass halfway. He thought there would be more.

"There will be," Charlene said. "But let's not wait around for it."

He held the glass to the light and swirled the fluid. "I thought it would be clearer."

"If you're going to drink it, you can stay here."

Timothy drove through the deserted streets as if they were a Le Mans course, his hands loose on the wheel, his foot holding the accelerator steady. They were briefly airborne after crossing the railroad tracks near the Pillsbury plant.

"Slow down, Parnelli," Charlene said. "This is supposed to be the easy part."

But the rest had not been difficult: only three hours from when the water broke until Jill crowned. Timothy's hands were at Charlene's back while she pushed. They breathed together through her contractions. The doctor, seeing how well they worked together and impressed by Charlene's control, agreed to bypass the cervical block.

Jill had an Apgar score of ten within five minutes of birth. She was a robust cryer, pink to her fingertips, arms flailing. A nurse photographed the three of them looking like ghouls as the sun began to rise.

During the six months she was home with Jill, not working, Charlene let her hair grow long. Timothy had never seen her with hair to the shoulders. Her freckles came back and her hazel eyes turned summer blue.

In the middle of the night, he would get up when Jill cried and bring her to Charlene sitting up in bed, propped by a half dozen throw pillows. At that time, Jill looked more like Timothy, with her thick black hair and dark eyes. Often, the three of them would fall asleep, nestled together among the zebra stripes and polka dots.

Timothy went back inside his office. He started to call Lauren again, to tell her he'd wait for her at his home, but hung up before the call went through.

Instead of meeting for drinks, they went straight to Lauren's condo. She lived in a new complex on the other side of Gardner Park, a trapezoid of sprawling fourplexes painted the colors of goose plumage.

"Wait," she said when Timothy slipped his hands inside her jacket. "Let's do three miles to put the day away."

He kept a gym bag with running gear in his car, so there was no easy excuse. Lauren was already changed when he got back inside.

Timothy didn't mind running with her. As hard as she trained, Lauren was helping him become faster. Besides, he loved to watch her stretch.

She sat with her back against the door, legs spread. Reaching for her toes, she ducked her head toward the crotch of her fuchsia shorts and bobbed a few times. Timothy touched the lawn with his fingertips, standing where he could keep watch on her.

The best part came next. Lauren flung herself down on the grass at the side of the complex and threw her legs over her shoulders until her toes touched ground. Then she inched them still further back and flattened herself into a vivid envelope. Timothy walked over to make sure she was doing it right, stopping for some hip twists along the way.

"Lecher."

She unfolded. They jogged to Gardner Park, warming up, and headed clockwise into the sunset.

Lauren's form was classic, her hands loose, gait even, a strong surge in her arm swing. Timothy was clunkier when he ran, his short legs hardly lifting, thick thighs making him seem to chug rather than run. But he was fast and had a good base of miles, the steady pace he could maintain always a surprise to runners who didn't know him.

A cobalt blue, springtime sky promised a storm within the hour. It was too humid for them to run hard.

"So how's Jill?"

"Resolved, I think. No messages from school all day."

"You shouldn't worry too much. Fourteen's very hard."

"And Fridays help," he said, beginning to work harder as they ran up the hill. Someone was inside the carillon practicing and Brahms rang through the park. "This is the day she gets to do whatever she wants between school and midnight."

"You're brave."

"Just hopeful."

They reached the top of the hill. Lauren looped behind him and they headed back down.

"A hundred years ago," he said, "you could see all the way to Colorado from up here."

Their first drink of the night was Gatorade. Lauren was flushed and soaked. She downed her drink in enormous gulps straight from the jar.

"What are you looking at?" she asked.

"I keep waiting for you to turn green from this stuff, like in the ad on tv."

"You weren't watching my throat, pal. I saw your eyes when I swallowed."

"Look, I have something to tell you," Timothy said.

She refilled his glass. Probing the back of her thigh with two knuckles, she frowned at him and tried to work out a knot.

"That sounds ominous."

"Not really. But it is a little awkward. See, I'm very concerned about your expenses."

She stopped the self-massage. "What the hell are you talking about? Expenses?"

"Your personal finances. I think it's important for you to manage them better, in case we decide to travel somewhere together. Say this winter."

"And this is your way of inviting me on a trip? What class." She dug into her leg again. "I do know something about investments, pal."

"I just like to plan ahead."

"Oh, I get it." She smiled. "You just want to take a shower with me."

"Well, it *would* save you money."

"Not if I understand your plan correctly."

It was still new for him. Timothy had never known a woman like Lauren before.

She, however, claimed to have known more than enough men who acted like Timothy did when they first met. At least he seemed to be changing now.

Timothy had fallen into the habit of referring to women by body type. It helped him to explain what had happened in his marriage. At the office, his comments were good for a few laughs and became reflexive.

Hardbodies, he'd say, were very risky, unless you understood how they got that way. For example, Career Mongers didn't make time for their bodies. They would diet to keep thin, but had no room on the schedule for fitness. Their hardness was simply tightness, it was soft underneath. So he shied away from Career Mongers after Charlene died. The Jockettes, those women he met at races or running in the park, had time to make their bodies hard but their lives often went soft. They took classes at night and did social work in the day.

He joked that it required careful probing. He complained that the way men and women allied had changed radically during the dozen years of his marriage, which explained why it was difficult for him to get back into the habit of meeting women and dating.

He tried this on Lauren after the first time they'd slept together. She corrected him, fast.

"What's this horseshit?" She sat up in bed and let the sheets fall away from her. "You live in a small midwest city and your sex life is strangers and running groupies. What'd you expect, Sally Ride?"

"I'm just talking about my own experience."

"And that's as far as you've gotten in six years? Hardbodies and Jockettes?"

"I started slowly."

"You really need some help." She stomped out of bed and stood with her back to him.

"That's what you're giving me, help."

"If it is, pal, you'd better get out of here and I mean now."

She was furious with him. Stalking around her bedroom muttering, she finally walked over to his side and slapped him. He thought lovers only got slapped in movies.

"I should have done that before," she said.

"I take it you don't agree with my theories."

"That's not a theory and you know it. It's office shtick. What bothers me is you thought I'd laugh at it."

"Just a little post-coital chatter."

"Don't be such a fool." Lauren leaned against the wall and folded her arms beneath her breasts. Her hip jutted toward him.

"Ok, here you are: Remember when I was late to dinner because something came up at work? You didn't call me for a month. What does that tell you?"

"I was busy."

"You were hiding." She pointed a finger directly between his eyes. "And another thing: You can only think of going to films, concerts, games. Events instead of encounters. What does that tell you?"

"Take it easy, Lauren."

"I'll tell you what that tells me. It tells me you buried your wife, but not your marriage."

Timothy got out of bed too. Lauren took a step toward him.

"A person might think that was nasty," he said.

"It might have been a little harsh."

"Besides, I had my wife cremated."

"Jesus Christ."

They stared at each other. "So where does that leave me?" he asked.

She came back to the bed and knelt beside him where he stood, taking his hands. "Still here, for now."

That was almost four months ago. He was still still there.

In the shower, they washed each other's backs and shampooed each other's hair. They embraced, chins on shoulders, and the cool water spilled off the dam their torsos made. That was all.

Dried, wearing only a thick towel around her head, Lauren pushed Timothy gently against the door. It clicked shut. With the fingers of her right hand, she barely touched the hairs on his chest, but it was enough to hold him still. With her left, she opened the cabinet and pulled out several fresh, scarlet towels.

"Stay there," she whispered.

Lauren squatted. She spread the towels along the shag like a red carpet, inching away from him. He stared, matching her intensity.

"This is the only use I can see for shag in a john," she said. Then she lay back and reached for him.

"Good thing we're both short."

He moved beside her and ran a hand from her hip to her shoulder. She was tight everywhere and her skin was very warm. As he stroked her, Lauren's body didn't yield to him. Instead, she met Timothy on her own terms.

She was active, demanding, but she was tender. He wondered where her sharp bones had suddenly gone and loved the feeling of her hands moving along his sides as they rocked together. Despite her power, she was soft wherever she touched him.

Timothy knew he would miss her this summer. That feeling, too, was new for him.

SUMMER BLUE

PART TWO

New York

6

WHEN TIMOTHY and Jill deplaned, Mrs. Packard wasn't waiting for them at the gate. They shouldered their carry-on bags, heading for the main terminal.

"Your grandmother's always late," he said. "We'll find her."

They walked past advertisements for Broadway shows, scanning the crowd for a glimpse of her. Mrs. Packard was very short, but wouldn't be difficult to spot if she dressed typically. Timothy hoped she wasn't wearing one of her home-made masks.

"MY GOD! LOOK AT YOU!" Mrs. Packard's contralto blared as if over the public address system.

They stopped to look around. Jill giggled.

"COME ON! I DON'T HAVE ALL NIGHT!"

"This is just like when I was a kid," Timothy whispered. "She can see me, but I can't see her."

"Isn't that her? There by the x-ray machine, in the Indian head-dress?"

"I remember that hat. It's made from the underfeathers of the rare sooty shearwater, or something. Be sure to compliment her on it."

"Look at you," Mrs. Packard said again after they embraced, her volume subsiding. "Just look at you."

"You haven't seen her in over four years, mother. Of course she's changed."

"It's you I'm shocked about, not Jilly. I expected her to be changed. But you! You look like seltzer."

"I'm healthy." He put his arm around his mother's shoulders, nudging her toward the baggage claim area. "Really, I feel fine."

"You look," she grunted, "like you need a good woman."

7

"THIS IS the beach," Timothy said.

It was the next morning. He and Jill were still on central time and had been up for hours.

"I figured that out."

"Your grandmother bought you a pass, so you can get on whenever you want."

"I need a pass to use the beach? Will they charge extra if I breathe?"

"The locals got tired of paying upkeep for careless tourists."

"It's not all that fancy a beach. I remember it used to seem bigger." She skipped ahead of him up the ramp and onto the boardwalk.

They began to walk west. "A dollar says you don't know what those are," Timothy said, pointing toward the shore.

"Those rocks? Of course I do, they're piers. No, wait a minute, it's coming to me: they're jetties."

"Hah! They're called groins. Jetties only get built at inlets. These are groins. And this whole area is a groin field."

Jill stopped and grabbed his arm. She looked in his eyes. "This is true?"

"A groin field."

She dug into her pocket and brought out some change, counting a dollar for him. Then she folded his hand around the coins and skipped off.

"That's worth a dollar, easy."

They walked for a few minutes in silence. Elderly men sat on benches watching the surf. Two boys, Jill's age but looking years younger, pedaled by and whistled.

She wore cut-off white jeans over a striped one-piece swimsuit which showed through in a way Timothy didn't like at all. Her hair fell to the middle of her spine.

"Hi bozos," she called.

"There are a few rules," Timothy said after they'd walked about a half mile.

"So I'm finding out."

"These are your grandmother's rules, not mine. I have to live with them too. Like no sand in the apartment. So you've got to clean off in the public shower room downstairs. Leave your sandals at the door, make sure any shells you pick up get rinsed, that sort of thing."

"So far, no problem." She turned around and began walking back toward Mrs. Packard's apartment. "You know, this sounds just like the first day at school, go over the rules and make sure you know where the auditorium is. I'm hungry."

"That's another rule. No cooking."

Jill rolled her eyes. "Can I maybe use the toaster?"

"And last: no boys upstairs."

"You think I'd do that?"

"No."

"Does she?"

"No."

"Then why the rule?"

8

IT WAS early afternoon. Timothy and his mother were eating lunch in the kitchen of her apartment, which was roughly the size of the photocopy room at his office.

The tv's sound was turned low, so that it provided only background murmur. But the tv in her bedroom was still on loud enough to be heard in the kitchen. An old movie on cable. Timothy thought he heard Burt Lancaster's voice.

"What's wrong with cottage cheese?" Mrs. Packard asked.

"I'm just watching my fat intake, Mother. Nothing's wrong with cottage cheese. For you."

"You could use some intook fat, if you want my opinion."

"Cholesterol, remember? Cholesterol's why you've been a widow three times as long as I have."

"You're not a widow, Timmy. You're a widower."

"We're going to argue semantics?"

Timothy walked to the refrigerator for a piece of fruit. A jet roared overhead—her apartment was on the flight path to Kennedy and Timothy hadn't become accustomed to the noise again.

He leaned against the built-in oven, flipped a pear from hand to hand, then bit in. He knew she preferred that he sit, to use a plate and knife.

"I was only trying to illustrate something," she said. "If a widow stays a widow, that's no big surprise, especially at my age. But a widower? One so young? This is an unnatural condition."

"I've met lots of women since Charlene died, mother. I date. Please, I need time for Jill now anyway."

"Not so much time that it stops you from living your life." She seemed close to tears. "You nearly went crazy that time, when she was . . . you know."

"That was normal behavior, Mother. A temporary withdrawal. I was hardly crazy."

"What do I know, I'm half a continent away from you. But I read that even a swan finds another whatsit, another cygnet, when his wife dies. And they're famous for mating for life."

Timothy smiled. He got a plate from the cupboard and a knife from the cabinet. He sat beside his mother again, patting her hand.

"I think I just figured you out. There's someone you want me to meet, isn't there?"

"Would one date hurt? Maybe dinner, then a show? I'll babysit."

"Don't let Jill hear 'babysit.' She just turned fifteen."

"I know she's fifteen: half of her is twenty-one and the other half nine, so on the average you're right. I'll play Scrabble with her, a penny a point."

There was laughter from the small den beyond the kitchen, then cheering. Timothy realized that the tv must be on in there too. A game show.

"Who's the girl?" he asked.

"It would hardly even be a date. You remember little Janie Delery?"

"You can't be serious."

"It's been a long time since high school, Timmy. At least you two might have something in common, not like that trickster from California that you married, God rest her soul."

"Mother."

"Well."

9

THE TWO mile long boardwalk was a patchwork of planks. The older planks were a drab color Timothy associated with World War II, the gray of big ships. The newer planks were blond, vulnerable looking.

A long section was being replaced after damage by a hurricane. Windows on the old hotels near this part of the boardwalk were still crisscrossed with tape to strengthen them against the storm's winds. Timothy had to slow down when he ran through the construction area, which was so restricted that he risked bowling over elderly walkers.

The boardwalk was an ideal place to run. Soft and yielding, it didn't bother his shins like the pavement of Gardner Park back home. On warm days, the sea breeze cooled him. The sound of surf was peaceful and there was always plenty to watch.

There was also plenty to remember, like that abandoned concrete watch tower midway along the boardwalk, built during the war to detect German invasions. Inside the tower, Timothy had made love for the first time. Zonnie Buzzle. God, what a name. She led him in through the trap door and scampered up the metal rungs in the wall, a bored tour guide. It was cold and dank inside, a very creepy place to drop your shorts.

Running back toward the apartment late in the afternoon, he saw a group playing volleyball in the soft white sand. Although her skimpy two-piece suit was new, Timothy had no trouble recognizing Jill among them.

He stopped. Jill's back was to the net, her arms were raised, and she concentrated on the ball as it was passed toward her.

She laughed, immersed in the game. He watched her deftly flick the ball over her head. It ticked and cleared the net, falling dead before a diving woman in a tank suit on the other side.

"All right, Jill girl," yelled a boy on her team. There was applause from her teammates.

"Point game," she boomed.

Timothy sat on the boardwalk, feet dangling over the edge and his arms on the bottom rung of railing. No one took any notice of him.

The boy who cheered was, on closer inspection, probably a fresh college graduate. Not a boy. Timothy studied him.

A good twenty-one, twenty-two. Certainly old enough to buy liquor. Tanned, long-armed, mustachioed. Timothy couldn't see his eyes for the wraparound sunglasses, but his face looked soft. He wore shorts, which were probably stolen from some friend on his college basketball team. Because the shrimp couldn't have made the team himself unless he had a deadly outside shot and had gained a quick twenty pounds since the season ended. Didn't look like a star. But the boy moved gracefully and came over to whisper something to Jill punctuated by pats on her butt.

Most of which was exposed by the new suit she had bought with hoarded allowance money. It was cut to fit her bottom like a thong fit a foot.

The boy went back to his place. He put a foot on the ball in the sand, spun it backwards, caught it on his instep, and kicked it up to his hand. All with a smile toward Jill. Anybody could do that, Timothy thought, given enough practice.

Jill jumped, hands above her head. "Drill it, André," she yelled.

André served overhand. The ball sizzled over the net with maybe an inch to spare, curved sharply downward, and hit the sand before anyone on the other team had moved.

As Jill leaped into André's arms with her legs circling his hips, Timothy stood. He jogged a few wobbly steps west, then circled back without looking at the beach and sprinted toward his mother's apartment.

10

TEN YEARS ago, little Janie Delery, ace speller and Treasurer of the Sophomore class, had become Jane Delery Brock. Was still Jane Delery Brock, she told him, but was no longer married to the asshole.

Timothy couldn't imagine the girl he remembered from Geometry calling anyone an asshole. Nor could he imagine her married.

"Neither could I," she said, laughing. "You should never do anything you can't imagine yourself doing in advance."

"But you kept his name?"

"I kept the name I used when I made my professional reputation."

"That's all right. Lawyers are supposed to have three names."

"No, attorneys are supposed to be stable. Now eat your little-necks."

It was a salt-tinged, wet Long Island night. Jane and Timothy ate outside, beneath an ultramarine sky overlooking a bay that was an even deeper blue. Everyone else ate inside the remodeled dining rooms of Mack's Clam Bar, but Timothy couldn't get enough of the old shore air. Jane didn't mind.

"Do you remember Allan Abernathy?" she asked.

"The math whiz? Of course."

"I saw him a few weeks ago, in Manhattan. It's strange, running into your past all of a sudden."

"So he's what, a big New York accountant?" Timothy spooned sauce onto a clam and swallowed it with little chewing. "That figures."

"No. He's selling hats."

"Like on a street corner? You've got to be kidding me."

"Not on a street corner, you nasty man. Abernathy's Haberdashery. We're talking mid-town, real haute couture. He wears a perm."

"How about this: I saw an article by Percival Collins last year," Timothy said as their chowders arrived. "It was reprinted in our local paper, with a big box around it."

"Percy the Pussy? I'm in shock. Who'd listen to anything he had to say?"

"Apparently all of Idaho. This chowder's good." He blew on it to conceal a smile. "Percy's editor of *The Boise Bulletin*, or whatever. Now who's being nasty?"

"It's *The Statesman*." Jane added crackers to her chowder. "Work for a Congressional Committee, you learn the names of every daily with a circulation above 20,000."

They ate slowly, keeping watch, enjoying the pace. Timothy had forgotten Jane had a cleft chin, had a birthmark which dripped down her shoulders like blood. She was all right.

"Did you see the sign on the bridge ramp, coming into town?" she asked.

"And couldn't believe my eyes." Timothy looked toward the sky. "Welcome to Long Beach. Home of Billy Crystal."

"He always said he was going to be a star."

Later that night, Jane and Timothy sat on the beach watching the water. It was high tide, but quiet. The ocean looked more like a big pool than "the steep Atlantic stream" that Milton wrote about. Freshman English.

They'd skipped a movie in favor of the beach, where both had spent so many eager evenings when they were young. What would Mrs. Packard make of this? Timothy sat with his back against Jane's for mutual support and watched the lights of a jet fade as it roared south.

"So tell me about your wife."

He didn't answer right away, thought about not answering at all. But Jane reached around for his arm.

"It's all right," she said.

"The odd thing is, I met her on a beach. Isn't that something? In San Diego, not long after I graduated from Cal Poly."

"That's right, weren't you going to be some kind of engineer?"

"I was going to be lots of things, Janie. Engineer, astronaut, four minute miler. Charlene was this high strung redhead, absolutely mottled by freckles. Talked like a William Buckley on 78 rpm. And she was a magician. Literally practiced magic. She put herself through UCLA making things appear and disappear. Wore a spangled, skin-tight evening gown and did sleight of hand at Rotary and Elks meetings. I was captivated."

"We all have our weaknesses." Jane laughed. "My ex used to make jewelry out of mollusk husks."

"My daughter would love the guy."

"She'd be about the right age for him."

They were still sitting back to back, but were also linked hand in hand. Timothy was glad they stopped at her place for sweaters.

"So," he continued, "we got married. I'm 23 and she tells me she's gonna get the fat cats. Count on me, I told her. We had to move to where the action was, which sort of explains why we were in Illinois. When we got there, she was the youngest lobbyist in the state, gungho. Till the day she left for Washington the first time, I thought a lobbyist just wrote impassioned articles for hippie magazines."

"So it was travel?"

"It?"

Suddenly, Timothy was back in Illinois on a late winter night a decade ago. He was calling the number Charlene said she'd be at, hearing it ring and ring. Her father had died; Timothy couldn't locate her to break the news. He tried all through the night.

"I was actually very happy," he said. "At least for the first half of our marriage. I thought she was indebted to me for helping to boost her career after we had Jill."

"What do you think happened?"

"Two things. Apparently I failed to appreciate that Charlene didn't share my happiness. And indebtedness wasn't the right concept."

Timothy turned his head to look away from the water, back toward the beach. Jane turned too. Their cheeks rested together, warm in the night.

"Only now," he whispered, "maybe the last fifteen twenty months, have things started to make sense to me again. Maybe a dozen years there, it was like I'd lost the tide charts. Every time I went out I got stranded somewhere."

11

"So when do I get to see Billy Crystal's house?" Jill asked.

They whispered in the kitchen, trying not to waken Mrs. Packard. Jill was being flexible about eating Raisin Bran every morning.

"Are you serious?"

"Yes I'm serious. I've already done your high school, the restaurant where you were a busboy, and the house you lived in when you were my age. I even saw the place where you fell off your bike and landed in the canal. But Grandma doesn't remember where Billy lived."

"You're being an angel." Timothy didn't know that Jill was giving his mother that much of her time, thought she'd been on the beach every waking hour. "But I don't see what's so important about Billy Crystal's house."

"Come on, Dad. He's a big star. You know, they made Abe Lincoln's house a national monument back home."

"Wait a minute. That's because Abe Lincoln was a national figure."

"So's Billy. Everybody knows who he is. Springfield just didn't have any famous actors to make their home into a shrine, so they had to settle for that silly poet, whatshisname."

"Vachel Lindsay. Who was a very important writer."

"Right. And my English class has to go visit his house every year. 'Boomlay, boomlay, boomlay, boom!'" She gulped her orange juice and smiled at him. "Just take me to Billy Crystal's house, all right?"

"Billy's just a guy I went to high school with, Jill. A guy I used to drink egg creams with at the Cozy Nook."

"I know. So why not write and get me his autograph?"

They drove the half-mile to Billy Crystal's childhood home in Mrs. Packard's Honda. Jill brought her camera along. Timothy just wanted to make a quick getaway.

"What was he like?" she asked.

"Fast, just like he seems on HBO. Real clever, even in first period when everybody's half-asleep. We drifted apart after our fathers died. I guess we didn't want to jinx each other's mothers. But he was a funny guy, a jock, always into a bunch of activities after school. Ok?"

"Did he have a lot of girl friends?"

Timothy, reluctantly, got out of the car to stand by Jill. She was determined to take a whole roll of pictures.

"I really don't know if he had a lot of girlfriends. Why?"

"Well, he's pretty sexy. I wonder if any of the guys I know'll grow up to be important, like Billy."

"He's just a comedian." Timothy took a picture of her on the lawn of Billy Crystal's house. "It's not like he's a world leader or a scientific genius."

"That's what I mean." She winked at him. "Who'd want to take pictures of some senator's house, some egghead chemist, you know?"

12

JILL WAS frightened. She knew him only a week, but already felt closer to André Fitch than to any male except her father.

They lay together on his blanket, not touching. Under the intense glare of the sun, they talked for hours.

Jill felt like she was roasting, barely holding within herself juices that would burst through if she were handled too roughly. Something like that. She was having trouble working it out exactly.

"You just don't seem fifteen," André had said the first time they'd kissed.

"Everybody says that." Jill tried not to talk too fast. "Right now, I don't feel fifteen."

"You have to tell me if I'm rushing you. Otherwise, I have no way to know." Then he kissed her again, his tongue deep inside her mouth.

"I'm not much of a student," she had said, "but I'm a good learner."

That was something Jill once overheard her father say about her. He'd been talking to a new girl friend, the skinny runner.

Now Jill sat up, suddenly uncomfortable. André's arm fell back to the blanket.

"What's wrong?" he asked.

"I'm too hot."

He studied her. A smile was getting organized within his thick mustache.

"I like it when you're hot."

"Really," she said. "Heat-type hot. I need to swim."

She dashed toward the water. André walked after her, watching her pick up speed. He understood that she didn't want him to intrude.

Picking her legs up higher as she splashed toward the breakers, flapping her arms like wings, Jill lurched past a group of waders. Not far from the rocks, she flopped into a wave and dove underneath, coming up on its smooth side in perfect control. Then she began swimming away from the rocks, cutting across the breakers parallel to the shore.

"What was that all about?" André asked when she finally came back in.

"I was groining." Jill said.

Later in the afternoon, André took her to the boardwalk arcade. As they walked, they shared a knish.

"What is this?"

"Jewish food," André said. "There's always a lot of Jews around here, see. That influences the food you can get."

Jill nodded. She shut her eyes and bit in.

"Oh, gross!" She spat a chunk of knish by her feet. "I thought this thing was going to be sweet. What's in here?"

"Potato stuff."

"Yuk. You ever have your mouth all set for, like, whipped cream, and then you give it potato stuff? Barf city."

André taught her to play ski ball, to spin the ball so it wouldn't bounce. She scored three fifties in a row and won a red plastic back scratcher.

Then he showed her how to aim a dulled dart so it would break the half-filled balloons. He won a small stuffed panda by knocking metal bottles off a table with a baseball, throwing it hard enough to win despite the table's thick rim meant to keep the bottles from rolling off.

They agreed to meet at the ferris wheel after Jill ate dinner.

"You think your father would let you eat with me one night? I'd buy."

"Let's not mess with a good thing," Jill said. "Wouldn't want my dad to start worrying."

"He doesn't know about me?"

"I don't think he's ready to know about you yet, André." She kissed his cheek and headed toward the apartment. "Let's just leave well enough alone."

13

"YOU EAT," Mrs. Packard said, "like a hummingbird. You hover, go bip-bip-bip, and goodbye."

"I'm just not hungry tonight, Grandma. Last night you told me I put too much food in my mouth at once, tonight I don't eat enough."

"A fresh hummingbird, yet."

Jill let out a long sigh. She put down her chopsticks and reached for a fork.

"Watch."

She jabbed a slice of pork, dipped it in sauce to coat it, and buried the meat in her rice bowl. Smiling first at her grandmother, then at her father, she chewed slowly and cooed in mock pleasure.

"I give up," Mrs. Packard said, though not unhappily. It was a tone Timothy didn't remember from his childhood.

"So why the hurry again, Jilly?" he asked.

Jill saw her grandmother's eyes shift quickly between them. Timothy's held her own.

"A bunch of kids are going to meet by the rides after dinner. Nothing special."

"I'm glad you've found things to do," Mrs. Packard said. "It's given me time to talk with your father. Except, of course, he's not around much either. I'm thrilled that you two came to visit me."

Jill sat back, glad the focus had switched. She turned to face her father.

"And just where have you been going every night, young man?" she teased.

"The rides. Wonder why I never bump into you there?"

Where Timothy had gone last night, though, was hardly to the rides. It was something he couldn't begin to explain. Because actually, last night he went to 1959.

The first hint came when he noticed *Ben-Hur* was playing at the Nassau downtown. He was walking from his mother's apartment toward The Hawser Tavern to watch a Mets game and drink some beers. But on the bridge over Reynolds Channel, about mid-span, he was suddenly back in the year of the 49-star flag.

He stopped on the metal grate and looked around. East, where there were supposed to be tennis courts, Worthington Ford took up four long blocks. On the west side, Blum's Hardware sprawled where he'd seen a new McDonald's earlier in the week.

Timothy remembered the talk in school. Batista was out and Castro was in now, so there was fresh optimism about Cuba. He'd done a report on how the St. Lawrence would open the Great Lakes to the Atlantic.

He realized that his father was still alive. Maybe not at home, this might be one of those times when he'd moved out for a while, but at least alive. Timothy could go see him, talk about what had been happening to him these last few years.

He turned back toward Long Beach, feeling a little dizzy. From where he stood, Timothy could see the dozen traffic lights strung between the bridge and ocean swaying in the breeze. Each light was red. He hadn't realized how much the wind had come up.

He reached to the railing for support. It was as though he'd been breached in some way, begun a minute splintering along the hollows of his bones. Timothy worried that he might fall through the grate and into the water.

14

TIMOTHY AND Jane took the train into New York City. A few museums, lunch in Little Italy, maybe a couple of galleries or a tour of the twin towers. It would be a cut above the old high school field trips, she promised. They could even spend the whole afternoon in bookstores if they wanted to.

Jill got to stay behind, but only by promising to spend the entire evening with her grandmother.

Based on what André had told her, that wouldn't be a problem. They would be back by 4:00, easily.

He was waiting for Jill at the east end of the boardwalk. She walked the few blocks to meet him quickly because it took her an extra ten minutes to get her hair right. She arrived out of breath.

André spit out his gum when he saw her coming. Something about him looked different today. Was his mustache trimmed? Hair trimmed? He seemed sharper at the edges.

"Look at that," he whispered when they hugged. "The Paradise."

He was pointing to an old hotel ten stories high and thin, like half of a building. The name was written in neon script within an entrance of stone painted azure. Above the entrance, all that remained was the steel work of its superstructure.

"There was a fire last year," André said. "Now they can't decide whether to tear it down and rebuild, or just leave it like this."

"I bet my Dad could sell it. This has to be a good place to have a hotel, right on the beach. Someone would want to buy it and make his fortune."

"Well, apparently nobody wants to buy it."

"My Dad could make someone want to. It sure looks sad, just hanging out like that."

"Sad? I guess. Looks bombed out to me."

André had borrowed a friend's car for the day. It was a jeep-like vehicle, open on the sides and top, and he had it crammed with pillows, blankets, and a cooler.

Jill loved to smell the salt air. She put her legs on the dashboard and held her hair up with her hands.

They drove east toward Bayshore and the ferry to Fire Island. Although talking was difficult over the noise of the wind, Jill could tell that André was excited, which made her feel powerful.

"You'll love it," he yelled. "There's a little village called Lonelyville. I think I want to kiss you on the shore of Lonelyville, with our feet in the water."

Jill slid closer to him. She liked the patient way he treated her, the way he took time to say sweet things.

On the ferry, they stood at the prow holding hands.

"Let's look for whales," she said.

"You can look if you want. But any whales are a good sixty miles east of here."

"We could talk about music. Are you into old-time rock?" When he didn't answer, Jill looked in the direction he was looking. She could see the island. "I thought I heard you singing while we were in the car."

"Am I into old-time rock?" He looked at her as if she'd just walked up next to him. "I'm like an expert. We all get off on it during finals week, break the tension."

40

"My dad turned me on to the Beatles when I was little. We've got lots of tapes."

"All right, test time: let's see who can name the most Beatles' songs with love in the title. Name it and then sing a couple of phrases."

Jill rolled her eyes. "Let me go first. Can't Buy Me Love."

"She Loves You," André said.

"Love Me Do."

"All You Need Is Love."

"All My Loving."

"Oh no," he said. "That's loving, not love. They're different. Half a point is all you get."

"Ok, then 'P.S. I Love You.'"

"And I Love Her," he said. "Love To You, Words Of Love." His face hardened and he seemed to be looking right through her. "It's Only Love, Love You Too, You've Got To Hide Your Love Away."

"Ok," Jill said. She suddenly wished they were on their way back instead of on their way out. His tone frightened her. "Ok, you win."

She imagined it was another world, the Planet of Blue Mist. The people here spoke only Touch. Their skin was especially tender because there was nothing in their world to toughen it.

Fire Island seemed so isolated from the mainland of Long Island that Jill felt she was finally starting her real vacation. Forgetting the Planet of Blue Mist, she imagined it was a coral atoll in the south Pacific, one of those places like Fiji or New Guinea. Someplace where, when you arrived, it was automatically tomorrow.

André spread his blanket behind a low dune and pulled Jill down with him. She curled against his long torso, ready when he wanted to kiss her.

But he didn't want to kiss her. Instead, he put his hand on her back, pulling Jill close, and slid it down inside the back of her shorts. He moved quickly, sure, snaking the hand down her buttocks and between her legs.

She tried to draw back, but his arm along her back was too strong, like a brace. She moved her head away, looking toward the sky, gasping for breath like a swimmer too long submerged. The hand kept moving, pinching her flesh, insinuating itself. She never guessed that a guy might come at you that way, from behind.

"André, please. I don't want this."

He didn't answer. He also didn't stop.

Going with her momentum, André pushed Jill onto her back. Suddenly, without her knowing how, his hand was inside the front of her shorts.

He was moving quickly, but he wasn't exactly hurting her. The hand was searching, homing in. Jill was having trouble breathing because of André's weight and because he was covering her mouth with his.

Jill was seeing it all as if from a distance, maybe from as far away as in the water. It seemed to be happening in slow motion, gracefully, and in utter silence. Why wasn't there breathing?

She wanted to scream, but she wasn't quite certain this was the right time. Maybe she could still get him to stop without resorting to the scream, like a frightened child. Maybe it was all a misunderstanding.

Jill tried to wrap a leg around him, to change the balance. But she was having trouble thinking clearly now because things were speeding up. She felt deeply chilled and lay back down.

André eased up, freeing his hand from her crotch and trying to pin her arms over her head. He must have thought she was ready to go along, because he released her hands and reached to lower her shorts.

All Jill could think about was how she was going to get to her grandmother's apartment without having to go back to Long Beach with André.

Instinctively, she scissored her legs against his middle, breaking his hold. Then she rolled over him and tumbled away, kicking sand as she scooted up the dune.

"Get away," she commanded without losing control of her voice. "I mean it André. You could go to jail for this shit."

He rose to his knees, panting. "Take it easy. I didn't mean it."

"Then what the fuck did you mean? Your hand was in my pants."

"Calm down."

"I'm fifteen."

"It's all right, Jill. I know how old you are."

"I'm five fucking teen." She was on the verge of tears and didn't want to give in. "And you are goddamn rushing me now."

"Nobody dragged you here, Jill. I thought you understood what was going on."

Now, for the first time, she was ready to scream. It wouldn't be a scream of panic, though, but a scream of rage.

Instead, she glared at him, biting her lip, feeling proud to have gotten away yet also ready to throw up. She wanted to take a shower.

"So did I, you prick."

She ran up the beach toward the ferry slip.

15

"JUST LOOK at this move," Mrs. Packard said. "Oxygen. That's one; and eight tripled is twenty-five; plus four, six, seven, and one tripled is ten. So thirty-five points down. Also, I get eleven more for turning wide into widen. Not bad, forty-six points."

"You get all the good letters," Jill muttered.

"There's plenty of time. You'll probably get the q and the z."

"Wait a minute. Don't you spell oxygen with an a?"

"That would be oxy-gan, dear. The g would be hard."

"No, ox-a-gen. There's an a in the middle. Can I look it up?"

Mrs. Packard handed Jill the dictionary. She watched her granddaughter flip through the pages, having difficulty zeroing in on the o's and then the ox's, handling the book like an explosive.

Something obviously was troubling Jill, something more than her low score in the game and her difficulties with spelling. The girl wouldn't meet her eyes, wouldn't talk about her day, wasn't interested in dinner.

Mrs. Packard had surreptitiously scanned Jill for scars or bruises.

She saw none, nor any evidence of harm; only the vivid, unreadable signs of long crying.

She vowed to have a talk with her son. Jill's behavior and lack of academic achievement were just two more examples of how badly Timothy needed a woman around.

When the phone rang, Mrs. Packard was relieved.

"It's for you, dear. A boy." She handed the receiver to Jill. "I mean, a man."

Jill carried the phone into the den before speaking. Mrs. Packard spilled the game tiles back into their paper bag, grateful for an excuse to stop playing. She tried to avoid making noise with the tiles so she could hear Jill's end of the conversation.

"No," Jill said.

"I won't touch you," André said. "I promise. I just want to see you, and explain things."

"You don't need to explain anything. I was there."

"Just answer this, then. Why did you go with me, if you didn't want to get it on?"

"Adventure, excitement. I don't know, André. I've got to go now."

"Don't hang up. Please." He was breathing heavily, as if he'd just dived for a volleyball return. "I'm really sorry if there was a mistake. You know, my sister's your age."

"Then I feel sorry for your sister. I bet you peek at her while she's in the shower."

"You don't understand."

"My grandmother wants me to get off the phone. She's expecting a call."

"Will you meet me at the ferris wheel?"

"Just get off my case. I don't want this."

When Jill came out of the den, Mrs. Packard was nowhere to be seen. Jill opened the refrigerator and poured herself a glass of milk.

"Would you come in here?" Mrs. Packard called.

"Where's here?" Jill was still thinking about André's voice, his invitation to meet at the ferris wheel. "I'm not exactly psychic."

"Hallway."

44

Jill couldn't see her grandmother, but heard the sound of plastic bags rustling in the closet. Mrs. Packard was deep inside, standing on a step-stool in a space cleared among winter clothes.

"You should have let me climb up there," Jill said. "Be careful."

"Here, take this." Without turning or looking, Mrs. Packard handed down a package wrapped in layers of saran wrap resting inside two plastic freezer bags. "If I get down without falling, this will be a miracle."

Jill held her hand until Mrs. Packard was safely down. She plopped onto the couch and patted the space beside her, where she wanted Jill to sit.

"Do you know what these are?" Mrs. Packard asked.

"Some kind of dishes? Oh my God! They're those old-time records, the 78s. Where did you get these?"

"They're not so old, dear. And they're mine."

"Who's on them?" Jill opened the bags and drew out the disks. "They're so hard."

"That's what I mean, they're mine. They're of me, singing." She folded her arms across her chest as if daring Jill to doubt her. "Your grandmother, 'The Melody Girl.'"

Jill put the stack in her lap, careful not to damage them. "You?"

"I had a radio show in the 1930s. WBNX Presents: The Melody Girl of the Air. You didn't know? I played the piano and sang. For fifteen whole minutes."

"Can I listen?"

"What do you think I got them down for, to toss around like a frisbee? If we listen to them, it'll double the size of my all-time total audience. I was on opposite Rudy Vallee; my own parents didn't even listen to me."

The record was scratchy and the voice sounded far off, as if they were hearing music from the apartment above. Mrs. Packard's voice was higher than Jill expected, almost a soprano, but fierce. Slow it down to 45, she thought, and this could be Janis Joplin.

They listened to all three records, holding hands, keeping silent even as the records changed. Mrs. Packard looked at the window, through which she could only see the dark.

"I recognized that last one," Jill said.

"Can't help lovin' that man of mine," Mrs. Packard sang, her voice now deep and throaty. "I used to sing it to your father at bedtime. But I didn't think they still played it."

"I don't think they do, either. But Dad used to sing it to me too, every night when I was little."

16

"WELL, I think Jilly's having problems with a boy," Mrs. Packard said the next morning, when she was alone with her son.

Jill hadn't gone out as usual, so Mrs. Packard sent her downstairs to put in a load of laundry. She was talking to Timothy through the bathroom door.

"What makes you think so?"

"A woman knows these things. Besides, I spoke to him. He sounded about your age."

"If there's a problem, she'll tell me." Timothy tried to sound confident. "She always does."

"When would she do that? You two are never here at the same time."

"That's your fault." He tried to lighten her mood. "You set me up with Jane."

"But I didn't set Jill free to do whatever she wants to, wherever and whenever she wants to. That's your doing."

Timothy tried not to sound alarmed. He knew there'd have to be a good reason for his mother to approach him on the subject. Unless she was convinced Jill was in trouble, Mrs. Packard simply wouldn't risk interfering in his life again, as she had during the years with Charlene. Twice a month he would curse and argue with her long-distance, threatening to get an unlisted number if she didn't stop pestering him. Charlene was fine, he would tell her. They were fine together, she shouldn't worry so much, marriages had their cycles. That had taught him you shouldn't tell your mother things you didn't really believe yourself. They always know.

"Mother, I have to let Jill bring it up, if she has a problem."

"What for?" Jill was angry, pouting.

"Because you've never been there."

"I've never been to Paris either. Let's go to Paris instead."

Timothy had thought of it earlier in the week and the idea wouldn't go away. He hadn't been to his father's grave in twenty years.

He'd never taken Charlene there, but he felt it would be important to go with Jill. He wasn't certain he could find the plot without help.

"It wouldn't take two hours."

She shook her head.

"Come on, Jill. A rainy day, I mean it's not like you'd be going to the beach instead."

"That's not it. I just don't want to go to some spooky goddamn cemetery on my summer vacation. We're supposed to be having fun here."

"Are you?"

"Am I what?"

Jill glared at Timothy. She looked so much like Charlene then that he thought he'd lose his temper, flare back at her like a match lit by another match. He was astonished at how automatic his response was. He looked away.

"So forget it."

"What's with a cemetery, anyway?" Her eyes were icy. "Remember, we just tossed mom's ashes in the lake, for Christ's sake. I thought you said that was good enough."

17

WITH HER short legs and enormous bosom, Mrs. Packard was nearly horizontal when she drove the Honda. Jill sat beside her, elbow out
the window, enjoying the breeze.

It was the next morning. During breakfast, Mrs. Packard had suggested a trip to Roosevelt Field.

"I didn't know you liked sports," Jill responded.

"I loathe sports. Sports are absolutely barbaric. I went to watch
your father play in a football game once, when he was just a year older
than you are now. That was entirely enough for me. I had to watch
some elephant run into him so hard it knocked the poor boy unconscious for two days. Popped the ball right out of Timothy's hands and
when I saw it bounce away I thought it was his head." Mrs. Packard
sat with her toast poised in front of her mouth, slowly shaking her
head. "No, dear. Roosevelt Field is a shopping mall."

"A shopping mall! I can deal with that." Jill bounced up from the
table, perkier than Mrs. Packard had seen her in several days. "Let's go.
When do they open?"

"The question isn't when do they open, but when can your grandmother be ready to leave. It takes quite a bit of art to adjust this complexion for actual viewing."

"You. Look. Mahvelous," Jill said.

"I will be ready to walk out of here by 11:00. This is a promise."

She was true to her word. They drove east, along a wide boulevard
curving to match the shoreline which Jill could see to her right.

"Do you know what's there?" Mrs. Packard asked, pointing with
her chin.

"The ocean."

"I mean all the way out there. If you went straight out south and
kept going till you hit land again, where would you be?"

"New Jersey?"

"Haiti, dear. You'd be in Haiti. Like Paul Gauguin. Do you know about him?"

Jill shook her head. "Wasn't he an explorer?"

"I suppose you could say that."

After a few more curves, Mrs. Packard tried again. Jill wasn't being moody, maybe she was just tired.

"Here is where you father went to high school."

"I know, I know. I've been there already. He made me promise I'd go."

"Did you also know he saved a girl from a burning building when he was a student? Right over there, in that delicatessen." The car swerved when Mrs. Packard pointed.

"It looks like a new building to me."

"The deli *is* brand new. But it used to be one of those greasy-spoon cafes and the school kids would walk over for lunch. One day the place caught on fire. Big blazes shooting right out the windows like in the drawings of hell, it was awful. The newspaper said the fire started because the griddle ignited and burned right up the wall, which was stained with twenty years worth of grease. Your father was inside and he got out all right, with his mouth still full of a braunschweiger sandwich. But then he ran back in and dragged out this little girl, I still remember her name: Donna Glaze. She'd tripped and hurt herself against one of those big stools around the soda fountain. People just ran right by her. Timothy was a real hero. The mayor gave him a fancy plaque later."

"He never told me about that."

"Just remember that story the next time you leave your school for lunch."

Between the school and the parkway, the boulevard narrowed. Then it straightened as it passed through Lido Beach, several blocks of old homes with sloping lawns and curved, private driveways.

"And this little neighborhood is where a lot of the story *The Godfather* takes place."

"I didn't know that."

"These are very important facts, dear. After all, this is your homeland."

"Sort of."

"What, sort of? A girl has to know about where her family comes from, where her roots are. Without roots, you know, a tree would just topple over in a strong wind. Anyway, it's true, most of what happens in that Godfather story. For some reason, those mafia people decided to settle right here, where regular people are trying to live. Did you ever read that book?"

"I saw the movie."

"So did I, I'm sorry to say. Terribly gory. But it had my favorite actor in the whole wide world, Mister Marlon Brando."

"Which one was he?"

"Why, he played the Godfather, of course." Mrs. Packard stopped to pay the toll. She looked over at Jill to see if her granddaughter was teasing, but it was clear that she was serious. She was also engrossed, and Mrs. Packard was feeling very proud of herself.

"You liked the guy? I thought he talked funny."

"Some critic, you are. Nevermind." She rolled up the window. "This toll booth is where the one son got shot all to pieces."

"I remember when that happened. I had to look away."

"Let me tell you a story about Marlon Brando," she continued. "Back in the fifties, he was new. No one had heard of him. Your grand-father, God rest his soul, and I went to see him in his first big play. I'll never forget that night. The play was called *A Streetcar Named Desire* and I practically had to drag him to see it. He wasn't a very cultured man, a very refined man, your grandfather.

"But something about Marlon Brando really struck him that night. He was very moved and I think to this day that I saw a tear when that big, hulking brute fell down on his knees for love of his sweet-heart. His Stella.

"Do you know that play? Don't they make you read it in school?"

"I saw it on tv last year with my Dad. It was pretty goofy, if you ask me."

"Well, there's a certain kind of man, dear, that has a very hard time understanding what a woman wants and needs. Your grandfather, unfortunately, was one such man. And Marlon Brando played another one that night. No wonder it reached Mr. Packard. You have to watch out for men like that."

Jill looked at her grandmother without responding. Mrs. Packard watched the road, checked her rearview mirror, but didn't look at Jill.

"How much further?" Jill asked.

"About fifteen minutes. If I don't get lost."

At Roosevelt Field Jill was suddenly infused with energy, as if the floors carried a special charge. She darted from store to store, chattering and quacking to Mrs. Packard like a duckling.

"This is too much for me," Mrs. Packard said after a half hour of wandering. "I'm going to get a cup of coffee. Why don't you meet me over there, by the directory."

"When?"

"Is 1:30 all right?"

"I won't even be started by 1:30! What time does this place close?"

"I suppose there are a few things I could shop for." Mrs. Packard ignored Jill's question. "Let's say 3:00. Would that give you enough time?"

Jill rushed at Mrs. Packard and kissed her cheek. "Oh thank you, grandma." She put an arm around her shoulder and squeezed, as if her grandmother were an old buddy. Then she dashed off.

"Wait a minute. You don't have a watch on."

"I'll ask someone the time. Don't worry."

"Don't talk to strangers. There must be clocks on the walls somewhere."

Mrs. Packard found the nearest restaurant and collapsed at an empty table. Suddenly hungry, she ordered an English muffin with extra jam to go along with her coffee. She watched people stroll past, her thoughts turning inward, and forgot to thank the waitress when the food arrived.

She'd always wanted a daughter. When Timothy was born, she didn't need the doctor to tell her this would be her only child. Vern Packard had made that quite clear. In fact, her husband didn't even want her to have Timothy. Without asking, he'd arranged for an abortion at some doctor's office in the Battery section of Brooklyn. But Mrs. Packard refused, threatening to leave him. When the baby turned out to be a male, she felt betrayed, as if she'd risked her life's savings on a well that turned out to be dry.

An hour later, Jill reappeared. She seemed closer to the child Mrs. Packard remembered from four years ago.

"Grandma, this is Bonnie Wheel. I met her in the record store. Bonnie's going to be a sophomore in the fall too. At where is it?"

"East Meadow," Bonnie said.

Jill snapped her fingers. "East Meadow East Meadow."

"Pleased to meet you," Mrs. Packard said. "Too bad Jill didn't find you last week. She's about to go away again."

Mrs. Packard could not believe this child was the same age as her granddaughter. She came up to Jill's shoulders and was bony. Even her bleached hair was the color of bone. Inside a frame of pouting, crimson lips were teeth pointing in several directions like a harrow.

But their styles were the same. Dressed in layers, bedecked with hand-made jewelry, smelling of tea rose. They'd found each other at a glance, Mrs. Packard was certain, like long-separated sisters.

She could hardly understand them because they talked so fast. Bonnie seemed to be addressing her, though, so Mrs. Packard nodded.

"Then Jill goes 'I'm leaving for Michigan in a week or two' and I'm like, Wow, I just get to meet you and now you're going to Michigan?"

Jill laughed as if this were the funniest improvisation she'd heard in her life. "Bonnie's the only girl I've ever met besides me who knows all the words to 'Born To Be Wild.' We sang it in the store and everybody was looking at us."

"That's nice, girls."

"Could I have an extra hour, grandma? Bonnie wants to show me where she gets her clothes."

Jill's eyes were open wide. Her hands were folded in front of her chest as if in prayer and she vibrated like a junkie from this need to be with her new friend.

"Of course, dear." Mrs. Packard opened her purse and took out a few dollars. "And go buy yourself a souvenir. I'll be waiting right here."

As Jill skipped away from her, Mrs. Packard had to turn her back. To focus herself, she scanned the counter and tried to count the different kinds of pastries stacked in the display.

The waitress caught her eye. Mrs. Packard shook her head slowly, but the young woman sashayed over with a fresh pot of coffee and a smile.

18

Jane Delery Brock was pleased. She grabbed Timothy's hand and led him down the Court House steps.

"I was going for a settlement the whole time," she said. "A jury trial would have been too great a risk. Whew, you can't get much closer than this."

"But the lady was full of shit."

"Of course she was full of shit. They couldn't find a single doctor to testify that she'd had a real injury. But pain is pain. You can't disprove a person's pain."

"A jury would've seen through her."

"I wasn't about to bet on it. All a jury needs is to see the cervical collar and hear her tale of woe. Then they put themselves in her place. Here's this lifelong clerk-typist claiming she can't work anymore, she can't go square dancing, she can't weed the garden. And there's my rich client, driving a new Volvo, and saying he was only going two miles an hour. I'd have lost the case."

"And so the insurance company forks over fifty-five grand to the clerk-typist and everybody else's rates go up a couple percentage points."

"That's the way these personal injury cases work, Tim. You don't often beat whiplash. Especially when it's compounded by no more square dancing."

"Personal injury. The guy I'd like to meet is the one who sets up those value tables, where you lose one hand or one foot and it's $35,000 but one hand and one foot is $80,000."

They reached the parking lot, still holding hands. Jane unlocked the passenger door of her Audi, then walked around to the driver's side. Before getting in, she looked across the top of the car at Timothy, who was gazing over the rows of cars at the Court House.

"What is it?" she asked.

"I was just thinking about when Charlene died. Her mother and I had a terrible fight in the parking lot outside the hospital. The woman was in a rage. I remember she wanted to sue the doctor for malpractice, hold the hospital liable, go after the association that Charlene worked for. 'Somebody has to pay for what happened to my child,' she told me. When I said Charlene simply ignored the signs until it was too late, her mother tried to kick me. She walked right over and took a swipe at me, soccer style."

Jane slid behind the wheel. She leaned over and opened his door from inside.

"Get in."

When Jane was aroused, the birthmark on her shoulders turned vermilion. Her speech softened nearly to a whisper, as if her voice were coated with a film of mist.

"That feels wonderful."

"There's no need to talk," Timothy whispered. He put a finger to her lips.

They were in the bedroom at the back of her house, which overlooked dunes frizzed with salt-marsh grasses. It was a low part of the beach, given to flooding even during a modest storm surge.

Two candles flickered in the room, which she had opened to the warm, windy night. Beyond the wind, Timothy could hear the ocean. It was a childhood nightsound that he'd all but forgotten.

He hadn't been this comfortable in a long time. Jane shut her eyes and stopped speaking. She inhaled deeply, then let her breath out loudly, lips forming a soft O.

Standing at the side of her bed, bending over, Timothy worked almond oil into Jane's long, naked back. With his fingertips, he probed the flat triangle of muscle from her shoulder to upper back, stroking and stroking until the knots eased. He rotated her arm in its socket.

Inching down toward her waist, he thumbed each vertebra, then rubbed it softly between his fingers like a coin. He slid his hands gradually from her neck to her buttocks. Then he knelt on the bed, stretching to whisper in her ear.

"Take a deep breath again."

He stood to knead the backs of her thighs, flexing her legs inch by inch until they bent without resistance, rolling her ankles until they no longer made a cracking noise. The only time his hands weren't in contact with Jane's skin was when he stopped to put a little more oil on them.

He took her hand and relaxed the tension between elbow and wrist. He locked her fingers in his, tugging gently with his other hand.

When he'd finished with her back side, Timothy climbed onto the bed beside her and stretched out along her flank. Jane opened the eye that faced him.

"Turn over," he whispered.

"Why don't you put a tape on the machine, something with lots of reed."

"Just turn over. We can listen to the wind."

She turned over, her arm circling his back. He could feel her breast against his biceps.

"The issue is, I'm ready to make love." She nipped his ear. "And I just thought: reeds."

"The books all say you shouldn't break contact during a massage."

"That's the trouble. You thought this was a massage." She slipped an oily hand up Timothy's thigh and gently cupped his balls. "Now please put on some music. At least I didn't think flügelhorns, or you'd have been over by the tapes for a good hour."

When he returned to her bed, Jane was flat on her back. Her hair was fanned out on the pillow. One knee was cocked so that she seemed tilted toward him, but not splayed, not too far ahead of him.

Timothy knelt on the bed, ran his hands along the back of her lifted thighs where they were still oiled, and then bent between them. Jane's fingers groped for and found the sides of his head, buried themselves in his hair.

"I don't suppose you'll stay the night?"

"I'm not sure the Packards are ready for that," Timothy said as he sat at the edge of Jane's bed. "My mother, my daughter, or me. I really shouldn't."

"When will I see you next?"

"How about tomorrow night? I think it's high time you and Jilly said hello."

"We could have dinner here." She reached over for her purse. She rummaged through it for her calendar book, then checked her schedule. "Good, I'm clear. Let me fix a meal for you. And let me be on my home turf, that'd be better. But please, let me not have to deal with your mother at the same time."

19

"WANT COMPANY?" Jill asked.

It was the next morning. She was sitting in the living room, flipping through yesterday's afternoon newspaper.

Timothy had slept later than usual and emerged from the den wearing only his briefs. He was surprised to find Jill still around.

"What are you doing cooped up inside?" He stood in front of the couch smoothing back his hair, fighting down a yawn. "With this bright sun, I had you figured for the beach."

"If you don't want me around, just say so."

"Whoa. Who said I don't want you around? I was just surprised to see you." He walked back into the den to put on his jeans.

"Here's some juice," Jill called.

"I just dreamed that you were lying on a very small blanket, or maybe it was just a big towel, all alone on some enormous beach. The water was an unreal shade of blue, almost the color of eggshells. But the tide was coming up and you were fast asleep."

Timothy came into the living room again and took the glass of juice Jill offered. He sipped it like hot coffee, frowned, blew as if to cool it off.

Jill laughed. "Wake up, Dad."

"Ease up on me, I had a hard night." He downed the juice and put the glass on the knick-knack shelf, forgetting about it immediately.

"So I figured. When Grandma and I got back from shopping, we waited for you for dinner. Then after dinner, we waited a while more, playing Scrabble. I finally went to bed around midnight."

"Then you just missed me."

"A man of your age. . ." It was part of their old game, but she didn't have the desire to play it out this morning.

"So tell me, how've you been doing?" he asked when she faltered.

Jill flopped onto the couch. "A couple of days ago? While you were in New York with Jane? Well, I had a bad day. Since you asked." Jill sank back against the armrest. When she'd settled, she bit her lips, fighting tears. "Oh damn it." Timothy thought she looked like a child on Christmas morning whose first gift was a pair of grown-up style bedroom slippers.

"I'm sorry. What happened?"

"Like I said, I had a very bad day."

"Your grandmother thought something was up. She was worried about you."

"Yeah, that was great. She was watching me every minute, like some goddamn nuclear physicist just waiting for me to blow up. That was exactly what I needed, you know?"

"Jilly."

"Jilly Jilly." She turned her head away from him. "I went to the beach with this guy I met. And he went crazy on me, just about ripped my skin off." She looked back. "It was a little scary, that's all."

Timothy went pale. "Well, I mean, did he force you to do anything you, I mean, are you ok?"

She made a sound like a whale clearing its snout. "Nothing I couldn't handle. But I don't think I'll go down to the beach for a few days. Fucking savage is probably lurking around there waiting to take a bite off my ass."

"Who was the guy?"

"Just somebody I met on the beach. Don't worry. You don't have to do anything."

"I don't know what to say, Jill."

She knew he would ask who the boy was, want to find out where he could find him. She also thought he would tell her to tone down her language. But then Timothy surprised her. He reached out to touch her face.

"Men aren't all like that," he said. "Believe me. You've just got to watch who you get alone with."

"Gee, thanks. Grandma said almost the same thing the other day and she didn't even know about this. All I know is nobody told me a guy goes after you like a one-man SWAT Team."

Timothy squatted down beside the couch. Jill closed her eyes, shook her head as if to clear it from a blow, and leaned back. He kissed her brow and smoothed back her hair. He felt like crying.

"So what do you want to do?" he asked.

"Leave."

"Leave? You mean like for a day in the city, Fifth Avenue, the Village and that?"

"I mean leave leave. Like to Michigan."

"When?"

"How long does it take to get plane tickets?"

20

NOTHING OPENED Timothy's mind like long, slow distance. The runner's LSD.

He ran west on the boardwalk for two miles until its end. Then he went down the ramp and looped onto the sand. It was too soft and dry for running, but once he got to the shoreline the wet sand was better. The tide was coming in. He turned back east and picked up his pace.

From there to Point Lookout would be a good five miles more, if the beach was open all the way. He figured that would be time enough to sort things out.

A: This was Jill's vacation. B: They'd been here a little more than two weeks. C: She says she's ready to leave New York for Michigan. So far so good.

But D: Timothy wasn't ready to leave.

Also E: He hadn't decided exactly where they would go in Michigan. The more he looked at the map, the less he felt like being there. He'd talked Michigan over with Jill a few times before they left, but she was no help.

"I've been thinking we shouldn't stay in the same part of Michigan we used to stay in," he had said, unfolding the map in their dining room.

"Fine. Where did we used to stay?" She glanced at the map where Timothy was pointing and then looked away. "All I remember is cheese."

"Your mother loved this part between the Thumb and Thunder Bay. That's why we bought the cabin there. You've been to all these little towns: Sebewaing, Pinconning, Au Sable, Alpena. Don't you remember those names?"

"Alpena I remember. I used to think it sounded funny, like maybe it was a dirty word."

"We used to go to the cheese festival in Pinconning. That's why you remember cheese."

"So what's wrong with staying there? As long as there's sun and a beach, I'll be all right."

"Memories. Bad feelings. I associate Lake Huron with a time that my life wasn't very happy."

"I always thought you liked it in Michigan. What were you so unhappy about?"

"We'll talk about it sometime. We'll look at the photo album and I'll try to tell you. But for now, let me get away with saying the idea of going back to Lake Huron doesn't thrill me."

"Then why'd you suggest it?"

"Beats me."

"Well, it's not like there's only four places we could stay up there. Looks like a big state. Just pick someplace. I trust you."

Timothy remembered the feeling of frustration that these conversations left him with. She really didn't care where they went. She didn't understand his mixed-up feelings, especially since he'd always sheltered her from knowing about their problems.

He suddenly found himself splashing ankle deep in water. He hadn't been paying attention to the tide. He adjusted, moving a few yards up from the foamy edge of the waves.

So it really wasn't an issue of where they would stay. Timothy knew that. He'd call his office and get a recommendation. It was an issue of his not wanting to leave here right now.

Jane. Talk about surprises. Timothy had come to New York expecting a couple of weeks with his mother, running the boardwalk and the beach, which he loved, maybe a Mets game or two, and lots of reading.

But what was going on? Last night, briefly, he and Jane had talked about it. They were standing by her window, looking at the night.

"In high school," Jane had said, "I didn't like you very much."

"In high school, I wasn't very likable. All I did was study math, run, and beat off."

"Doesn't sound like you've changed a whit in twenty-three years."

"I sell houses now."

Jane kissed him. Then she put a hand out the window as if testing for rain.

"Tim, I could never live away from here. I tried to once. But even with someone I loved, I don't think it would work."

"It's funny, how people think. I was just thinking that I could never live here, even with someone I loved."

"That sort of limits our future, wouldn't you say?"

Timothy wrapped his arms around her. "I'm way out of the habit of thinking about my future. My zone still seems to be the past."

"For want of a better word, I'd say that's poppycock. You're just scared."

"And you're not?"

"Of course I am. It never works when a guy's mother sets you up."

Timothy slowed to a jog. Just a few hundred yards ahead he could see the back of his mother's apartment.

It didn't require a ten mile run after all. He walked up the beach, under the boardwalk, and back to the apartment.

21

JILL WAS waiting for him when he got back upstairs. She still hadn't gotten dressed to go outside.

"That was fast," she said.

"I was a little tired."

"I can see that. You look like old celery. No offense, I heard that one on the beach last week." Jill brought a towel for him from the bathroom. "You had a call while you were out. You'll never guess who."

He wiped his face and neck.

"Was it Jane?"

"That's one wrong."

"My office? Great, maybe the Lattner house sold. I listed it and Jerry Monroe was going to handle the sale, one third-two thirds. We could use the extra money."

"And that's two wrong."

Timothy frowned. He didn't mind playing Jill's games, but he was stumped.

"At least get me some water while you're bugging me."

She sauntered to the cupboard, then the freezer, then the sink. A smile threatened to overrun her stern expression.

"It was your sweetheart, Dad." She handed him a large glass of ice water. "I'm surprised her name didn't come right up. You do remember Lauren Hazeltine, don't you?"

"When?" Timothy asked.

He'd reached Lauren in her office. It wasn't a good connection, though, because her voice sounded like she was overseas.

"End of the week. And I could stay on in the city after the seminar. That way we'd have the weekend together," she said.

"What rotten luck." Timothy actually snapped his fingers. "Jill and I just made plans to leave here for Michigan. We'll be gone by the end of the week."

Timothy turned his back to the den door, where Jill suddenly appeared. He was facing the entrance to the kitchen, where his mother now loomed. He put a finger in his ear to block out the din they didn't make.

"Too bad I didn't know sooner," he told Lauren.

"I just found out, myself."

"That's a shame, really is a shame. But I guess it won't work out. What about when we get to Michigan I send you a card, let you know where we are?"

"Fine. You do that. But I don't think there'll be a program up there in Michigan on changing regulatory policies in the thrift industry."

"You could take a few days off for a vacation."

"Not right after I take a few days off for a seminar. Some of us have regular jobs."

"So we'll work something out later."

"Maybe."

When Timothy hung up, Jill and his mother were staring at each other, not at him. He sat down.

"Nothing like a run to clarify my thoughts."

"I hear you're leaving in a couple days," his mother said.

"I hear we're leaving in a couple days," Jill said, imitating her grandmother's inflection.

"Jill," he said, turning to face her, "You were right. I think we'll be leaving in a couple days."

22

TIMOTHY AND Jill walked the three miles to Jane's house along the beach. It was another warm, windy evening. He was reminded of the candles flickering in Jane's bedroom and of her hand reaching out of the window.

Ahead of them, lights from buoys marking the bar flickered in the dusk. When he was Jill's age, this had been Timothy's favorite time of day and summer had been his favorite season of the year.

Even the beach itself liked the summer. Gentle swells would sweep the sand upward, steepening the beach so that it seemed to be reaching out to the sky.

Winter was another story. Winter would flatten the beach to spread the energy of its storm waves over a larger area. Timothy never wanted to greet a new year on the shore, like the other kids did, because he found the beaten, prostrate duneline depressing.

Now, with Jill beside him and the red sunset fading, with Jane's house suddenly visible as they followed the curve, Timothy felt peaceful. As before, now that he'd made up his mind to go, this became a difficult place to leave.

Jane was waiting for them outside. She sat in a lawn chair that was sunk to its knees in the sand. Her back was to the house and her view of the ocean was unimpeded.

She wore a white plastic hat with a floppy brim, a Columbia University tee shirt, and cut-off jeans. From a tape player she had balanced on the bedroom window sill, they could hear John Lennon singing "Come Together." It was one of Jill's favorite songs.

Clever woman, Timothy thought. She had dressed for the jury. Jill will like her.

Through heavy binoculars, Jane was scanning the horizon. The strap hung on her tee shirt like a necklace.

"Take it easy, Jane," Timothy said. "Don't rush around on account of us."

Jill started to sing along with John Lennon. When they reached the chorus, she stomped a foot in the sand and belted out: "Come together, right now."

Jane dropped the binoculars in her lap. Catching the beat perfectly, she added her voice to Jill's, reaching skyward as they sang "Over me."

They smiled at each other. "What were you looking at?"

"First, a couple of fishing boats heading around for the marina. Real exciting. But then, the sunset. I'm convinced if you watch the horizon and see the exact moment the sun sets, you'll have good luck for seven times seven days."

"Did you see it?"

"Nah, you guys came around the horn, so I watched you instead. I've got enough sunsets this summer to be lucky until I'm fifty-nine ."

"Do I eat it or drink it?" Jill asked.

"It's cold yogurt soup. 'An elegant starter for that light summer dinner,' the magazine says."

"Oh fun, what's the little green hairs floating in it?"

"Dill, Jill."

This cracked them up.

"So what was Billy like in high school?"

"Let's see. He was very popular. We all had a crush on him. I remember he was in the senior play and there was a scene where he had to kiss Melinda Collier on a couch. Now Melinda was stunning, the majorette, right? Huge boobs, long blonde hair, turned-up little nose. But she was five inches taller than Billy, at least. So we drew up a petition demanding that Melinda be dropped from the show because it would make Billy look foolish. But we couldn't decide which one of us would get to play the part instead, and we dropped it. I don't know what he had, but we all wanted it."

"It must be amazing, seeing him in the movies and all."

"Sometimes, in his stand-up routines, he uses the real names of people from school. I keep waiting for him to talk about me. But the thing that's amazing now is how many girls he must have dated and how many guys were his closest friend. Everybody I run into says they were at his Bar Mitzvah."

Jill cleared the table and helped Jane bring out the salad. She refilled Timothy's wine glass, stopping behind him to kiss the top of his head.

"Try some of this," Jane said. She handed Jill a dish with a small mound of chilled ratatouille. "And don't ask what it is till you're done."

Timothy hadn't spoken since the meal began and neither Jill nor Jane tried to force him. Jill thought he must be feeling sad because they would be leaving soon. Jane thought he must be lost in memories.

He watched, not hearing the words but only the female voices, the pleasure. Timothy understood how much of value Jill had missed, despite his attention and love. He was silent because he was unable to speak.

They were walking on the beach after dinner. Jill had an arm through her father's and a hand in Jane's.

"We leave the day after tomorrow," Timothy said.

"I know. Jill told me when we were doing the dishes." She stopped walking and the chain of contact broke. "It's not a surprise Tim. I never expected you to stay for long."

"It just came up. We only decided today."

"Look: I understand. You weren't deceiving me and I wish to hell you'd relax about it. I have the feeling we'll keep in touch."

"I'm going to write," Jill said.

"Maybe we can work something out later this summer. You could take a few days off for a vacation."

"I bet you say that to all the girls you leave behind."

"He does," Jill said. "I heard him."

23

MRS. PACKARD was back inside the hall closet. She must have been working at it for several hours, because there was a stack of plastic-wrapped dishes on the card table nearby.

Timothy recognized them immediately. In one bag were saucers, in another soup bowls, cups in a third. She was struggling to haul down the dinner plates when he arrived.

It was his grandparents' china. He remembered eating holiday dinners on them at their apartment in the Bronx. Off-white and burgundy bordered, decorated with blue thistles and pink roses, the delicate china brought back memories of endless Seders and gut-busting meals followed by long games of Casino.

"You should have these," Mrs. Packard said.

"I can't lug dishes around with me all summer."

"So we'll send them to the airport and one of your friends can pick them up."

"They might break."

"I've got ten years worth of excelsior stored in boxes in my closet. We'll pack so they wouldn't break if you dropped them from the moon."

"Mother, you might need them again."

Mrs. Packard turned slowly on the step-stool to stare at her son. Timothy was afraid she'd lean back as if against the sink, her normal position for such discussions, and topple off into the winter clothes.

"You and Jilly are the only ones I have left that I would eat with off china. And you're leaving, I don't know when we'll see each other again."

Timothy looked away, his eyes coming to rest on the array spread on his mother's card table. In their dusty bags, the china looked like table settings for a feast of ghosts.

"Is that it?" he asked.

Mrs. Packard reached out and Timothy helped her down. They embraced. He could feel her nodding against his chest and then she was sobbing.

SUMMER BLUE

———————————

PART THREE

Michigan

24

OLD MISSION Peninsula is a mutant finger on the hand of lower Michigan. Flecked with pear and cherry orchards, jeweled by luxurious homes, it pokes twenty miles north into Grand Traverse Bay.

Michigan 37 is a narrow highway leading to the tip of the peninsula and Old Mission Lighthouse. The lighthouse is perched midway between the North Pole and Equator.

Fine, Timothy thought. Right there. A place of balance.

It took all day to get from Mrs. Packard's house to the Holiday Inn in Traverse City. The plane was late leaving LaGuardia. They sweated on the runway for an hour and a half. Then they had to wait three more hours for the loud, crowded commuter flight across Michigan.

They reached the realtor's office at 5:15. The door of the old storefront was locked and the blinds were drawn. Timothy knocked on the glass, rattled the knob, tried to peer around the edge of the blinds.

"I don't believe it," he muttered.

The sign said summer hours were noon to four, and by appointment. He guessed the summer trade in a town like Traverse City got booked before early spring, which would leave little to do in July except handle complaints. No wonder there was nobody around.

"I should have called ahead."

"Dad, it was all kind of sudden. Why don't you have a beer, relax." She patted him on the shoulder. "Let me look around downtown. We can try again in the morning."

Jill left him at The Whitefish Lounge, promising to be back by 6:00. From the corridor beside the men's room, Timothy called the realtor's office. He rasped a terse message onto the answering machine for the agent whose name he'd been given—time of day, name, number where he could be reached.

Then he called her at home. He figured she wouldn't mind, since they were both in the business. With a name like Leah Bell, and with her reputation as a regular in the Million Dollar Sales Club, he imagined that she would always be ready for work.

Leah Bell's recorded voice boomed like a side-show barker's. Waiting for the tone, Timothy tried to remember where his friend said he'd met her. Was she the one he met in Reno that time, the one who'd been an actress?

Once he got started talking, Timothy couldn't stop. Amazing, what a day of travel can do to you.

"This is Timothy Packard calling, Leah. I'm a realtor from Illinois and I work with an acquaintance of yours named Jerry Monroe. Jerry speaks very highly of you and he suggested I get in touch when we arrived. My daughter and I just got to town on vacation and we're looking to rent a small cabin with lakefront for about two weeks. I'd appreciate it if you could call me, tonight if possible."

He chugged a second beer, feeling logy from sitting too long and eating too much airplane food. He needed a shower, a shave, a change of clothes. By the time Jill returned to The Whitefish, Timothy was waiting in front, leaning against its wall like a vagrant.

In their rented Datsun, Jill and Timothy drove out to the lighthouse. It was not yet dark.

The motel clerk had told them Old Mission Point was particularly beautiful on warm evenings. She promised to make a note of any messages.

They met a truckload of migrant workers halfway out the peninsula. The crew was heading back from the orchards, looking tired as the truck pulled into the parking lot of a cafe that served beer. Otherwise, Timothy and Jill seemed alone.

"We'll find a cabin in the morning," Timothy said. "By this time tomorrow, we'll be all set."

"I'm in no rush. A few days by the motel pool would be all right with me."

"I appreciate that you understand about the beach. I don't like to break my promises."

"It's ok, really."

"The more I thought about it, the less I could see dredging up bad memories, spending vacation time in a place that would sadden me. This is new, up here. It'll be better for both of us."

Jill nodded. "It's ok."

She understood that her father needed to explain. He needed to be sure she accepted his reason for changing their plan. The deal had been three beaches, and now he was talking about some lake where there might be nothing for her to do.

But after a quick tour, Traverse City looked all right to her. It had lots of small shops and places to hang out, and she'd seen several kids around her age in a park at the mouth of the bay.

They were dressed right. They had portable tape players and head phones, and they were laughing.

"I like it here fine," she said. "I wouldn't mind if you got a place for us that wasn't too far out. Then you could read or fish, or whatever you want to do, and I could spend some time in town when I got bored with nature."

"We'll see what's available."

Jill gazed out into the bay. Timothy settled for her silence.

He watched his daughter as she quickly forgot his presence. She seemed to be changing almost daily, thinning, becoming more striking in her angular beauty. And she had a way of keeping to herself without seeming to exclude him.

Jill was staring across the bay. Timothy thought she must be trying to see all the way to Lake Michigan, trying to see across the Upper Peninsula and Lake Superior, north into Ontario and beyond to Foxe Basin, across Baffin Island to Baffin Bay and the top of the goddamn world.

25

THE WHITE Saab pulled up before the motel with its front wheel on the curb. Timothy bent to smile through the passenger window before trying the door.

Leah Bell looked like a computer-enhanced image of Marilyn Monroe at age fifty. There was even the pouf of platinum blonde hair, a small mole on her left cheekbone, that neat parade of teeth when she smiled back at him.

The body, even while she was seated, was obviously luxurious. Her skin was creamy. She had enormous round eyes, oyster-colored and moist. She favored blues in her dress, reds and orange for the accents.

As she leaned over to unlock the door for Timothy, the eyes were also frightened. He thought she seemed to be pleading that he not see where she was weak. It had been a long time since Timothy saw a style like hers.

"Do put that list away, cutie," she said, straightening as he sat beside her. She pointed to the steno pad he held in his hand. "Tell little Leah what you're after and then just leave everything to me."

"I went through the morning paper at breakfast. Just in case."

"Just in case what? I told you on the tellie we'd find your dream place, didn't I?" She patted his thigh while looking in the rearview mirror. "Now don't be vile."

Timothy put the note pad in his breast pocket. "I always look at the classifieds."

"Buckle up, Mr. Packard." Leah said as she pulled onto the highway.

"I'm sure no friend of Jerry Phillips wants a cabin that's already been listed in the newspaper."

"Jerry Monroe."

She was, simply, a stunning woman. Even this close, she looked half her age and evoked responses Timothy thought he'd conquered:

72

protect me, cherish me, use me. And she did everything in her power to confound those responses.

He was a little dazed. She smiled at him as if recognizing her impact, then slowly—almost regretfully—turned her attention back to the road.

Here she was, showing bedrooms and living rooms to a widower on vacation. As a realtor, he thought, she was close to unfair competition. Yet she was so long accustomed to inhabiting men's fantasies that she seemed to doubt her own substance.

That could explain the voice. He'd never heard anything quite like it.

Her speech aspired to the vulgar. She whined, joked, blared, and blathered; she sounded like Peggy Cass with a midwestern accent. Driving with her left Timothy little room to think about what he was seeing.

Leah changed the radio station after every commercial. She talked to traffic lights and street signs, to other drivers, to the Saab itself. She checked a map folded and clipped to the sun visor while she drove on the narrow, curving roads of the county. From time to time, there was a fact thrown in about the town, about the cabin they'd just seen with mosquito netting torn off the porch, or about the room they'd lingered in while he poked the paneling, but Timothy often missed it.

She showed him five cabins in two hours and each one was exactly what he'd said he wanted. She ambled through each with reckless grace.

They headed back toward town shortly after 2:00. At the outskirts, she pulled into a small shopping center and jammed the car into park before it came to a stop. They rocked in place while she spoke.

"I simply must have an iced coffee," Leah said. She licked her lips. "Perhaps you can tell? I am a woman who needs constant rehydration."

"Then let me buy. I want to go over my notes, anyway."

He got out, scooted around to Leah's side and opened her door. She emerged awkwardly, as if not quite accustomed to gravity.

"Yes, I saw you scribbling in that little book of yours. It was very touching."

"I didn't want to get the cabins confused later. This helps me keep them straight."

"Really, Tim." She touched his biceps on her way through the door. "They're all very much alike. Go with your gizzards, I'd say."

Timothy wished he'd brought Jill along.

He chose a cabin on Star Lake, only one mile from downtown. Jill would like that.

Star Lake was a broad body of water that narrowed to five points. They would be at the northern tip, cut off from the water skiers, and shaded from the midday heat.

Their cabin was set steeply down off the state road. Its roof was about level with the asphalt and maybe thirty yards away from it. The cabin was the last in a group of four and was the newest, though it appeared to be the oldest. They were well hidden among the first-growth trees.

Above the entrance, burnt into a cedar plaque, were the words "Fons et Origo." Leah said they were probably the names of the owners' children. The mailbox at the edge of the highway said "Quintana."

The cabin was larger than they needed, but Timothy's gizzards liked the rough-hewn exterior and African artifacts on the walls. While standing in the kitchen, he could look through the thick stand of hickory and imagine that the site had just been hacked out of unexplored wilderness.

A dented canoe was tethered to a stump, its paddles roped to the seat. There were fishing poles and tackle in a shed behind the cabin. Timothy had been fishing twice in his life, never since puberty.

Leah had said the nights would be cold. She'd pointed to a cord of wood on the porch.

"You'll need a fire," she said. "And if you think of it, bring in some dry kindling."

"There's no tv?"

"You couldn't get decent reception anyway. But there is a radio in one of the bedrooms and there's a phone in the bathroom."

"And I suppose the toilet's in the kitchen."

"I don't build them, Tim, I just rent them."

Later, when he showed the cabin to Jill, Timothy wished he'd given *her* gizzards a chance to react before he'd written the check. She looked stunned.

"If I wanted to go to summer camp, I'd have said so."

"The realtor said this one was the quietest point on the lake."

Jill frowned. "Who lives in those other cabins?"

"Leah didn't say." Timothy opened the cupboards and drawers, something he'd forgotten to do the first time through. "We can move in Monday and stay two weeks."

"Good. That gives me the weekend to learn my way around downtown."

26

THE ELIASONS, Terrence Delannoy and the Sharpes lived in the other cabins. Timothy and Jill met them within the first two hours, when each came by to say hello. They didn't see them again all day.

The Eliasons were from Indianapolis. They had two small kids and an older girl named Corrie who was with them as a mother's helper. Margaret Eliason said Corrie would come by after dinner, when the children were in bed.

"You'll love her."

Terrence Delannoy had his friend Richard visiting from St. Paul for a month. Apparently, Richard played piano.

From the porch where he went for wood, Timothy could hear Richard playing Chopin. Later, it was a Scott Joplin rag. He was surprised Leah hadn't mentioned him. Having Richard nearby might prove better than having a radio.

The Sharpes would be leaving on Thursday. They had owned their cabin since before the others were built and would have sold it a long time ago if they'd known their hide-a-way was going to turn into a subdivision. Mac Sharpe thought his son's family would be staying in the cabin for the next three weeks. He planned to be out of there well in advance of when the brood arrived.

Despite her grumbling, Jill liked being at the cabin. It smelled woody, she thought, and was pleasantly cool. She called it Fonzie and Oregano, and cooked a tuna casserole for their supper.

"I've been thinking," she said when the food was ready. "You know what this is an excellent time for?"

"For reading Charles Dickens?"

"This is an excellent time for you to teach me how to drive."

"Good casserole."

"I mean it. Out in the boonies, nothing to do. None of your usual excuses. Besides, it's in your best interests. Only a year till I get my license. You should want me to have a lot of practice."

"It's not even our car, Jilly."

"One more good reason."

"And you don't have a permit."

"Who cares about that? Cops probably don't cruise all the way out here unless there's a murder or something. Come on."

She wouldn't ease up. Timothy promised to think about it.

"Let's go for a canoe ride," he said when they were done with the dishes.

"A canoe ride? You have to be kidding."

"That's what people do on lakes. Especially at sunset."

"If you row."

"Paddle."

"The point is, I don't do any of the work. But I will provide the music."

"Music?"

"*Hot Rocks.* Through the magic of my boom box."

"Couldn't you bring along some Bach too?"

"What group is he with?"

"You're sure in a good mood."

"It's the great outdoors."

27

WHEN THEY got back, Corrie was sitting on the porch in a loop of light. Timothy saw her first and felt a rush of relief. There would be a companion for his daughter.

Jill walked up to meet her while Timothy tied down the canoe. Corrie's head tilted toward the sound. Had someone mentioned that the girl was blind?

Seated on the steps, hands folded on her drawn-up knees and chin resting on her hands, Corrie looked elegant. Her thick black hair was swept around to one side and fell over her shoulder.

Jill guessed nineteen. But nineteen was old for a mother's helper.

Corrie stood as Jill walked out of the darkness. She was tall and thin, but not lanky. Jill admired her looks, her composure. There was something foreign about her appearance, something worldly about its focus.

Corrie wasn't blind. In fact, her eyes moved as if to see everything in the world. Their eyes met, quickly scanned each other's face and clothes, then met again.

"I like your jacket," Corrie said.

"Did you make that necklace yourself?"

Corrie nodded. She pointed to Jill's tape player. "Let me guess. Talking Heads?"

"I look like the Talking Heads type?" Jill sat down and Corrie joined her. "Where'd I go wrong?"

"I was going to say Bruce Springsteen, but I didn't want to risk offending you. In Indiana, he's always The Boss."

"The Stones, actually. We were in the boat longer than I expected. My dad hates The Stones."

"They all do. They've hated every good group since The Ink Spots."

"You know what? We just came from my grandmother's in New

York. I found out she used to have a show on radio. She even played me some of her old records. It was pretty amazing."

"Boy, I'm glad you're here. There's no one to talk to except the little brats and the dilts."

"Dilts?"

"Adults. Groans." She pointed toward the lake. "As in grown-ups."

"So what's there to do?"

"Not much. You could come over in the morning, we'll tire the brats out and haul them downtown for lunch."

"You must be Corrie," Timothy said. The girls hadn't heard him approach. He leaned against the porch railing beside the steps.

She smiled, gazing in his general direction. She looks tired, Timothy thought. Children can do that to you.

"Corrine Gable, Mr. Packard. I'm the Eliason's *au pair*. I suppose you figured that out, though."

"From Indianapolis, too?"

"Anderson. It's not far. I heard about the Eliasons from some friends of my mom. At church."

"Must be a nice way to spend the summer. Up here, on your own."

"It's not bad." She stood up to leave. "Beats Anderson."

"I'll walk you back," Jill said.

28

JILL KNEW she'd never get the Eliason kids straight. Three days, and she still wasn't sure which was which.

The little girls were about fifteen months apart, six and seven. Both were tow-headed and both were the same size. Their mother dressed them in matching outfits, down to the tiny pink running shoes.

"What did they do, cast them?" Jill asked.

"You can tell them apart after a while," Corrie said. "Miriam has the crooked teeth, Mary has the longer bangs."

"What about from the back?"

"It really doesn't matter. They both come when you call one of them."

They were in the park by the bay downtown, pushing the children in swings. Boys appeared to be everywhere, popping out from behind trees to say hello or skateboarding along the seawall to wave at them. Corrie seemed to know most of the boys by name.

"Who's your new friend?" one of them called.

"My sister Elizabeth," Corrie told him.

"This is Rachel," she told another. "She's a student over at the music camp."

"Meet my friend Grace Deface," she told a third. This one wore a leather vest over bare skin and was at least twenty-two. "She's from home."

After the first day, Jill always wore shorts and a halter top. It might be cool by the cabins in the morning, but the days got brutally hot. Still, Corrie dressed for spring. Jill wondered why her friend didn't fade, as she would have dressed like that in the midday heat.

They continued to push Miriam and Mary, ignoring their cries to go higher.

"These nice Bible names, too," Jill said, still trying to master their identities. "Did you go to the same branch of church as the Eliasons? To the same sect or whatever it's called?"

"Listen, Jill, none of that stuff I said the other day was true. I didn't meet the Eliasons through church. My mom's been lapsed so long she's out of the club. I was placed with Eliason, there wasn't any friend."

"Placed?"

"Yeah. By the court. It was either the Eliasons or The Farm."

The kids hopped down because Jill and Corrie had stopped pushing. They dashed over to the slide.

"You lost me back at the church."

"That with your dad the other night, it was just a story I told. Probably not one true fact in the whole thing. My last name isn't even

Gable." They followed Miriam and Mary toward the slide. "Hey, take it easy, kids!"

"What farm? What court? Slow down."

"Just forget it."

"I mean, was your mom trying to get rid of you for the summer or something?"

"Hardly. I was about to be sent to the youth farm downstate. For frequent offenders."

Jill touched Corrie's arm and stopped. "What are you telling me?"

"Some truth."

Jill skipped ahead, then spun around to look at her. "So you had a little trouble, right?"

Corrie laughed. "You might say that."

"What was it?"

"Mary, hold her hand!"

Jill looked over at Miriam and Mary. There was one more thing she wanted to know.

"You were doing drugs?"

"Was. But I've been clean up here." Corrie gathered her hair and held it up off her neck. What Jill wouldn't give for such a long neck, such long thin arms. Corrie had scratch marks on the back of her arms and a few on her legs, as though a cat had gotten rough with her. "Whew, it's warm."

"Then why don't you wear summer clothes?"

"You really want to know?"

"Oh, God, don't tell me!" Jill started to walk again, this time more quickly. "Not needle tracks."

Corrie laughed. "Needle tracks? You're really out of it, you know that? I mean, like from Mars. Nobody shoots up any more. They snort, or they get into the pipe."

Jill tried to steady herself. She couldn't tell if she was frightened or excited.

"Then what is it?"

"It's just that I'd feel funny." She pointed to her chest, then cupped her hands and shook her head. "I'm seventeen and there's nothing here. The titless wonder. So I dress loose and long."

"But you're so pretty, Corrie. What wouldn't I do to have your legs? I don't believe this."

"Boys don't want pretty. They want tits."

"You're too much. I see how the boys flock around you."

"That's another thing. And I was in trouble for it back home, too."

They were interrupted by Miriam and Mary running over to grab their legs.

"We're hungry," one of them whined.

"But you just ate lunch," Corrie's voice softened when she spoke to the girls.

"For ice cream," said the other.

They trudged up from the park. Corrie had a girl by each hand and Jill trailed a step behind her.

"Do the Eliasons know?"

"They've got my whole record. I told you they're part of this program I'm in."

"And about here?"

"There's nothing to know about here."

"Corrie, why are you telling me all this?"

"So you'll know."

Jill shook her head as if trying to clear it. She followed Corrie and the kids to the ice cream store in silence.

Know? she thought. I don't even know your last name.

29

THAT NIGHT, after the kids were in bed, Corrie and Jill walked over to Terrence Delannoy's cabin. It was a cool night and Jill had slipped jeans and a sweatshirt over her day's clothes.

She enjoyed being with Corrie during the day, but she relished being with her at night. That was when Corrie seemed more like a big sister than a new friend. It was also when—with Miriam and Mary out of the way—Corrie seemed likely to say just about anything.

"I go here a lot," Corrie said. "Terry always has the most interesting guests. The Eliasons said there was—I couldn't get over this—there was a real minister with him when we first got here. The last one, before Richard, was this heavenly looking dancer from Chicago."

"What is he?" Jill asked.

"A zoologist."

"That's not what I meant."

"I didn't think it was. Make sure you check out the stuff he's got hanging on the walls."

In black jeans and a sleeveless black tee shirt, his muscular back to the door, Richard sat at the piano. He was looking toward the bronze wrestlers above the fireplace while he played. In the stark light of a naked bulb, his shaven head shone with sweat.

Corrie shut the screen door gently and sat down beside Terrence Delannoy on the floor. He smiled at her from beneath a drooping mustache, but his eyes weren't focused. He seemed hypnotized.

"It's a Polonaise," he whispered. "Number 6, in A-Flat."

Corrie put her hand on Terrence's shoulder. "Sounds like dance music."

"It was, originally. Stately and formal dance music."

Jill sat on a director's chair near the fire place. She watched Richard's long arms move easily, like wings, and then she watched Terrence lean back against Corrie's legs like an old lover.

When he was finished, Richard spun around and smiled at the girls. He didn't seem to mind how Terrence and Corrie were sitting.

"Chopin has such variety," he said. His voice was plush, a cushion of sound. Jill thought his smile was for the music, not for the guests. "So many moods, so many styles, such an assortment of architecture."

"Yes," Terrence said, still whispering. "Chopin appeals to everyone. Just like our Corrie here." He ran his fingers through her hair. "Something for every taste."

"Could I have some of your fancy coffee, Terry?"

He rose immediately. "Richard, play a little pop for these young girls while I make them cappuccinos, will you?"

"If you make another Irish for me."

"Consider it done."

Richard closed his eyes as Terrence walked away. The girls watched him. He went through a few facial contortions, screwing his eyes shut tightly, pursing his lips, dilating his nostrils. He gagged a little, coughed. It seemed as if he were undergoing some kind of transformation. Still seated on the stool, he bowed his head, settling.

Then, with his head still down, he spun quickly around again, stopping himself by bringing his hands down hard on the keys in a resounding chord.

Corrie squealed with delight, clapping her hands. She recognized Richard's act and knew the song from its opening crash.

She dragged Jill over to the piano. They rested their elbows on its top, touching each other's fingertips as if passing along a field of force.

"Sing along, now," Richard said. "Help!"

"I need somebody."

"Help!"

"Not just any body."

"Hel-l-lp!"

30

TIMOTHY RAN up to the main road and turned north. The paved surface did not have enough shoulder to run on and was not as yielding as the boardwalk had been. He would pay for it with aching shins in a few days.

At least there wasn't much traffic. He stayed close to the edge, listening for cars he wouldn't be able to see around the curves.

He'd dressed light, remembering how warm the days were. But in the early chill, he had to run hard to get warm and could see his breath whisked back across his face.

The road curved, following abandoned railroad tracks. He could hear dogs. They seemed to be beyond the tracks, but as the road swung east he could tell they were actually on his side of the road.

Timothy didn't want to meet a loose dog that wasn't used to runners. He checked his watch, figuring that another couple of minutes would make it three miles out. Then he would turn back.

A Doberman the size of a deer burst out of the weeds to his left and came toward him. A line of froth settled on its nose. Timothy froze.

The dog stopped too. It trembled and began to bark again, bearing his teeth. But it didn't advance.

"Nice doggie."

Timothy decided to grant the dog his territory, three miles or not. He backed up, looking over the dog's ears down the road, smiling.

"I'm out of here, Dobe," he said, hoping it sounded soothing. "See the nice man go backwards? It's been sweet. Bye bye for now."

The dog didn't come after him. When Timothy had backed through the curve, he turned and began to run again. Slow and easy, trying to get his breath back. He was tight, suddenly cool again.

Then he heard another dog barking. This one sounded like it might be just around the curve.

"Don't listen to him," he said to the memory of the first dog.

Timothy crossed to the track side of the road and continued running. Another Doberman, this one chained to a tree, was frothing at him from the field. It stopped barking and gripped a metal food bowl in its mouth, watching Timothy pass, snarling, jerking his head with rage. Timothy could see the dog's slobber flying around its head.

The rising sun glinted off the bowl.

Back at the cabin, warming in a long shower, Timothy thought it would be nice to run with a partner again. He almost always ran alone.

At home, of course, there was Lauren. But running with her wasn't exactly relaxing. It had the constant byplay, the underlying presence of sexual possibility, an energy of its own to impose.

Timothy had no close male friends. Jerry Monroe at the office was someone he could talk to over coffee, but they seldom got together outside. Besides, Jerry could hardly walk to his car, much less run.

Timothy had joined the Road Runners Club and was a member of the Y, but never had time for meetings. The people he met as clients were always in transition, moving in or out, happy to deal with him for a small part of their lives but not likely to become permanent companions.

When was the last time he'd had a close male relationship? College track team, maybe.

His first year with the power company, Timothy worked with Johnny Holladay Moore on a project and they'd become close. They put together a plan for replacing the substation near Pleasant Plains.

Twice a week from November through March, Holladay drove them out to the little town, always stopping for breakfast on the way. He had plans.

"This is my last winter," Holladay told him. "This time next year, I'm in Tucson."

"What's in Tucson?"

"This morning in Tucson? Seventy-eight degrees. This morning here? Minus two. Minus thirty if you count the wind chill."

"Never happen," Timothy told him. "For every ten guys thinking like you, there's probably half a job. How would you live?"

"String wire. Not that, I could learn to mine copper. They do a lot of that. Or electronics. The Silicon Desert. Whatever it takes, pal."

They went out together on New Year's Eve that year. Charlene was away, visiting her family in California. Holladay had no special plans.

The following Monday, he was gone. Timothy waited for him at the motor pool until 9:00, then went upstairs to check.

Holladay called a week later from Pittsburgh, where the wife and son he'd never mentioned had been living. He was about three years behind in support payments. Among the choices he'd been given, going back home seemed the smartest.

Timothy called once, a few weeks later. That was it. He never heard from Holladay again.

Timothy shut off the shower and stepped onto the sodden wood floor to dry himself. He hadn't thought about this much before. All his friends—at least the few people he thought might be classified as friends instead of acquaintances—were women.

31

JILL AND Corrie were at a table in the playground behind McDonald's. They'd bought a bag of fries to share, but only Jill was eating them.

"No wonder you're so thin. I never see you eat."

"My appetite comes and goes. If I eat too much sometimes, it just makes me throw up."

Miriam and Mary rocked on toy horses that had thick blue springs for legs. The girls never squealed. They showed their delight with polite giggles.

It was the first cool afternoon since Jill had arrived in Michigan and she was shivering in her sleeveless shirt. Corrie kept looking beyond Jill's shoulder, announcing events on the street like a parade broadcaster.

"There's Felix Quintana. Look at the lovely flowers on Felix's Hawaiian shirt! The Quintana's have a chain of buffet restaurants here in Traverse City. It's his uncle that owns your cabin, Jill.

"And next, twerpy Marcus Ridley carrying his skateboard because they won't allow it on the brick streets of beautiful Traverse City. So what's Marcus doing? He's rolling it along the walls just to hear the sweet noise of the wheels. Somebody told me Marcus has a little pail that he keeps upside down beside his toilet at home so he can hold one foot up like it was on a skateboard when he pees.

"Oh my God, there's Jack and Tina, arm in arm in arm. Jack and Tina have been going together since the second grade. They no longer have last names. Tell me, Jack and Tina, how do you do it? Is it the matching sweaters and matching shirts? The positive and negative braces? Sorry, Jill; no offense meant.

"And now, sports fans, it's Robbie Aswell. Robbie is Mr. Traverse City High, King of the Apple Blossom Festival and President of the Student Body. Of course, this student has a lovely body, but flawed. It's covered in those gross little bumps. Can we get a close up of that? Isn't it a shame? Robbie could go to any university in the country. He's the quarterback, you know what I mean? No one plays as well as Aswell. But he's probably got acne even on his dick."

"You kill me, Corrie," Jill interrupted, laughing. "I mean, how do you know all this? You're supposed to be from Indiana."

"This is a small town." Corrie looked distracted. "And besides, I've been around it all summer."

Suddenly, she stood up, watching Robbie Aswell until he turned the corner. Her brows knit, then relaxed, as if some problem she'd been puzzling over had just been solved.

"Hey, watch the kids for me," she said. "I want to get us some Diet Cokes, ok?"

Corrie was off before Jill could answer. Jill watched her through the window. Her tall image moved gracefully through the restaurant. She went out the door on the other side without stopping to place her order.

32

"YOU BUSY?"

"It's July, Tim," said Leah Bell. "I'm never busy in July."

"Well, I'm at The Whitefish and I don't feel like going to my cabin."

"You're at The Whitefish at noon? I didn't have you figured for a lush."

"This is where it gets complicated. I'm in my running shorts, I need to take a shower in water that comes out with enough force to get the soap off of me, and I'd like to spend the afternoon looking at commercial property."

"Now that's a new one." She guffawed, then paused to catch her breath. "Listen, my ex used to call from The Whitefish at noon, too. Near the end, when his voice was shot, I could swear it was his liver that spoke."

"Could you spare the afternoon?"

"I didn't know you were thinking about investing."

"I'm not. I was thinking about getting into commercial sales. I thought maybe you could give me a primer?"

"A primer? Son, I don't do kinky." Leah laughed again, her voice so loud Timothy had to hold the phone away from his ear. "You know how to get out here?"

"Yes. You pointed it out when we were looking at cabins."

"You must have a good memory."

"For houses I do."

Timothy parked in Leah's driveway ten minutes later. He had a change of clothes in the back seat.

He wondered what it was about this woman that made him call her almost every day. They wouldn't be lovers, he was fairly certain of that. Besides, he wasn't interested in an affair right now. He was still trying to untangle his feelings about Jane and Lauren. And he wanted time for Jill, although his daughter was always wrapped up in the life of some new friend and had little time for him.

He'd promised himself to be on the lake every day—to fish or canoe or swim—but so far he hadn't done it. He'd promised himself to listen to more classical music, to read a classic novel every two or three weeks. But so far, he hadn't gotten past buying a used copy of *David Copperfield.*

The only new thing he'd managed to do at least once a day was call Leah Bell. It was more than comradeship, two colleagues at ease with each other. Timothy liked being with her. She'd begun to tone down her act a little.

He grabbed his clothes and got out of the car. Leah was standing in the doorway, leaning against the frame while she watched him approach.

The walls in Leah's bathroom were decorated with fifties kitsch. One was papered with news clippings, playbills, and catalogue pages. A poster of Yma Sumac, the haughty chanteuse who claimed to be an Aztec princess, hung behind the door. Some people believed in her story, others said she was really Amy Camus from The Bronx. No one knew for sure.

Leah had soaps in the shape of toy Edsels and Chevy Bel-Airs. There was a decoupage of old 45-rpm records, shellacked into the shape of a disk, hanging over the toilet. There was an old issue of *Life* on top of the hamper with a picture of Adlai Stevenson on its cover.

Timothy's first reaction to all this was to moan. But as he changed his clothes, he stood close and read the labels of the 45s: The Platters, Cogi Grant, The Elegants, Elvis. It made him feel at ease, on familiar ground, as if he and Leah had grown up together. He sang as he showered, hitting all the high notes.

When he came downstairs, Leah handed him a glass of orange juice and led him down a short flight of steps. They sat together in her living room.

"This is all I've got that isn't booze or full of fizz. I use it to make screwdrivers."

"It'll do just fine. I had about a gallon of water at The Whitefish."

"Did Mac Wilson charge you for the water?"

"Nah, we're buddies now."

"So what's this, you want to go into commercial? Is that right?"

"I've been thinking about it."

"Well, here's little Leah's checklist: down there where you live, what're the hot businesses?"

"Tourism, for all the Lincoln stuff. Some education. Services. Most of the industry's gone."

"They got a shopping mall yet?"

"Four."

"Office space."

"Yes."

"Lots of restaurants?"

"All Italian or Chinese."

"You know what?"

"What?"

"I think this idea of yours was just a come on, wasn't it? You hoped I'd walk in on you in the shower."

"No, I'm serious."

"Then listen to me. Don't go into commercial real estate."

Leah drove him on a circuit of the city, pointing out new commercial properties and giving him their histories. She was less nervous than on the day they looked at cabins. This time she didn't fiddle with the radio and she didn't talk to traffic signals.

"I see lots of new office building," Timothy said.

"Yeah. Most of it's vacant, too. But you can't see that from the car."

"What's that, over by the trees? The A-frame with a warehouse behind it."

"That was going to be where the world's finest cherry brandy got made. Grand Traverse Distillery. The plan was impeccable. Take the best fruit—Michigan cherries—which grow right here in the area. Bring in authentic pots from Germany, all kinds of filters and genuine oak casks. Nose around the Alps and the Pyrenees to learn how to make brandy right. It was a lovely tour. Trouble was, the stuff they made here tasted like syrup at the International House of Pancakes. Closed without selling a bottle."

"Too bad."

"That's what my ex thought. He was a major investor, along with some old-time local families like the Aswells and the Boynes."

Heading back toward downtown, they drove past an abandoned construction site on several acres with a clear view of the bay. The huge hole behind a chain-link fence was nearly filled with rainwater. Timothy turned to face Leah, his back against the door.

"You planned this whole itinerary carefully, didn't you? Vacant offices, a dead distillery. Then let's wrap it up with a tour of the little commercial property that couldn't."

She chuckled. "Nothing uglier to an investor than hole in the ground with no bulldozer nearby."

"Ok. I'll reconsider."

"Buffalo," she said, pointing to a herd on a hill. "You ever think about raising buffalo down there in Illinois? The meat's better than cow."

She drove through downtown by the scenic route, following the bay. Several of the motels already had the No lit up above their Vacancy signs. As they approached the entrance to The Whitefish parking lot, Leah patted him on the leg.

"Stick with what you know," she said.

"That's easy for you to say. You're driving the Saab."

"The residential market's coming back. I read about it in the paper."

She got out when he did, her Saab idling loudly. Timothy thanked her for the afternoon.

"People will always need houses," she added. "That's what I say." Then she got back in and drove away.

Timothy turned to where his car was parked and saw Jill sitting on the trunk. The two little Eliason girls were playing with her boom box and Jill was crying.

33

"FANCY MEETING you here."

"Where were you?" Jill wiped her nose. "I've been sitting here for hours."

"I was looking at buildings."

"Is that all you were doing?"

"No. There were buffalo, too."

"Sure, Dad. Even I can do better than that. Who was that lady?"

"That was no lady, that was my friend Leah." Timothy wagged his eyebrows like Groucho Marx, but Jill wasn't going to be amused. He put his arm around her. "Ok, what's the matter?"

"I don't know. I mean, I honestly do not understand what's going on." Jill looked down at the kids. "Corrie asked me to watch these two while she got us some Diet Cokes and then she never came back."

"When was that?"

"Noon. Now it's almost 5:00."

"That's strange. But to me it doesn't sound like crying time."

"Maybe it doesn't to you. But Corrie's my friend."

"There's something you're not telling me. Do you think she's in trouble?"

"No. No trouble. She only disappeared."

Miriam and Mary had stopped playing and were staring at Jill.

"I'm sure there's a simple explanation," Timothy said. "Now should we try to find her, or just go home?"

"It's not home."

34

THE NEXT morning, while Timothy and Jill were eating breakfast, Corrie knocked on the screen door. She walked in smiling, holding the door so it wouldn't slam.

Jill looked at her, looked at her father, and dropped her spoon into the cereal bowl with a clatter.

"Abracadabra."

"Sorry about yesterday, Jill."

Corrie came over to their table and sat down opposite Timothy. He pointed to a plate of toast.

"Hungry?"

Corrie shook her head, continuing to talk. She didn't take her eyes off Jill.

"It was really weird. I ran into this friend of the Eliasons at the counter. We went outside and just got to talking. Then before I knew it, it was dark out. Didn't you see me?"

Jill gaped at her as if watching a magician perform.

"I was at those round tables with the umbrellas," Corrie said. "Anyway, thanks for watching the kids."

"It's all right."

"How about we rent a movie and watch it this afternoon on the Eliason's VCR?" Corrie asked. "I could use a quiet day."

"My dad and I were going to try fishing."

"Fishing? Nobody catches anything in Star Lake, it's jinxed."

Jill studied Corrie for a moment before responding. Timothy thought she was trying to make herself be angry, or trying to stare Corrie down. It made him uneasy to see his daughter doubting this friendship. It also made him uneasy to hear Corrie rattle on.

"Dad," she said, still watching Corrie, "tell her that story about the guy you went to engineering school with. The one who used to go out and zap the worms whenever he wanted to go fishing."

"God, Jilly, Lew Yancey. I haven't thought about Yancey in years. Why do you want to bring that up?"

"Corrie just reminded me of it, that's all. Talk about fishing and jinxes."

Timothy shrugged. "Do you know anything about night crawlers, Corrie?"

"Not much. I know you buy them in a bait store and they're supposed to wriggle a lot."

"Sometimes, and true. This friend of mine at school refused to waste his money buying worms. Besides, he was a science whiz. So when people told him he couldn't catch night crawlers except at night, and except when the ground was moist, he saw it as a challenge. That's when he came up with a worm zapper."

"Don't forget about the sprinkling can," Jill said.

"Right. Whenever he wanted to go fishing, Lew would get out the sprinkling can that he used in his garden. He was just like Mr. Wizard—you know Mr. Wizard?"

"A famous fisherman?"

"Skip it. First, my friend Lew would wet down the dirt behind his house. Then he'd find two metal rods and knock them a few feet into the ground. He'd take an old piece of cord, like from a toaster, fray the ends, and wrap the wires inside it around one of the rods. Then he'd plug the other end into a socket, which sent a charge between the two rods that was conducted by the wet ground.

"Pretty soon, all these night crawlers would come wriggling up into the air and he'd just scoop them into his bucket. I never went fishing with him, so I don't know how good he was on the water, but he was a wonder at catching worms."

When she was sure he was finished, Corrie sat back in her chair. Timothy smiled at her.

But Corrie's stare had begun to unnerve him. She had a way of looking plundered, as if her insides had been scooped out while you sat there thinking she was solid.

"Yuk," she said.

"I think it's neat," Jill said.

35

"WHAT WAS that all about?" Corrie asked.

"Worms."

"Worms give me the creeps."

They sat on the gunwales of the canoe. Miriam and Mary played in the shallow water behind the Eliason's cabin, trying to catch minnows in plastic buckets. They splashed and plunged headlong after shadows.

"Lies give me the creeps."

"Don't be mad at me. Please, Jill. I told you what happened."

"You didn't run into any friends of anybody at any counter in McDonalds."

"You mustn't have seen me. What I told your dad was the truth."

"Corrie! I watched you march right through McDonalds and out the other side. So tell me what's going on, and tell me the truth, or just leave me alone. I can get along fine by myself, you know."

Corrie didn't answer right away. She looked in the general vicinity of the kids, but wasn't watching them.

"Would you believe I'm having an affair with Mr. Eliason?"

"No I wouldn't."

"Would you believe I'm in counseling and that Terrence Delannoy is helping me? I had to go talk with him."

"No."

"Would you believe I'm doing crack again? Some guy named Santa meets me in the alley behind the comedy club to sell the stuff."

"No."

"You really should start believing me, Jill."

"About what?"

"Take your pick."

36

At first, Jill didn't see the man. He was leaning against the graffiti-covered wall of the club, blending into it as if by camouflage.

When he spoke, her body went rigid. Only her head turned toward him.

"Ho-ho-ho," he said. "What have we here?"

In an instant, the man's image was burned into Jill's memory.

Dreadlocks hung behind the Detroit Tigers cap pulled low on his fore-head. He wore wraparound shades that miraculously stayed up on his bridgeless nose.

"Hi you, daughter. I'm Santa." The voice was mostly breath. "Actually, Eddy. But they call me Santa. You lookin for me?"

"I'm not looking for anything," she managed to say.

All Jill could see of his face was a thin mustache and flash of teeth. Where were his ears? She thought he could be either twenty-two or sixty.

"Then what you doin back here, you're not lookin?"

"All right. I was just looking for a friend."

"You see? I knew you was lookin for me." Santa used his elbows to push himself off the wall, but didn't approach her. "I am your friend."

He wore a sleeveless tee shirt that exposed thick shoulders and arms. He held his hands out to her, palms together and opened them as if offering jewels. Inside were small chunks, like white rocks tipped in black.

"Want a jump, babe?"

Jill backed up. She tried not to look in his hands.

"What is that? Is that crack?"

"Oh no, it ain't no crack." He snickered. "It's only a little dried up bakin soda and water, spiffed with a pinch of poppy seeds." He closed his hands and shook the rocks like dice. "Like a fuckin bagel."

"I've got to go meet somebody."

"But you already met me. Ho-ho-ho, and I'm so glad to be your friend." He shook his hands again, rattling the chunks. "Say, maybe you ain't got a pipe. Is that it?"

"No. I mean yes."

He snorted and said, "Shit, I got you a nice pipe. Got it right here in my front pocket. Why, I bet you can see it, too, you look close. Reach in and take hold of Santa's pipe now."

Jill was too scared to answer. She kept backing up until she reached the wall. They were behind Clippers, at the edge of downtown.

"Now, you got a lucky thirteen dollars, we could get you high for days and days. Seein as how you're a beginner and all. Oh yeah, that'd last you days and days." Santa had the smile of an anteater.

She didn't know if she was supposed to talk, scream, or bolt by him. They'd been over it in school, seen films, talked about it in little groups. But Jill forgot.

Then she saw Corrie walk into the alley. She almost collapsed with relief.

But Santa saw in Jill's eyes that someone had appeared. He thrust his hands into his pockets and turned around slowly.

"Be careful!" Jill yelled.

Santa pointed a finger at Jill like a gun. "Keep it down, daughter," he whispered.

"Leave her be, Santa," Corrie said.

"Well now, if it ain't our own darlin Corrie. Our little coriander spice." He shrugged his shoulders, took out his empty hands. "I hope you ain't abusin the shit. I mean, I wasn't spectin to see you here again till maybe Wednesday."

"Just forget it."

"You usin that much, I hope you're all prayed up. I hope you right with the Lord. Listen to Santa now: you overdo and you overdie."

"You know him?" Jill's voice was pinched in her throat. "You know this guy?"

"I told you about Santa the other day," Corrie said. "You really should start believing me."

Santa rocked back on his heels, looking from Jill to Corrie. "I thought you brung me a nuther customer, daughter."

Corrie reached her hand toward Jill, who walked around Santa and grabbed it. "I am really glad to see you."

"Ok," they headed toward the street. "You're glad you saw me, but now I want you to forget you saw me. Just remember that I came."

Jill felt that friendship meant being there when someone needed you. It was like being the other cop in the squad car, a partner who popped in when you were in the worst trouble, no thought for their own life.

So she would no longer doubt anything Corrie told her. They were true friends and, even if her stories didn't always hang together, hey: Corrie was somebody she knew she could count on. That had been proven now.

After dinner, they went to see Terrence Delannoy and Richard in their cabin again. Music drifted down toward them as they walked.

Standing at the screen door, Jill and Corrie could see that Richard wasn't playing the piano. Flute music wafted from speakers hung among the beams.

Richard sat sideways on the bench, back to back with Terrence Delannoy. Each had a knee pulled up toward his chin so that his heel rested on the edge of the bench. Their backs nestled against each other's for balance and their heads were just touching.

"Let's not disturb them," Jill whispered.

Corrie didn't answer. She stared at the two men framed by the screen door, her brows furrowed.

Then, without looking in their direction, Terrence crooked a finger and beckoned them in. When the door creaked, Richard's eyes rolled in their direction.

"Corrie," he said in his silken voice. "And was it Gillian?"

"Just Jill, I'm afraid."

"Would you prefer if it was Gillian?"

"Oh, I think so. Gillian sounds so much fancier."

"Fancy?" Terrence said. He smiled at her. "Or perhaps it sounds flashy?"

"Royal," Richard said.

"Flowery," Terrence added. "You could say Gillian was more flowery. That would fit. What about you, Corrie, what does it sound like to you?"

"Rich." Corrie glanced at Jill. "Gillian sounds richer than Jill."

"That's good. How about glittering?"

"Flamboyant," Richard said. "It would be a bit flamboyant on you, my dear."

"Not tawdry, I hope," Terrence laughed. "Or gaudy?"

"No," Jill said. "Like a jewel instead of a stone."

There was a silence then, everyone smiling. Jill sat on the same director's chair by the fire place that she'd claimed during the previous visit. Corrie looked around, then sat on the floor at Jill's feet and leaned back.

Jill tried to place the way the room smelled. It wasn't incense. She thought it might be some kind of berry, or perhaps a spice, the tangy odor of cloves. She sniffed like a beagle, nose to the ceiling.

Terrence had been watching her. "Cinnamon candles. Think of winter mornings, your mother sprinkling cinnamon on two thick slices of buttered bread. Lovely, isn't it?"

"My mother's dead," Jill said. She spoke softly, as the others were speaking, but her voice was steady. "And anyway, it would have to be my dad in the kitchen."

Terrence touched Richard's elbow with his own and then stood. The movement was graceful and slow enough so that Richard could straighten his leg without losing balance.

Terrence stretched his arms like a gymnast before the start of a routine. Richard smiled up at him.

"Cappuccino again?" Terrence asked, looking at Corrie.

"I'd love it."

"Me too," Jill said.

Richard shook his head. "I won't need it."

From the kitchen, Terrence called, "How's it going, Corrie?" Jill felt Corrie stiffen at her feet.

Terrence appeared at the kitchen entrance. "I mean, really. How's it going?"

"Three steps forward, two steps back."

"Nevertheless," he turned away from her, "that does add up to progress, right?"

"Just a dance, I think," she said, her voice edgy. "A slow one, too. I hate slow dancing."

"You prefer to do the Adolescent's Limbo?" Richard asked, barely audible. "The Teenager's Twist."

"But not the Loser's Lindy," Terrence called. "Not the Bunny Hop."

"Stick with the theme," Richard said. "The Recoverer's Waltz, the Mainliner's Mambo."

"The Mashed Potato," Jill said.

"Oh shut up," Corrie said, burying her face in her friend's lap.

37

TIMOTHY COULD feel it coming on again for days, like a virus. First there were the dreams.

He dreamed of his wife and her winter-coated back as she walked onto the plane for another weekend away. Wind swirled dry snow around her body like a corona.

Then he dreamed that she was aboard the Broadway Limited as it pulled out of the train station. She was seated on the side he couldn't see from the platform. He was waving, holding the toddler Jill up against his hip. He told Jill to wave although they couldn't see whether Charlene was waving back.

He dreamed she was swimming out into Lake Huron. She moved smoothly through the calm water, fading from sight.

The dreams had her walking away, running away, turned away. He woke at the bed's edge, having pushed the pillows onto the floor.

Timothy had no trouble recognizing the pattern. He'd even pushed the pillows off to the left side again, the side Charlene had slept on, just as he used to when she was alive and always away from home.

And there was the music. Songs insinuated themselves while he ran, bringing back an image of himself sitting in the old recliner ten years ago, unable to face going to bed alone again.

Then, on the car radio, he heard a local commercial for an unfinished furniture store. It was backed by the song "We'll Meet Again." This was a song he and Charlene would sing together in the car, early in their marriage, when he drove her to the airport for another business trip.

Or he would walk by Terrence Delannoy's cabin at dusk and Richard would suddenly switch from Chopin to Prokofiev, Charlene's favorite. Love for Three Oranges.

At The Whitefish last night, a jazz group called Impromp 2 had played "Blinders." This was the last song on a tape Timothy used to listen to in bed when Charlene was away. He would have a novel folded open at his middle and a last cup of brandy balanced on its pages.

He'd had to leave The Whitefish. By late afternoon, Timothy knew there was only one thing for him to do. Go to the phones, talk to the women.

"So how was New York?"

"Lonely without you," Lauren Hazeltine answered. "I mean, there's so little to do there on your own."

"I just wondered if you'd had some time to get out." Timothy fiddled with his telephone charge card, tapping it against the shelf that held local directories. "See the sights."

"Not this trip. But I've seen the sights there dozens of times before."

He tapped out a tune that had come back to him during the day. *Just the two of us, we can make it if we try. Just the two of us, you and I.*

He'd run into Traverse City the long way, pursued by this song. He brought nothing with him but the charge card, cabin key, and a folded five dollar bill in his wrist-wallet. It wasn't a well planned trip.

The beer he chugged before calling Lauren made him feel muzzy. He was sipping his way through a second.

"Probably too hot to sightsee anyway," he said, sounding like Eeyore fretting over his fate. The conversation wasn't going as he'd hoped.

"I'm busy right now, Tim. Did you call about something specific?"

"I didn't know. Well, why don't you come up here for a while? Say, this weekend?"

"I see. This must be the 'later' that you referred to last time. Are we 'working something out' already, since we couldn't pull off New York?"

"You're a real turn-on over the phone."

"Sorry. But I can't leave here now. That weekend I spent in New York was my summer vacation this year. Besides, next week's the County Fair."

"Oh boy. I didn't know you were on the Jersey and Holstein circuit."

101

"How quickly he forgets." She covered the phone and said something Timothy couldn't hear. So she wasn't alone, maybe that explained her tone. "I've got to go pretty quick. You remember the 5 k race at the Fairgrounds? I've been working out on the track ever since you left, 400 repeats at eighty seconds each. I intend to win this thing."

"For what?"

"I take it you wouldn't believe for self-actualization. First prize is a weekend for two in St. Louis. Would you be interested?"

"Depends on which weekend."

"As I understand it, that would be up to me. Look: I've got to go, Tim. We can talk about this some other time."

"Make it after Labor Day and I could come with you."

"Right. After Labor Day. You can just look at this weekend as an investment. You do without my company now and get the payoff in a couple of months, like a short-term note."

When he tried to call Jane Delery Brock, Timothy forgot to dial the area code. Then he dialed his security number incorrectly and the computerized voice instructed him to try again.

Unlike Lauren, Jane seemed pleased to hear from him. It made him think again that he shouldn't have left New York when he did. He'd allowed Jill to talk him into fleeing from her problems. Except, he knew, that wasn't exactly what happened. And if anybody fled, it was him.

Jane's voice, mingling with static, recalled their easy intimacy backed by sea wind. He felt himself relax.

"Nobody writes anymore. You and Jill both said you'd write."

"We said we'd sunbathe, too. You can't count on anything people say anymore."

"Even yourself. I'd vowed never to date any man I knew before turning forty. Then you showed up."

"I didn't know you were so much older than me."

Jane laughed. Timothy sipped his beer, let the silence linger.

"Maybe you shouldn't have left here so soon," she said.

"I was thinking the same thing. But Jill was ready and this is her summer."

"My recollection is she didn't have to slap a full-nelson on you. You were ready too."

"Jane, I want to tell you I really did enjoy our time together."

"So did I. What is it, are you lonely?"

"I would call it sealed. When was the last time you were in Michigan?"

"Let me think. I once spent an entire week in Indiana. There was a course in mediation and arbitration techniques. Isn't Indiana part of Michigan?"

"So I take it you're not interested in flying out for a visit."

Jane paused. When she spoke again, her voice had softened. She sounded like she had after the massage. "It would be much too soon."

"There's another way to look at it. I was thinking how close it gets to being too late."

"Tim?"

"What?"

"Don't ask me to come to your cabin in the wild. Invite me to your home and I'll try to do it. There really is plenty of time."

"Sure. You've never known winter till you've been in Illinois in December."

"One more thing. If you're ever in the neighborhood, drop by."

"We're doing fine, Mother. Stop worrying."

"Then why did you call?"

"Just to see how you are. To say we appreciated the visit. I thought you'd be glad to hear from me."

"I am glad. Why wouldn't I be glad? Is something wrong with Jill?"

He cupped the mouthpiece and spoke into his hand. It was an old trick to change the timbre of his voice. "There is nothing wrong, Mother. I promise."

"She had a bad time here. I'm afraid it was something with a boy. You can tell me."

"She hasn't talked about that. And she seems all right here. Sometimes it's best just to let things pass. Besides, there's a girl about her age nearby."

"That's very nice." Timothy could hear wild cheers from the television in the background. She must be watching a game show. "So tell me, are you really in Michigan? I thought it was primitive out there, still the frontier. No phones and no toilets."

"Actually, I'm in town now."

"In town? This sounds like a movie with Kirk Douglas."

"The real reason I called is I forgot my bathing suit. It was in the bathroom, drying."

"Also your lurid paperback with the purple cover. I'll send it along with the trunks when your wanderings are over."

"What book are you talking about?"

"It's right here. Something called *Forever*."

"That's not my book."

"Well it's certainly not mine. Wasn't too bad, though."

Timothy would have let it ring for an hour, working on his beer, listening to the noises from the bar. After four rings, Leah Bell's booming voice greeted him over static.

"Don't worry, you've reached Leah Bell, just like you wanted to. I'm just not available to talk with you right now. I might be out with a client or I might be in with a friend, you never know. But why don't you leave your name, phone number, and message when you hear the little beep. I'll get back to you when I can."

"Leah, this is Timothy Packard. I was just trying to see if you . . ."

"Tim?" Leah broke in. "Damn it, hold on a minute." He heard her fiddling with the machine, which screeched as she tried to turn it off. "I don't know how to de-activate this thing once it gets started."

He listened, knowing she wouldn't hear him if he spoke.

Leah slammed the phone down on the kitchen counter twice as if trying to beat it into cooperation. In a moment, she picked it up again. "Ring me right back, ok?"

"Sorry about that," she said when he called back. "The damned machine has more buttons than an accordion."

"Sleeping Bear Dunes. Leah, you've been holding out on me. I mean, don't you think I ought to see this amazing sight while I'm in the area?"

"You want to see a pile of sand?"

"When we were in Arizona once, Jill and I drove miles out of the way just to see a meteor crater. We're talking about a hole in the ground."

"Then you just get in that nice little rented car of yours and take Route 72 west for a half hour until you get to a place where there's this nice sand. There's a great big sign and everything. I'm a realtor, not a tour guide. Call me when you get back and maybe we can have a drink."

"Actually, I was looking for something to do during the day."

"I wasn't. I'm busy the entire afternoon. Why don't you call me later."

He had to dial directory assistance to get his sister-in-law's phone number. He'd left it in his wallet at the cabin. Then he couldn't remember if Natalie still used her married name or had gone back to Galloway.

When he first knew her, Nat was fourteen. Jill's age.

Like her big sister Charlene, Nat wanted to be a performer—a mime rather than a magician. At their wedding, she stood throughout the ceremony leaning against a fence no one else could see. Winds no one else felt kept gusting an invisible hat off her head.

Now she worked at a kite shop in Cannon Beach, a small tourist town five miles from her home on the coast. She acted in plays there and taught classes in mime. The last time they'd spoken, to set up this summer's visit, Nat had just gotten back from a weekend of windsurfing in the Columbia Gorge. She made him promise he'd try it.

While the call went through, Timothy tried to compute what time it was in Oregon. He hoped she'd be home from work and was surprised when she answered on the first ring.

"Hello?"

Timothy couldn't speak. Natalie sounded exactly like Charlene, with the same open tone, the same breathy emphasis on the first syllable, the same forced glitter of expectation. He'd forgotten.

"Nat?" he murmured.

"Is that you, Allie?"

"No, it's Tim." When she didn't respond, he added, "Timothy Packard."

"I wasn't expecting to hear from you for another week or two."

"This isn't really hearing from me. I just called to touch base, make sure we were still ok. Who's Allie?"

"Someone who also calls me Nat. Most people call me Natalie now."

He remembered that Charlene had shifted to Char and back to Charlene every few years, whenever they'd relocated. And she also had a friend named Allie. No, that was Ellie. Ellis Farry. When Timothy first heard his wife talk about Ellie in Chicago, he'd assumed it was a new woman friend. But Ellie, it turned out, was the only white member of the feared Black Curtain, the invincible Chicago Bears defensive backfield. An Ivy-Leaguer, no less, with a degree in economics from Brown. They'd met in the jewelry section of Marshall Fields.

He went over the schedule with Nat. She'd already arranged three days off work and offered to meet them at the Portland airport.

"We'll rent a car. Looks like a nice drive."

"It is, especially through the Coastal Range. But it'll take you a couple hours."

"We have time."

After he hung up, Timothy strode out of The Whitefish trying to move as though nothing had happened to upset him. He turned left, where the road to his cabin was, then reversed himself and began walking toward the bay. Finally he circled the block, broke into an easy trot, and with his head down chugged the wrong way out of town.

38

TIMOTHY SAUNTERED out of the cabin after dinner, rolling down his sleeves. He was actually humming, something he never did. What was worse, he was humming a song from his childhood that he had come to hate, and now the words were there too. Keep this up and pretty soon he'd be crooning to the quarter moon. "Many a tear has to fall, but it's all in the game."

Because of his boundless capacity for trivia, Timothy knew the whole story behind this song. He knew the tune was composed in 1912 as "Melody in A Major" by Charles Gates Dawes, a putterer on the flute who was better-known later as Calvin Coolidge's Vice-President. Or as a winner of the Nobel Peace Prize for his work settling Germany's World War I reparations. Dawes's melody, given lyrics the year after he died, had been widely recorded—Sammy Kaye, Dinah Shore, Carmen Cavallaro—before Tommy Edwards used the new-fangled stereo recording technique to make it a hit in 1958.

To stop himself from humming, singing, or thinking about Charles Dawes, Timothy inhaled deeply the fresh lake air and set his mug of coffee on the porch railing. The water glittered as daylight, stretching itself like a lazy cat, settled to face the evening. "All in the wonderful game, that you know as love."

What was that called, when you sang the same song over and over to block your thoughts? Sure, as though he'd have some *useful* information stored up there with song lyrics and vice presidential minutiae. "And your heart will fly away."

Jill came out of the cabin to sit beside him on the steps. She smelled of dish soap, charcoal smoke and energy. It would be light for a few more hours.

"I'm glad you gave me this evening," Timothy said. "I was missing you."

Jill looked out over the lake. She could hear the swarming sound of a speedboat, but couldn't see it around the point. "Corrie was busy tonight. No need to get sappy on me."

"So I'm just a stand-in?"

There was no point in acting offended. Timothy had waited three days for this. On the way out of the cabin, he'd slipped the metal ring onto his finger, hiding the Datsun's keys in his palm.

"Where we going?" Jill asked, standing to stretch.

"Into the unknown," he said, flipping her the keys.

Jill stumbled backwards, her mouth opening wider than her hands. She juggled the keys, then swatted them against the door like a horsefly, and bent to retrieve them. A driving lesson? Unbelievable.

"This is acceptable," she said, trying not to smile. She skipped across the ten yards between porch and car.

Jill slid in behind the wheel, bounced a few times, and rubbed her hands together around the keys like a crapshooter. Then she grew still, concentrating, eyes shut tight.

As Timothy buckled up, Jill fiddled with the rear view mirror, rolled down her window, adjusted the side view. Then she grabbed the wheel, scrunched her neck down into her shoulders, and said, "vrooom vrooom."

Timothy wanted this to be serious, but he had to laugh. "Use the square key. The other's for the trunk."

She turned the key and the Datsun lurched toward the lake.
"Oh yeah," she said. "The clutch."

"Wait a minute. Let's not rush into this."

"Just watch me, now. I know what I'm doing." Jill depressed the clutch and moved the gearshift. "This is neutral. You're supposed to wiggle the stick around to show that you're a hotshot." She demonstrated this principle. Then, without looking at the knob for help, she solemnly moved through the gear positions. "Now here's first, vrooom, and here's second, vrooommmm, then third, vroooooooooom, and, mmmmmm, smooth old fourth. So do I pass this part?"

"Where's reverse?"

"Dad, chill out." She twisted to look around the headrest, held the clutch at its contact point, and rolled backwards neatly. "How about you turn on the radio?"

"How about you just drive?" Timothy said.

Where the driveway met the road, she stopped too far back to see if any cars were coming.

"All clear?" she asked.

"Pretend I'm not here. You've got to do this on your own."

"Roger. Over and out."

Inching forward, rocking back, gunning it to inch forward again, Jill stalled the car. Then it began rolling back down the driveway as she depressed the clutch and accelerator, trying to restart it. She slammed on the brakes and it stalled again.

Timothy didn't say anything. Jill moved her feet away from the pedals and let them drift down toward the cabin. He reached over and lifted the hand brake gently so the car wouldn't lurch to a stop.

"A temporary setback," Jill said.

They repeated two-mile pentangles from their driveway to an old barn to a flashing red light at the top of Camel Hill to the sign for the village of Grawn to the T in the road and back. Jill felt ready for a greater challenge. The last time around, she'd even hung an elbow out the window and steered down the hill with one hand.

"Nothing to it," she hummed.

"Doing just fine."

"You sound surprised."

"Relieved is more like it." He checked his watch.

"The night is young," she said, her voice deep and breathy. "And it's rude to look at your watch when you're out with a woman."

"It's almost eight."

"Good. What's next?"

"I thought this would be enough for the first time."

"Oh please, Dad." She was a child again. "There's nothing at the cabin. Besides, it could be a long time till I get another shot at this."

"You sound like little Jilly eight years ago at the State Fair. Pleeeese, Daddy, just a few more rides."

"I WANT ANOTHER COTTON CANDY!"

"Ok. Let's go to that abandoned distillery I saw the other day. You know where it is, just outside of town?"

"I've been past it."

"We can practice turns and parking. Pull off here."

"Why?"

"So I can drive us to the distillery."

"Oh, come on. Let me."

"There's a four-lane highway on the way."

"I'll be careful." She turned with a tight, pleading smile and, he'd swear, even batted her lashes at him. "Come on, I'm doing fine. You said so yourself."

"Watch where you're going."

*   *   *

"I think the hardest thing is learning how to get around," Jill said. "I mean which roads to take, which exits. Memorizing what connects to what."

"Maps help."

"Maps are not cool. You just know these things."

"My father told me he always planned out his route before getting into the car. Even if he was driving to work, the same streets every day."

"Boring."

Timothy flipped their visors down as Jill headed west toward the distillery. The sun was warm on his thighs.

"The first time I tried to drive to New York City by myself, I ended up in Oyster Bay."

"Where's that?"

"The north shore of Long Island. Farther from where I was going than from where I began."

Timothy leaned back and tried to relax. Jill was being conservative, driving in the right lane and at the speed limit.

"The highway traffic was crazy," he continued. "Cars jumping from lane to lane, everyone going sixty-five. And the signs were so confusing. I kept looking for 'New York' and none of the signs said 'New York This Way.' They don't even call it New York, but what did I know? All I saw were destinations I didn't want: Queens Midtown Tunnel, Throg's Neck Bridge, LaGuardia Airport. So about an hour after I thought I should be there, I got off and started to free-lance. I'd have gone clear past Oyster Bay too, if it wasn't for the Long Island Sound."

"So how'd you get back?"

"Asked directions."

"You mean you didn't have to hitch-hike and get beat up by a motorcycle gang or anything?"

Timothy cleared his throat. "The distillery's at the bottom of this hill, you'll want to get over to the left. It really happened, believe me."

Jill swung wide on the turn, but handled the downshifting well. At the deserted A-frame that still said Grand Traverse Distillery, she stopped and set the brake. Timothy could hear the river behind the empty building.

She turned to face him. "So tell me."

"Tell you what?"

"The moral of that story. *Timothy Packard Takes A Drive*."

"I was remembering when I learned to drive, that's all. It was like you said. You get taught how to make the car move, but not how to get it where you want to go. The mechanics instead of the mysteries. I'm just agreeing with you. No big lesson."

"Sounds a lot like love, you know." She released the brake and put the car in gear.

"Now that's a new one on me."

"I mean, people tell you about sex, what goes where. They teach it in school. You'd think love is like putting together a model fort or something. This goes there, add a little epoxy, and it takes overnight to set. Nobody tells you a guy's going to want to stick his tongue in your mouth."

She began driving the two-lane roads that had been built for the distillery's visitors. There was a solid line painted down its middle.

"You're on the wrong side of the road, Jilly."

"Pretend we're in England."

About a half hour later, they were ready to leave the distillery. She had parallel-parked between two imaginary cars, using a log as the sidewalk. She crossed a pretend downtown with its yield signs, bus stops, and railroad crossings. She drove a straight line in reverse.

"Don't give me directions, Dad. See if I can get back on my own."

"Fair enough. But you were supposed to turn right there, coming onto the road."

"I know. I just wanted to practice a u-turn."

As they went by the distillery again, Jill rolled up her window. The evening was cooling quickly.

"Did I tell you I met the guy whose father used to own this?" she asked. "Corrie knows him."

"I heard the story too. The woman who showed me Fonzie and Oregano told me about it. What's his name, again?"

"Robbie Aswell. He's ok, but Corrie makes fun of his complexion. Kids use this place as a hang-out now—it's supposed to be a good spot for rafting."

"I wondered why it wasn't more overgrown."

"Let me ask you something. You've been seeing a lot of this realtor lady. When do I meet her?"

"You're keeping track?"

"Word gets around. This is a pretty small town."

"Well, nobody tells me what you're up to. How come they tell you about me?"

"You just don't know the right people, I guess."

Timothy was silent for a moment. "She's just a friend. I wasn't thinking you'd need to meet her at all."

"You like to meet my friends."

"That's different."

"Somehow I knew that's what you'd say."

"Well, it is."

Jill shrugged. She drove up behind a car that was going too slowly in the right hand lane, but did not pass. Their turn-off was only a half mile ahead. Looking through the back window of the car in front of them, Timothy saw that it held an elderly couple. The woman in the passenger seat was sitting as far away from the driver as possible, leaning against her door and looking steadfastly out of her window. In the back seat was a smaller head, which Timothy at first thought was a child but then realized was a dog. It sat exactly midway between the couple, the top point of an equilateral triangle, and gazed at the road ahead. Timothy remembered driving with Charlene and Jill in almost the same positions, each of them lost in their own thoughts, each of them as far as possible from the others within the confines of their car. He shook his head like a boxer after taking a hard right cross to the jaw and it occurred to him that he did understand what the Michigan part of their trip was about.

Timothy looked at Jill and smiled. "Ok, right. We could cook dinner for her tomorrow night, if you can be free."

Jill nodded. "That would be nice." She turned on the directional signal, checked her rear view mirror, executed a neat turn onto the narrow road to the cabin.

39

THE NEXT time Jill saw her, Corrie looked preserved, like one of those Iron-Age women pulled from a Danish peat bog. Her skin seemed leathery and misshapen, a worn pouch sagging around its cache of jumbled bones. At first, she wondered if it was really Corrie.

Jill was walking along the water's edge toward the cabins. Corrie, looking out at the lake, didn't notice the movement nearby. Jill slowed down, trying to bring her friend's face into focus, to figure out what was wrong.

Corrie didn't look battered, just steeped. The expression on her face was mild. She seemed not quite at peace but not animated either. Her lips and eyes were half-closed, like the sleeping or like the dead.

Jill stopped short, as though walking into a hot-wired fence. Wearing bikini bottoms and a man's dress-shirt, Corrie was straddling the prow of the canoe, her long legs spread wide and her heels dug into the sand.

It was a stunning pose, hot and unconscious. This must be the way Corrie liked to be when there was no one to see her. Jill thought this was the first time she'd seen Corrie open and natural. But yet, her face looked so strange.

Jill grasped something about her new friend that frightened her. This person on the prow of the canoe was someone Corrie was trying to escape, not someone she was trying to find.

Despite what she said, Corrie dressed and moved to cover herself up, knowing men could not ignore her and she was too needy to cope with their attention. It had cost her dearly.

Jill felt as if she were being granted a peek at the truth of Corrie's struggles. Beautiful as Corrie looked, Jill knew she did not want to be her.

Corrie stared across Star Lake as if looking for a signal. She didn't hear Jill approaching.

"What's wrong with you?"

Corrie turned slowly, as if still uncertain that she'd really heard anything. Jill couldn't tell if Corrie recognized her.

"Oh. It's you." She looked beyond Jill to see whether anyone else was coming. "Nothing much."

"But you look, I don't know, soggy or something. Like you've been crying for a month."

Corrie puffed her cheeks and exhaled loudly. "Nope."

"Then what, your period?"

"I fell down the stairs, Jill. I got stung by hornets. I got Elephant Man disease. Cut myself shaving."

"Corrie, talk to me."

"This you do not want to hear."

Jill walked past her and turned toward the water. She didn't stop until she was shin deep in the lake. Then she faced her. Corrie wouldn't meet her eyes.

"Try me."

"Fine, I'll try you. But you'll be sorry. Eliason came on to me again last night."

"No."

"Ok, have it your way. Eliason didn't come on to me again last night."

"Mr. Eliason?"

"Snuck up behind me like he was on patrol. Shit, and just last week he agreed we would stop. So there I am leaning back on the porch steps, holding in this humongous hit, chest out to here. I'm really starting to rush. All of a sudden he puts his face next to mine from behind. Talk about coming down fast. I never heard him, and then he's got his hands over my tits and I'm choking to death. Smoke's coming out of my ears, I'm coughing so bad. What does he do? Puts his hands over my mouth. It feels like I've been shitting lung all day."

"But he's older than my father."

"That matters a whole lot."

"God, it must've been so scary." Jill tried to imagine some fat old man materializing out of the night like that, his face suddenly against hers.

"I could have sworn they were already asleep, him and Margaret. Like for hours."

"And you're sure it was him?"

"Up close and personal, as Robbie Aswell says. Believe me, I know Kenneth Eliason when I smell him. Besides, that's how they do it when they're forty, by tricks. He knows the pipe makes me horny."

"I don't believe this."

"You've got to stop saying that." Corrie moved her head in Jill's general direction. "The first time Eliason did it to me was the day we got down here to the cabin. He drove eighty the whole way in his Beemer, never stopped. We beat Margaret and the girls by two hours."

Jill didn't know what to say. She stood in the water and hugged herself.

"And I thought he was Mr. Cool," Corrie added, "driving like that, giving me stuff to smoke, giving me extra money all the time. 'Buy yourself something nice, Corrie.' Like it was for clothes instead of crack. He really likes the effect that stuff has on me."

"What does it do?"

"Aren't you listening? It makes me horny. Maybe you don't know what that is? Makes me want to fuck. Even fuck a guy like him. The pipe makes me feel like opening myself up so I'm inside-out, so I'm raw to the wind. At least until it makes me want to curl up and die."

"So you're on drugs again."

"This is true." She turned her face toward the lake. "Though that's not exactly worded right. Two, three weeks already. But the word you're after is 'dirty.' I'm dirty again. Robbie told me he heard about a way to get clean, though."

"How?"

"That's what I don't know yet. Robbie says I have to go with him to find out."

"Go with him where?"

"Ha!" Corrie shook her head. "Now it's my turn: I don't believe you."

He thought Leah might dress down for the occasion. He thought she'd go casual, maybe a pants suit or a summer-weight dress in cool pastels with a serape against the evening chill.

When he saw her through the screen door, which she tapped lightly, Timothy realized he didn't know this woman at all. Jill went to greet her.

If he'd seen a photograph of Leah taken from a distance, he'd have thought she was a Catholic Cardinal. Wrapped in a loose, red robe over a matching skirt, she even had on a small red beret that kept her blonde hair hidden. A red hood hung to the middle of her back. Protruding through the armholes of her robe were the floppy white sleeves of her silk blouse.

"This must be Jill. Timothy Packard, your daughter is simply stunning. Why didn't you show me a picture so I'd be properly prepared?"

"Pleased to meet you, Mrs. Bell."

"Oh dear." Leah shrugged out of her robe. She pulled off her beret and shook her hair loose. "It will have to be Leah, you know. Unless you're willing to let me call you Ms. Packard all evening."

She marched into the kitchen, where Timothy was putting the stuffed game hens into the oven. She picked up a spoon and stirred the vegetables on top of the stove, bending over to sniff them.

"Not bad. That would be gvetch, isn't it? I'm very knowledgeable about Middle Eastern cooking. It comes from having grown up in West Virginia."

"I thought a gvetch was someone who complained all the time. This is ratatouille. I just learned how to cook it when we were in New York."

Jill brought over a cutting board loaded with crackers and a wedge of cheese. She placed a small knife beside the cheese and sat opposite Leah.

"Your mother cooks exotic foods for you? Timothy, how sweet."

"My mother is above cooking. I learned this from a friend."

"Oh. I see."

"It's not what you think. An old high school friend."

Leah turned to Jill, a smile firmly in place. "So what do you think of our little town?"

"It's friendly. I'm enjoying it here."

"Fall. You should see northwestern Michigan in September, October. Trees, sailboats. It blazes."

"I like your outfit."

Leah stared at her for a moment as if assessing her tone. Then she smiled, her extravagant face instantly becoming radiant.

"Tell me about this summer of yours. I hear you're on some kind of tour. It's what, a reward for straight A's I suppose?"

"Something like that," Timothy said from behind them. He chuckled.

"More of a bribe, you might say."

"How old are you, Jill?"

"Fifteen."

"My goodness."

Leah cut the cheese in half. As she spoke, she continued halving each chunk until a pile of squares lined the perimeter of the cutting board.

"When I was your age, I was married. Can you believe that? I tell you, growing up in West Virginia when I did, fifteen wasn't even that young to be a bride. My husband escaped the mines, though. Raymond was a mechanic, some kind of genius with any machine at all, so at least we lived without the dust and danger. Why am I telling you this?"

She looked up, caught Jill's eyes, and looked back at the cheese. "Oh, I remember," she continued. "Raymond threw me out a year later because I couldn't get pregnant. That's when I left West Virginia and never did go back. I'm fifteen, semi-divorced, an eighth grader for Christ's sake."

"What did you do?"

"I'm getting there. I did sort of what you and your dad are doing. I mean, that's why I bring this up. I went places. Sat down with an atlas in the school library and made a list of every state beginning with the letter M because my maiden name was Mason. Then I started hitch hiking. Maine, Massachusetts, Michigan, Minnesota, Mississippi, Missouri and Montana. The Seven Ems. I got to Maine and Massachusetts, met Mr. Bell in Michigan, and that was that. Do you see what I mean?"

Jill wasn't expecting it to end there. She'd been almost hypnotized by Leah's softening voice, charmed by the simple shape of her story, and hadn't considered she might be asked to comment.

"Not exactly."

"Oh. Well, I mean you never know, you know?"

Jill nodded. She began placing Wheat Thins under each chunk of cheese Leah had cut.

"Sure," Leah said. "It was terrible that I was barren. But it turned out that it was good too, even though I never had a child. You see, I didn't get half way through the Ems before I kind of fell into my life anyway. Understand?"

"Yeah."

40

TIMOTHY TOOK two beers along to the Eliason's cabin. He'd only have to stay for a few minutes.

Earlier in the day, Eliason had waved him over when Timothy returned from his run. Tall and paunchy, with a florid face offset by his sparse blonde beard, Eliason held a steaming glass mug in his fist.

"A little Irish coffee to start the day?" he asked. His belly rested against the porch railing. "I've compounded it myself."

He walked slowly over toward Eliason's cabin as his breathing settled. Eliason took a step back, as if worried that Timothy might brush against him with his sweaty body.

"Just cold water, if you have any."

Eliason darted into his cabin and returned with a stein of tap water. He placed it on the top step. "If you're free tonight, you're welcome to drop by. We're having a little thing here for Marion, call-me-Mo, Sharpe."

Timothy gulped the water. "So he finally showed up."

"But much later than his old man expected. Mac always leaves weeks before Marion's supposed to arrive. Wants to take no chances."

"If Mo's such a pain, why have a party for him?"

"Oh, he's fine. It's just that he has two kids and his old man can't stand them. As a father of two myself, I can certainly see his point."

"Ok, I'll stop by."

"Say eight. Delannoy will be here too. I assume you've met him. He'll have his current friend with him. You don't mind?"

"Why should I mind?"

"Some people do."

"I look forward to it."

Eliason grimaced. "One more thing: I take it you don't drink Toonys?"

"Just beer."

"Afraid I haven't got any beer. Just the hard stuff. Beer makes you fat."

"I'll bring my own."

Now Timothy was trying to turn the short walk between their cabins into a hike. The Eliasons, the Sharpes, Richard, and Terrence Delannoy were making an astonishing amount of noise for six adults who hardly knew each other. Maybe it was because there was no music.

After meeting the Sharpes and greeting the others, Timothy was ready to leave. Mo Sharpe seemed pleasant enough, a landscape architect, short and lean with rust colored skin and a much larger man's baritone. His wife Molly wore a burgundy painter's hat and golfing gloves.

Eliason stood between the Sharpes, gesturing with the plastic spear from his martini glass. Two pimentos were cleaved by its tip. They coated the spear like a bloodstain.

"Economist, huh?" Eliason said to Molly Sharpe. "If that isn't something! Like I always say, there nothing a woman can't understand if it's explained to her properly."

Timothy had been anxious for companionship all week. But he didn't feel at ease with these neighbors.

He remembered that Charlene accused him of never feeling at ease with neighbors, or with anybody outside the immediate family. She said he belonged on the edge of town, in a ranch home with a high fence around it and a pit bull chained to the cellar door. Maybe she was right. Maybe he was, at heart, anti-social. He preferred to think of himself as reserved.

He felt a hand on his shoulder and turned. Molly Sharpe slipped her arm through his. She brushed a swaying hip against his.

"Was that your daughter with Eliason's *au pair*? She has lovely eyes."

She let him go and moved off to sit between Terrence Delannoy and Richard on the chaise longue. They made room for her. Richard accepted a few nuts from Molly's open hand.

Through the living room window, Timothy saw Eliason on the back porch. Martini balanced on the railing, he reached into his shorts pocket and held whatever he'd withdrawn out to his left. Then he waggled the hand as if shaking a thermometer down.

Corrie appeared beside Eliason, grabbing for his hand. He jerked it back, but wasn't quick enough. Timothy could see several bills flutter between them as they fell.

Eliason was smiling. Corrie looked ready to scratch out his eyes.

Terrence Delannoy came over to the fireplace. He turned and rested his shoulders against the mantle beside Timothy.

"I saw that too," he said.

"She looked upset. You know what it was about?"

Terrence looked through the window. "It's awkward, guessing about neighbors, isn't it?"

"Well, my daughter really likes that Corrie. I was just wondering what was going on, she seemed angry."

"I thought so, myself." He took a deep breath. "It might be good to see what your Jill knows about Corrie and our friend Eliason. He's a very troubled man, I think."

"How?"

Terrence shrugged. "I'm hardly an expert on these things. Besides, I seem to be the only one around who thinks that. So I could be quite wrong."

Timothy walked out the front door and stopped at the top of the steps to chug the rest of his beer. He popped open the second beer and strolled toward his cabin. It was getting hard to keep to two beers a day.

There was a shaft of soft, sunset light at the edge of the Eliason cabin. As Timothy entered it, he was almost knocked down by Corrie and Jill running toward the road. His beer went flying. The girls danced past him and, giggling, spun in a half circle so they could backpedal and watch him struggle for balance.

"Hi, Dad."

"Oops, Mr. Packard."

"Here's where I get it," Corrie whispered. "Used to be a dentist's office."

They stood next to the cherry-shaped sign welcoming drivers to Traverse City. It was at the eastern border of town, a mile beyond the Holiday Inn where Jill and Timothy stayed when they first arrived. The glow of streetlights hovered behind them, but where they were was a dark margin, cut off from the lights by an S-curve and dense trees.

"Which one?"

"With the white door."

"People just march right in? What about the cops, don't they know it's a crack house?"

"I don't know what the cops know."

When there were no car lights in sight, Corrie took Jill's hand and led her into the street.

"Santa rents the upstairs, where the dentist's mother used to live. He doesn't seem worried. He also doesn't call it a crack house. Calls it his base."

"He gives me the creeps."

"Santa's all right. At least he cares about kids, not like some dilts I could name."

Jill didn't respond. When a car rounded the curve out of town, she nearly ran from Corrie's grip.

"Easy," Corrie said. "This isn't the movies."

"I'm nervous."

She tugged at Jill. "You won't be, after a while."

They crossed the street holding hands. The front of the house was too dark for Jill to make out its number.

"If we buy only from him, Santa protects us," Corrie said. Her voice had changed, gone deeper. "I've seen him refuse to sell to this guy who was buying too much, so he wouldn't get real sick. I'll tell you one thing: I'd go to him for help if I ever got in trouble again."

"What's his last name? You tell me Claus, I'm going back home."

"I never asked. There are people in this world who don't need last names, you know. Cher, Buffalo Bill, Sting. I can't get over you, sometimes."

They went around to the side of the house where there was a narrow staircase to a second story kitchen. Corrie turned to face Jill.

"You don't have to come in."

"I want to."

"Ok. Just keep quiet."

Santa still wore his Detroit Tigers cap and wraparound shades. He'd added a tan leather vest over his tee shirt.

In his mouth, there was an ornately carved, deeply swooping pipe with a silver lid propped above its silver-topped bowl.

"It looks like a toilet seat," Jill whispered.

They could hear music through the door. Santa was nodding, bouncing one leg to the beat. On the other leg sat a laughing, white baby dressed in nothing but its diaper and reaching vaguely for the pipe. They couldn't be sure if anyone else was in the room.

When Corrie rapped on the pane, Santa didn't look at the door. He continued nodding, his body turned partially toward the corner of the kitchen they couldn't see. But one hand came away from the baby's side, the arm revolved slowly toward the door, and a finger pointed at them a moment. Then it curled to beckon them in.

He must have been able to see them out of the corner of his eye. Or in the mirror above the sink. As the door opened, he held up the finger to halt them. But in a hushed and friendly tone he said, "Ah, two more daughters."

"Evening, Santa," Corrie said, holding Jill back with her palm.

"You wait till this song be finish, Coriander spice." His voice was still mostly breath, but sharp enough to issue commands.

Jill saw a shadow move to her right and heard the rustle of a bead curtain. The baby knew whoever was leaving and followed the movement. It stopped laughing, reached toward the shadow, and began to bawl.

"Shit," Santa said. He spread a palm over the baby's head and cranked it away from the sight as if it were a doll. Holding the wriggling child at arm's length, he began to jiggle it on his leg. He bent close so it could touch his pipe. Nothing worked. He stood and turned toward the door. "Fuckin traffic, I'm tellin ya."

Corrie moved into the kitchen, but Jill lingered. Santa held the baby out toward Corrie, one hand cupping its bottom and its back firm against his forearm.

"Here," he said. "Do somethin with this while I turn off the music."

"I'm sorry."

"The fuck. Santa's got too much goin on tonight." He left the room, but instead of turning off the record he went into the bathroom. They heard him peeing, then heard the music become louder.

He came back into the kitchen and said, "Couldn't bear to turn off my sweet Max Romeo before he finish his 'Wet Dream.' You know this song, daughter? This is one rude number."

"You've played it for me, Santa. Look, I'm sorry to bother you. I can be fast."

"Ahh." He shook his head. "I just hadda pee. Makes me sour, fuckin pee all the summer time."

Corrie laid her money on the whiskey cartons that served as Santa's kitchen table. "It's thirty five bucks, all I've got right now. I'll get some more next week. You can count it if you want."

He smiled his anteater's smile at her and scooped the bills from the table. He folded one in half and used it to pick his teeth.

"I trust you, Coriander." He gazed at her while working his way methodically around his mouth. From where she stood, Jill could see Corrie's eyes. They never left Santa's.

"Please," Corrie whispered.

"You take back this ten, now. And I ain't sellin you any more this month."

"I need them all, Santa."

"You're too skinny, you know that? You could die on me." Santa was beside Corrie so quickly that Jill wasn't sure she'd seen him move. He ran a hand down her side and across her hip, jerking it back as if the bone had pierced him. "I don't need anybody dyin around here."

"It's not all for me." Corrie pointed over Santa's shoulder. "Jill needs some too."

Jill took a step toward Corrie, then froze. The look on her friend's face was like prayer.

Slowly, Santa turned toward Jill. He took off his shades, looked at her face, let his eyes roam over her body.

"I see," he said.

41

"JUST KEEP calm." Corrie pulled the latticework back in place and they settled in beneath the Eliason's porch. "There's nothing to worry about."

Jill felt that it was her turn to be the other cop in the squad car. Corrie had come through for her, now Jill would come through for Corrie. The problem was, Jill didn't know for sure what would constitute coming through. That did worry her.

She had let Santa think whatever he wanted to. She let him look at her with hunger, his eyes almost like hands on her body. At least he didn't try to feel her up, although she probably would have let him. And she hadn't contradicted Corrie.

Outside Santa's place, before they began to run into town, Corrie had stuffed the baggie of crack inside the waistband of her shorts. It stuck fast to her skin.

"It'll fall," Jill said.

"Never does."

"Just tell me why you need so much? Are you real hooked?"

"Just a little hooked. I figured to get as much as I could afford while I still had all that money from Eliason. Don't worry, this'll last a month at least."

Jill believed her. A month. That meant she would never have to go with Corrie to buy the stuff again because Jill would be gone next week.

They trotted the S curve back into Traverse City, hitched a ride to Grawn, then walked on the shoulder toward the turnoff for their cabins. They sang, making up lyrics to Madonna's "Like a Virgin," and skipped in sweeping figure-eights onto the empty road.

After fifteen minutes of walking, they realized that they'd gone past the turnoff for the cabins. By the time they reached Fonzie and Oregano, they were twittering like swifts.

Now Jill nestled beside Corrie and looked through the latticework at the lake. It was utterly smooth and seemed a more livid black than the sky.

"Who said I'm worried?" Jill whispered.

"Good. Here's what you do: breathe in as deep as you can and hold your breath till I say stop."

Jill did as she was told. She closed her eyes and pretended to be swimming underwater, trying to cross their leg of Star Lake without coming up for air. Her cheeks puffed like balloons.

After about a minute, she opened her eyes and looked at Corrie, who was engrossed in preparing her pipe. Jill let out a squeak, but didn't exhale.

"Keep holding."

By this time, Jill's heart was pounding. She could feel it expanding into her throat, which had begun to twitch. She was sweating, growing dizzy, tingling in her fingertips.

When Corrie finished with the pipe, she smiled at Jill and nodded. "Now."

Jill's breath gushed out. She flopped forward onto her arms, laughing, unable to inhale despite desperately needing to.

Corrie reached over and patted Jill's back. "Sit up." She crawled beside her, slipped both hands over her shoulders, and eased her upright.

"That's what it's like," Corrie whispered. "Only the rush goes on till your brain blows up. Amazing grace, all right. Knocks you right into another zone. Want to try some of it?"

Corrie crawled a few feet away from Jill. She shifted a mound of shells that she had piled against the foundation and located her lighter.

She crawled back carrying a small sleeping bag, rolled and knotted, clutched to her chest. Using the sleeping bag as a pillow, she propped herself comfortably, closed her eyes, and waited for her breathing to slow.

Her legs were out straight and draped over Jill's thighs. Several minutes passed. Jill watched as Corrie became very still. Only her open eyes suggested she wasn't actually asleep.

Then Corrie sat up. She folded her legs until the knees touched the ground. She lit the pipe and sucked deeply.

She inhaled in several stages, as though forcing her lungs to open ever wider and accept more of the smoke. Slowly, she eased back down, arms going over her head until they touched the ground behind her. The pipe lay in a sliver of moonlight that filtered through the latticework.

Corrie moaned. She lifted her chin slightly, almost as if expecting a kiss, and her eyes rolled back. Jill watched as her friend grew still at the center, only her knees flexing outward and her fingertips occasionally twitching where they'd come to rest among some small stones.

"It's the only time I feel pure," Corrie said.

"To me, you looked possessed, not pure."

"Those first ten minutes or so, there's nothing like it." They were on the porch of Fonzie and Oregano, whispering so they wouldn't waken Timothy, but not yet ready to part.

"I feel opened up," Corrie continued. "Like I could fuck a tree if I wanted to." She laughed and touched Jill's arm. "Which would be a big improvement over Eliason."

"How can you joke about that sleazeball?"

"Watch what you call him, young lady. Don't you know I'm the man's Love Slave?" She laughed again, then looked over toward the Eliason cabin, perhaps checking to see if he was sneaking up on her again.

"I'd be afraid," Jill said, looking after her.

"Well, I understand that." She tried to stifle another laugh. "But for you we could start out with a small tree at first."

"I'm serious. I'd be afraid the stuff would be too good and I would-n't be able to keep away from it. Or I couldn't afford all that I'd need. I don't know. I'm afraid to be desperate."

"I don't see that." There was a moment when neither spoke. Corrie sighed. "I mean, everybody's desperate."

"And the way you look, Corrie. I love how thin you are, but you never eat. You don't always look right. This can't be good."

"Bullshit. You sound like my mother." She sagged slightly, as if she'd been elbowed in the stomach. Then she smiled. "I look like I've always looked, that's part of the problem."

"Oh God, I don't want to hear this again."

Corrie sat on the top step, folded her arms over her chest, and gripped her shoulders. She continued as though Jill hadn't spoken.

"The pipe makes me feel like I can control my looks. One minute, I can be invisible and the men don't even see me. Then, if I want to, I can pop right into view. I can have these enormous tits out to here, so a man can't get his hands around them. It makes me feel things I can't even imagine otherwise. What's wrong with that?"

Jill shifted closer to her. She put her arm around her and rested her head against Corrie's shoulder.

"Your tits again."

Then, suddenly, Corrie began to weep. She turned so that Jill could wrap both arms around her and collapsed against her.

Within seconds, her face buried in Jill's neck, Corrie began to cry harder, shaking on the inhales like a baby having a tantrum. She tried to muffle the loud sobs and lost her breath. She gasped and began to slip out of Jill's grasp, seeming to liquify.

"What is it?"

Corrie couldn't respond. Her head was in Jill's lap. She sounded like an animal in a trap.

"It's always like this," Corrie said a few minutes later, when she'd regained control. "I get so depressed so fast."

"It's all right."

"Maybe not. It ends up with this awful noise, like a thousand windchimes in a tornado. My head just wants to shatter. Or sometimes there's a hoard of men running after me with their dicks in their hands like pistols. I can hardly stand it."

"You're ok now."

"Yeah, it doesn't last long. And I am getting used to it." Abruptly, Corrie stood. She shuffled toward Eliason's cabin, hugging herself as if trying to hold her insides in place. "See you tomorrow. Everybody's going to the river. We'll take the kids."

42

ROBBIE ASWELL was alone in the house. He had turned the track lights toward the center of the living room, where he sat slouched and spotlit on his mother's Herculon couch.

Robbie's head was against one worn arm, propped on a throw pillow. His butt was barely on the cushion and his long legs were stretched out underneath the glass coffee table.

Eyes tightly shut, lips compressed, he looked tortured as he plucked the strings of an imaginary guitar cradled in his lap. Most of the instrument's neck would have been sticking out behind the couch.

Robbie's head suddenly rolled way back, his hips lifted off the cushion, and he made wild sounds like a cornered cat. With his hand in the shape of a hook, he dug furiously at the air guitar for a few seconds. Then he subsided, dropping back into the shadowy flow, and his brow smoothed out.

From outside, Miriam and Mary Eliason watched him perform through the screen door. The girls held their hands to their lips, staring as though Robbie were a character in a video.

"Go ahead," Corrie whispered. She nudged Miriam in the back. Miriam in turn pinched Mary and they burst into the room, banging the screen door open.

Corrie and Jill followed them in. Robbie opened his eyes, but didn't seem startled, as though he were used to having fans charge at him.

"Well if it isn't," he said.

"I would've called, but we didn't have any change."

"No problem. I wouldn't have answered it anyway."

"I need to see you. Now."

Robbie nodded. Frowning, he laid aside his air guitar, reached over the couch arm to unplug it, and stood carefully to avoid tripping over wires. Then he gestured to his band, spreading his hands as if to let them know he was helpless to hold off these groupies.

"Well, here I am."

"Is your mom home or anything?" Corrie asked.

"No. She hates it when I get The Delusions together. She went sailing."

"Oh yeah, I remember. She got that job with Bibb, Freese. They should sue your dad for non-payment, handle the case for your mom free."

"So we're alone here, so what?"

"So you said you could tell me something." Corrie glanced at Robbie's face, then looked away quickly. She took a few steps toward the back of the house. "Remember?"

"By heart, Corrie. And I will tell you something new. I will tell you the musical lesson for today: Every Good Boy Deserves Fun."

"Come on, I know what you're talking about and you know what I'm talking about." She turned her face toward him again, then turned her shoulders and torso, put her hands on her hips. Her voice had a new rasp to it. "Stop playing games."

"Right. I see a darkened room." Robbie closed his eyes and held his hands out in front, swaying like someone in a trance. "I see a young couple whispering in the far corner. He has no pimples; she doesn't twitch. Ah, a deal is being struck! They get up, this couple, oh they're so tall and handsome together. They walk toward the door holding hands. What's that word I hear? 'Considerations,' he's saying. And she's smiling at him because she understands. Considerations. She understands perfectly."

Corrie looked at the floor while he spoke. She ran her right hand up and down her left arm.

"So like I said, I need to see you now."

"You, or the whole sorority?"

"Jill's taking the girls for McNuggets."

Robbie smiled. "Bye Jill."

They could not agree on the sauce. Miriam wanted barbecue sauce and Mary wanted sweet-sour.

The food server drummed his fingers on the counter. His name tag—Barry—was on upside down. Jill wondered whether he'd get fired if the manager saw it. Maybe that was why he was so nervous while the girls debated. There was a long line behind them.

"Can't we have one of each?" Jill asked.

"One order, I'm only allowed to give you one kind of sauce," Barry said. "Manager says so. Says extras turn into food fights in the playground."

"We got sweet-sour last time," Miriam whined.

"Did not," said Mary. "We got ketchup. Sweet-sour was the time before, when Corrie made us eat with that creepo skateboard guy."

"Ok. Make it two small Chicken McNuggets instead of one large. Give us one with barbecue sauce, one with sweet-sour." Jill handed each girl two dollars and put another dollar on the counter between them. "And a Diet Coke for me. You girls bring the stuff out when it's ready."

"I'll pay for it," said Miriam, reaching for the dollar.

"No, it's my turn," Mary yelled. "And I get to carry the tray this time."

Jill walked outside. She found a table near the playground and sat to wait for the girls. How did women stand being mothers? She didn't want to hear them utter one more screechy sound. She was ready to give them anything they wanted, if they would just shut up.

But as soon as she was alone Jill could see Robbie again. Without even waiting for her to leave, he had unzipped his fly and sat back down on the sofa.

43

WHEN CORRIE walked into the playground early that afternoon, she was smiling. Her hair had been washed and combed out. It was pulled into a pony tail held in place by a lavender ribbon.

Jill was beginning to recognize the smile. Corrie had been with the pipe again.

"You don't look so good," Corrie whispered as she sat beside Jill. Then she giggled. "Cretin duty doesn't agree with you, does it?"

"Corrie, you said Robbie knew how to help you. What's going on?"

"I would say that Robbie helped me. Yes, he did. Look how he cleaned and brushed my hair for me. We got this ribbon out of his mother's sewing box and he tied it for me."

"He didn't have anything?"

"Oh, he had something." Corrie took a sip of Jill's Diet Coke. "He's not like he seemed, you know. I think we just surprised him. He was trying to act cool in front of you. But he's really sweet. He cares about me a lot."

Jill took back her drink. She raised the straw to her lips, then stopped herself and put it back on the table.

"So he helped you?"

"Oh, yes. He told me his miracle cure for crack addiction." Corrie reached for the drink, held a huge mouthful to feel it fizzing, but then began to laugh and sprayed it out on the bench beside her. "But it's pretty sticky."

Later that day, as promised, Corrie and Jill took the Eliason girls to the river. They hitched a ride out to the abandoned distillery with a girl named Polly Wingate. Corrie said she knew Polly from church.

"My ass," Jill said. "You can stop with the church routine, ok?"

Corrie grinned. "Well, bless my soul!"

Polly appeared to be put together from two separate kits. She had the broad shoulders of a javelin thrower, a neck so extended it seemed segmented, and long ears made fully visible by her upswept coal-black hair. But her hips and ass were massive, her calf muscles thick as a line-backer's. The unlaced hiking boots she wore with her baggy striped shorts were a man's size ten.

Corrie had told Jill that Polly Wingate would do anything. She'd drunk a whole bottle of bourbon by herself in an afternoon. She'd sent a picture of herself naked on the deck of her father's catamaran to *Hustler*, with a poem supposedly written by her impassioned husband. She'd run for the City Council on a platform to legalize marijuana use.

She certainly drove like Janet Guthrie. Guys loved her.

The afternoon weather was perfect for inner tubing. It was sunny and hot, but not as humid as it had been all week, and there was a spicy breeze down by the water. The sky was deep azure and very high.

About a dozen people were already there and they had four thick tubes for riding the current. Several six-packs of beer held by ropes were sunk near the bridge pilings and guarded by a fat boy in a white bathrobe.

Jill knew several of the people by name now, and most by sight. The fat boy was Leon Boyd, a friend of Robbie's. He had once beaten the faculty advisor of the high school chess team in five moves. Leon seemed to be in charge of the beer and of whose turn it was to tube.

Leon's little brother Russell was the same age as Miriam Eliason. He had played with her a few times in the park downtown. Jill felt sorry for him. His pale, hacked hair made Russell's head look like a field of yarrow. Leon would cut it for him every week, trying to even it out.

Russell darted up to Miriam when the girls piled out of Polly's car. "Wanna help?" he screamed. "I'll let you help if you wanna."

"I'm not swimming," Miriam said.

"Me neither."

"You don't have to. I'm in charge of the bridge. See it over there? It's got a big rock at the bottom with a green rope around it that they catch onto. Everybody gets out there after their ride's over. They throw the tires up to us and we get to sit on them till they come out. They're pretty soft."

Russell was backing up as he spoke, his voice getting higher and higher, the words faster and faster. Then he turned around and darted toward the bridge.

Miriam and Mary squealed. They ran down after him.

Corrie watched them go, grinning at their antics. She didn't seem to recognize them.

"Be careful," Jill called.

"Stay dry," was all Corrie said. But she said it more to Jill than to the girls.

"Surf's up!" Leon Boyd yelled.

They turned to see Robbie Aswell come swooping downstream. He was lounging back within the tube's center, arms stretched, looking bored. He held his position in the current as if by magic, skimming the surface until he reached the green rope. Then he pulled himself to the bank.

"You see him in his house, you forget he's such a jock," Corrie said. "No one plays as well as Robbie Aswell, sports fans."

"Looks easy enough," Jill said. "All you have to do is sit there."

"Try it."

There was a shriek upriver. Everyone was laughing as Polly Wingate whirled into view, spinning in circles with her arms waving wildly.

Just before the bridge, Polly slipped out of the tube and disappeared. There were more shrieks.

She surfaced, but the tube had gotten away. It bounced off the base of the bridge and snagged against the bank.

Leon reached for it with a long bamboo rod he kept beside him for the purpose. He steered the tube over to Russell at the bank, who ordered Miriam to sit on it. Polly trudged up to a chorus of boos.

Next came Marcus Ridley, wearing only tie-died jockey shorts. He was spread across the top of the inner tube instead of riding in its center. His back was arched so that his hands and feet were out of the water.

"We have word from upriver," Leon announced, holding a leafless branch to his mouth like a microphone. "Ridley's been trying for the last half hour to stand on his tube like a skateboard. But he kept falling on his face. Tore his Bermudas right off on the rocks, which is how come he's got on his jockey shorts now. Let's hear it for the twerp!"

Corrie clapped and elbowed Jill. "Isn't it your turn yet?"

"Come off it."

"You never try anything, Jill. Go ahead, give it a rip."

"After you."

"God, Jill. Be bold!" Corrie elbowed her again. "Grab that ring!" She used both hands to shove Jill upstream. "Ride the inner tube of life! Take a chance!"

Jill stayed a few steps away from her. She continued to smile and tried to read Corrie's new mood. "I can't swim. It's my period. I'm allergic to rubber."

"If you're allergic to rubber, you're in a world of trouble, girl. You should definitely take shots."

"And what about you? I haven't seen you lining up for a turn."

"Can't. Got to keep on eye on those kids."

Miriam and Mary were having a ball. Russell Boyd coordinated the movement of inner tubes so that the girls never missed a turn. In exchange for this service, they let Russell walk up into the bushes with them and look inside the bottoms of their bathing suits after every five turns.

Corrie walked out on the bridge so she could look back underneath and see how the girls were doing. "You all right down there?"

"We're fine."

Miriam was sitting inside the center of a tube on the bank. The backs of her legs were up against the inner rim and her feet pointed straight in the air. Mary was higher up, near the bushes with Russell.

"We want you to try it," Mary called. "Then we'll hold your tire when you get done."

"Maybe later. I don't want to get wet now."

"You promise?"

Corrie didn't answer. She continued across the bridge to the bank opposite where everyone else was. Jill watched her go, saw her reach into the front of her shorts and dig around, saw her disappear among the trees toward the road.

Nobody noticed the riderless tube at first. Its color wasn't much different than the river's.

But when it hit the short run of whitewater a hundred yards from the bridge, Leon Boyd dropped his microphone. He put his hand on his forehead to shield his eyes from the sun and stared into the water. The sudden halting of his chatter caught everyone's attention.

They couldn't see anybody in the river. The tube squirted out of the brief rapids and swirled toward the bridge.

"Man overboard," Leon said softly.

As if hearing a signal, they all ran toward Leon, who was perched at the center of the bridge in his white robe. He continued scanning the river while the group converged around him.

"Ok, who's missing?" he asked. He looked around the group, mumbling names, adding them up. "There ought to be ten, I think."

"Robbie's not here."

"Polly?"

"Behind you, asshole."

"How about Brendan? Ok. Jessica, Kathy. Who else? Where's Corrie?"

"Over there," Jill said, pointing toward the trees. "She's not in the water."

"Anybody see Felix?"

"He left," Leon said. "With what's-her-name, Trendy Wendy. So its just Aswell?"

"Robbie can handle himself," Jessica said. "He'll be all right."

"We can't afford to wait and see. He could be hurt."

"Hey, where's the twerp?" Polly asked.

"Oh, Jesus. I forget about Ridley." Leon tightened the sash of his robe. "Wait a minute, he was the last one through. It can't be him again. Not yet. He's probably still walking up to the overpass."

"That's good," Brendan said. "Because I had gym with him and Ridley can't swim a lick."

"Here's what we do," Leon said. "Brendan, take a group up that side of the riverbank and Polly, you and Jessica take the rest up this side. If you see something, call out. Anybody bring a life jacket?"

"Let's just get started," Brendan said. He was the one in the group who'd had real outdoor adventures, who'd been to Outward Bound.

He'd gone mountain climbing where his father lived, in Washington. He'd hiked in the Appalachians with his older brother during Easter vacations.

"Take it easy, Brendan. We gotta think."

"You gotta think. I gotta go find Robbie. He could be drowning." He ran across the bridge.

"Anybody got a rope?" Leon asked. "Case we need to pull him in."

"There's one in my trunk," Polly said. "For tying it down when the lock was broke."

"Couldn't hang an ant with that," Brendan called from the far side of the bridge. "It's just thick string."

Several of the group had followed Brendan. Jill jogged off to join them.

"Polly, take this inner tube with you. He might need a float. I'll stay here and watch if he shows up."

Jill's group found Robbie Aswell a few yards from the overpass. He was lying on his stomach, in a patch of shade cast by the brick support.

Brendan saw him first and froze. Jill bumped into Brendan and the rest of the group bunched together with them, peering at Robbie's body.

His face was turned away from them. His hands were straight down at his sides, as if he'd been ejected head first from the river and landed on the bank without being able to break his fall. Nobody spoke.

"What should we do?"

"Get help, I guess."

"First somebody should see if he's dead."

"Good idea." Brendan started down toward him immediately, then turned to look up at the group. He'd turned pale through his tan and was trying not to tremble. "Wait. Anybody know CPR or something?"

"I do," Jill said. "My dad made me take a class." She started down after Brendan. "He's got high cholesterol."

Just before they reached the bank, the hillside became steeper. Jill was in front of Brendan and moving too fast. The best she could do on the sandy slope was flop onto her seat and slide down with her heels dug in.

She landed just beyond Robbie's head, kicking sand into his face. That woke him up.

When Robbie bolted to his feet, swatting at the sudden intruder, Jill screamed. His backhand to the shoulder knocked her down.

Twenty minutes later, back at the bridge, it was all good for laughs.

Robbie had been tired, decided to nap in the shade. But he didn't want to deprive his friends of one-quarter of their navy, so he'd sent the tube downstream for them. He apologized again for bopping Jill on the shoulder.

"No harm done," she said. "I guess boxing's not one of your sports."

Leon broke out the beer. He tossed one to Robbie, another to Marcus Ridley, a third to Brendan.

"To our gallant rescue effort."

"Come on, Leon," Jessica shouted. "Stop being Leon-the-Hard-On. I want a beer and so does Polly, even though we happen to be girls. You do know what girls are, don't you? Throw 'em over, it's been a bad day at the office."

He passed the beers to Jessica and Polly relay-style instead of tossing them. Jill took one too. She always forgot how nice beer was on warm days. Gulping it made her think of her father after a run. She hoped he was having a decent time himself.

Leon popped one for himself, looking around. "Hey, anybody see Russell? Kid loves the taste of beer, you should see him quaff the stuff."

Jill threw down her beer as though the can had burst into flame. She was in motion instantly.

"Oh shit," she yelled.

She shoved past the cluster of people and dashed toward the trees where she'd seen Corrie disappear an hour ago. They watched her fade from view.

"What's with her?" Polly asked. She'd been splashed with Jill's beer.

"Maybe she doesn't drink."

"Bet she smokes, though."

"She's been one jumpy bitch ever since I picked them up downtown."

"What do you expect, hanging around with Corrie?" Jessica said.

137

Jill came sprinting back toward the bridge again, alone. They heard her before they saw her.

She was yelling Corrie's name, repeating it, not listening for a reply. Jill's cries came so close together, it seemed impossible that she could also breathe. She was flushed and there was a long scratch where a branch caught her above one eye.

Jill reached the sloped surface of the bridge and stumbled, but she didn't fall. They stepped aside so she could run between them, but no one followed right away. She continued to yell as she recrossed the bridge. "Jesus Fucking Christ. She never came back. Jesus Fucking Christ."

Robbie was the first to understand what Jill meant. He stiffened, then flung his beer into the river and took off after her.

"Hey, wait up!"

"What's the big deal?" Brendan called. "Fuck, Corrie went off for a quick hit and fell asleep, probably."

They watched as Robbie hurdled onto the path beside the river and caught up to Jill. He grabbed her shoulders and their momentum made them tumble into the weeds.

"She's taking quite a beating today," Polly said.

"Life in the fast lane, here in bustling Traverse City."

Robbie was up, hopping out of his high-tops and jeans again. He was pointing at Jill. Brendan and Ridley cheered.

"Put it to her, Aswell."

Robbie stomped down the bank, flailing for balance. He stopped at the edge, peering in, checking for rocks. Then he pushed off into the water.

Leon Boyd hadn't taken his eyes off Robbie and Jill. He walked toward the bank, studying them as he moved, and shucked off his robe. It landed in the dirt at the end of the bridge, bringing up a puff of dust.

He began trotting toward Jill, who was now standing above the spot where Robbie had entered the river. Her hands were over her mouth.

No one had seen Leon run since the fourth grade. But there were no jokes. They'd heard what he'd mumbled.

"The kids."

They figured it had been about thirty minutes since anyone saw Russell Boyd or the Eliason girls. They tried to recall everything exactly.

Marcus Ridley remembered that he had snapped Russell's trunks after getting out of the river the last time. Then he had thanked whichever girl it was who gave him his tube and walked back upriver. He was sure that all three kids had been there then.

No one had seen them after Ridley. Leon was the only one who'd stayed by the bridge when Robbie was missing. But he hadn't been thinking about the kids then either. So it was a good half-hour.

Robbie found no sign of them in the river. Jill looked under the bridge for any clues, but there was nothing. She was no longer yelling Corrie's name.

"Maybe they went for a walk," Brendan said. "Hey, maybe they ran upriver after us and got lost. There's no reason to panic."

"Could be," Polly agreed. "But wouldn't they be yelling for help by now?"

"I checked back up there behind the bridge," Ridley said. "And I went through the woods a little. Called out Russell's name and all."

Leon stood thigh deep in the water, staring downstream. The river bent west about fifty yards ahead and then narrowed sharply into a welter of debris. They'd searched through there without success.

If the kids were in the water, Leon thought they'd have to be somewhere between the bridge and the debris. Unless they'd wandered upstream first and then fallen in.

Maybe it was time to get help. This could be really bad.

Brendan thought that was an overreaction. They'd look like fools, calling the cops because a couple kids wandered off for a half-hour.

Ridley thought they should try the woods one more time. Leon kept staring downriver.

"We're getting nowhere," Polly said, "I'm driving into town. Let Vic Hassey at TUSART decide. He's got experience with this shit."

"I'll go with you," Jessica said. No one else wanted to leave yet.

"We'll be back with Vic. Shouldn't take an hour."

"It doesn't make any sense," Leon was saying as the river flowed around him. "Russell wouldn't go in the water. Hell, he wouldn't shit unless I told him he could."

When Corrie walked out from the trees a few minutes later, Jill was looking right at the spot. Corrie smiled and waved.

Jill said nothing, didn't move. Then she scrambled up onto the bridge and walked slowly toward the middle, keeping her eyes on Corrie. She broke into a sprint, but almost immediately reined herself in and stopped at the far end to wait.

"What's up?" Corrie asked. "Looks like somebody lost the beer."

Jill held her hand up like a traffic cop. Corrie stopped. She raised her hand, pulled herself up to full height, and said, "How!"

"What are you, shitfaced?"

"Why Jill, how coarse. No, I'm not shitfaced. Not at the moment."

"Stoned? Splotto? Zoned out? What?"

"Barely awake, that's what. But refreshed by my nice little nap." Corrie finally stopped smiling. She moved toward Jill. "Hey, chill out, all right?"

"Stay there. Just stay put. I don't want you to come onto this bridge."

"What are you, the troll?"

"We need someone on that side, Corrie. And you're it. We've got the other side covered." Jill backed up the slope toward the middle of the bridge, still holding her hand in front of her. "So keep your eye on the water and just holler if you see Miriam or Mary floating by."

Corrie caught up to her before Jill reached the other side. "What's the matter with you?"

Jill had never hit anyone before. But she swung at Corrie, a real haymaker that Corrie blocked with her forearm.

"They're gone, you hear me?" Jill yelled. "Poof! While you were in there with your fucking pipe and Robbie was scaring the shit out of the rest of us, Miriam and Mary vanished."

Corrie was beginning to grasp what Jill was saying. Her eyes widened, her hands slipped down to her sides.

"But I was asleep."

"Well now you're not. And this is no dream."

Then Corrie and Jill crashed together, supporting each other as their knees gave.

The group at the river was watching them and didn't see Miriam Eliason come out of the bushy area behind them. Miriam was holding Russell Boyd's hand, but dropped it when she saw the crowd below them.

It was Corrie, the only one facing the bank, who saw Miriam and Russell first. She disentangled herself from Jill and headed toward them. Her face was contorted, eyes darkened by running mascara.

"Nice joke everybody," she screamed.

As soon as he saw Corrie coming toward him, Russell turned and raced back into the bushes, certain he was about to get punished for having snuck off. Miriam backed up a few steps, then plopped down on the ground to await her fate. She tried not to cry.

There was a moment of cheering. Then Leon climbed up after his brother. Robbie, standing a few feet out in the river, threw himself backwards and sank slowly into the water.

"I *told* Polly to cool it," Brendan said, punching a fist into the air. "Now she's gonna feel like a fool, she drags her beloved Victor the Frogman out here for nothing."

"Just can it, Brendan," Marcus Ridley said. "She was trying to help."

"Who's gonna make me, Ridley? You?"

Ridley ducked as Brendan tried to shove him, coming up under his arms and knocking Brendan backwards. But Brendan clutched him to his chest as they fell, did a simple back roll, and flung Ridley into the river.

He came up sputtering. "You could've killed me, asshole. There's rocks all over the place here."

"Come on out, let me try again."

Five minutes passed before Leon Boyd emerged from the bushes carrying Russell on his shoulders. But he wasn't smiling.

He couldn't find Mary. Russell said Mary hadn't gone with them. Just Miriam. He didn't know where Mary was.

44

THE TRAVERSE Underwater Search and Rescue Team pulled Mary Eliason's body from the river just before midnight. She hadn't drifted far from the bridge, but she'd been deep.

TUSART's theory was that after Miriam and Russell wandered away, and the teenagers had gone to find Robbie Aswell, Mary tried to reach into the water for something floating by—maybe an inner tube, a tree branch, something she thought might be a turtle—and she toppled in. No one saw her, no one heard her. She couldn't swim and she was gone in a few seconds.

Miriam wouldn't say why she'd gone into the bushes with Russell Boyd. Russell insisted he'd had to go to the bathroom and that Miriam just followed him. Then they sat down to rest for a while and talk. They might have fallen asleep in there, he couldn't remember.

After Russell and Miriam came out of the bushes, the group had searched another twenty minutes for Mary. Then they decided to give up and leave the job to TUSART.

They reasoned that it was probably too late to help the girl anyway. Everybody said the whole thing was just an accident, that nobody killed her. The best thing they could do was simplify the situation, let the authorities concentrate on what was important: finding the kid.

Brendan took the empty beer cans back into Traverse City, disposing of them in various dumpsters throughout town. He'd found loose matches by the bridge and put them in his pocket, rounded up discarded snack wrappers, scoured the area to remove any signs of their presence.

Robbie had to ride back into town with Brendan. He hoped that whatever Corrie was going to do she would not do while driving his car.

Because by the time Polly Wingate arrived back at the river with Vic Hassey and the police, Corrie had already fled in Robbie's car.

Most of the others were gone too. It was so quiet in front of the Grand Traverse Distillery that Vic wondered whether Polly's story was a lie.

With Russell wrapped double in his white bathrobe, Leon Boyd waited for the rescue team in the parking lot. They sat on the trunk of his car. He rubbed his brother's back, trying to keep him warm and awake while they talked about going fishing next weekend.

Only Ridley had stayed behind with them. "I mean, what can they do to us, you know?" he said. "It's not like we pushed her in and held her head under."

Corrie knew that Robbie kept his car keys behind the sun visor. She had no trouble finding them or starting his car, which he kept well tuned. She dumped his clothes on the ground and locked her door.

Jill, carrying Miriam Eliason against her hip, went after Corrie. The child wrapped her arms around Jill's neck. She seemed calm and sleepy, and Jill thought she might not realize that her sister was actually missing.

They reached the parking lot while Corrie was dumping out Robbie's clothes. Jill yanked open the passenger door and got in. They fishtailed over the gravel and careened onto the highway.

Corrie regained control and drove just below the speed limit, gripping the wheel rigidly, knuckles white, jaw muscles so tight it looked like she had the mumps. She didn't check her rearview mirror or look to the sides when they came to intersections.

"I didn't know you could drive," Jill said.

Corrie didn't answer. At the stop sign where 113 and 37 joined, she reached into her shorts, pulled out her baggie, and chucked it backhanded into the bushes.

They went straight to Robbie's house. Corrie jumped out with the engine still running and left the door open.

"Wait there," she ordered. "I won't be forty seconds."

Corrie found the box that Robbie had shown her earlier in the day. She dumped its contents on Mrs. Aswell's sewing room floor. Grabbing some ribbon, a few packets of needles and a small container of pins, Corrie ran back to the car. She flung the things on the dashboard, put the car in gear, and made a screeching u-turn.

They drove toward the high school. Corrie got fouled up with one-way streets, but finally pulled into the lot behind the public library. She checked her watch.

"Just made it. Stay here with Miriam, all right? This won't take long either."

Jill obeyed silently. She had no idea what Corrie was up to.

Inside, Corrie ran upstairs to the reference room. She was looking for an encyclopedia or some kind of health guide. A librarian was tidying the tables in the far corner.

"We're almost closed," she whispered.

"I just have to look one thing up. Please, where's the medical section? It's an emergency, I might be pregnant, I've got to figure this out. Please?"

"Over there." The woman turned back to her tables.

Corrie found a paperback copy of *Mosby's Medical and Nursing Dictionary*. There were several inserts with the kind of illustrations she was after.

"Oh my God, oh no!" she moaned, ripping out two pages while her voice covered up the sound. "What am I gonna do?"

Corrie folded the two pages so they fit in the palm of one hand. She left the book on a table and ran out of the room. She knew the librarian wouldn't look up, wouldn't risk meeting the eyes of such a troubled teenager.

She got back in the car. Resting her head on the back of her seat, she caught her breath, then unfolded the illustrations and put them with the other things on the dashboard.

She drove out of town, turning toward their cabins.

"They've got to know by now," Corrie said. "Probably everybody knows."

"Polly passed us on 113, going the other way. Didn't you see her? The cops too. Sure they know."

"I mean Eliason and Margaret. I mean Terry and Richard. Your father too, probably. Someone must've called already, right?"

"Maybe."

"So I want to drop Miriam off. But I don't want them to see me. Take her in, will you?"

"What about you?"

"What about me? I can't face Eliason. Delannoy. Any of them. First I've got to get clean."

"You can't run from this. I mean, they'll think it's your fault."

"My fault?" Corrie snorted. "I'll probably get the electric chair."

Jill didn't know what to say. She hadn't thought about Corrie's legal situation. Could she really go to prison over this? Was she on some kind of probation? Jill wasn't certain that Corrie's account of being placed with the Eliasons was true, or that she'd really been involved with the courts. She didn't know which of Corrie's stories to believe.

"I know what I'm doing," Corrie continued. "It'll only take a couple minutes. I understand how, it's real easy. Robbie told me all about it."

"This is crazy, Corrie." They had passed through Grawn and were just a few minutes from the cabins. "You can't just cure yourself, some kind of instant thing. You dry out, or whatever. What'd he give you, a bunch of pills?"

"You don't know shit, you know that? You know absolutely zero about this. That's what you know."

Jill saw the junction ahead, where they would have to turn. Corrie was going pretty fast. Jill wondered if she was just going to zip past it, keep driving until they ran out of gas.

"I never said I knew anything about the stuff. It's only that we've got to do this right."

"We?"

"Yes. I want to help you."

"And I told you how you can help me." Corrie made the turn, jamming on the brakes. "Are you taking her in or not? Because otherwise, I'm throwing her out of the car. Because I am not coming within fifty feet of Mister Kenneth Fucking Eliason. Not ever again."

They were approaching the driveway leading down to their cabins. Corrie took her foot off the accelerator, but didn't brake.

"Well?"

"Let me walk Miriam down to the end of the driveway. You wait for me. She doesn't know what's going on. I'll stay just until she gets into her cabin, then I'll come with you."

Miriam had fallen asleep during the drive from Traverse City.

Corrie glanced behind her, then pulled onto the shoulder across the road from the driveway.

"I don't need your help."

"I want to come with you. You don't need to be alone tonight."

"What'll your father do if you don't come back on time?"

"I don't know. But he'll listen to me when I explain it. I can make him understand."

"Bullshit. All right, be quick."

Corrie couldn't think of any other place to go. She drove by Santa's place four times.

Jill recognized the white door of the old dentist's office on the second swing past. She checked the upstairs windows, but no lights were on.

That didn't necessarily mean Santa was out. He probably spent a lot of time sitting in the dark. She hoped they weren't going inside.

Corrie parked four blocks east, on a deserted street where a tavern called The Pit had burned down in the winter. No one was likely to find the car there for a while. She put the keys back behind the sun visor and grabbed the packages she'd thrown on the dashboard.

"Come on, then. This'll have to do." Corrie took off her shoes. She flipped them in through the open window of the car. "Just be quiet."

"You're sure he's in?" Jill asked, following Corrie down the block.

"No, I'm sure he's not in. But he'll be back."

"How about if I check?"

"Do what you want. I'm going to be down here, under the steps. That's where I like it."

Jill went up the narrow staircase and peered into Santa's kitchen. The only sign of life was a huge cat standing on the sink, licking at a pile of dirty plates.

When she came down again, Jill found Corrie seated with her back straight against the wall and her legs folded under her bottom. The stairs sliced the evening light into strips along the ground, but Corrie was already in semi-darkness.

The items she'd collected were arrayed in front of her. Her eyes were closed, her hands palm up in her lap.

"I've got to get quiet. I've got to relax," Corrie whispered. Jill was panting. "Just settle down."

"Ok." Jill sat in the shadows. "I'll try not to breathe."

"Now listen. Robbie told me about Positive Energy. You know what that is?"

"Sure. Like feeling happy."

"No, it's more than that. This is a very scientific thing. They can prove it exists, he said they can even measure it."

"So what did he do, give you a jar of the stuff?"

"Something better. He gave me knowledge. He told me how to release the Positive Energy inside myself. It works on the spirit, I think he said. He saw a show on it once."

"Corrie, I know what he showed you. He was unzipping his fly before we were out the door."

"Shhh. I'm trying to relax now." Corrie kept talking in a breathy monotone. "Robbie said that in China, out in the country where they didn't have money for doctors, the Chinese people figured this all out. The peasants. They learned how to make a chemical come right out of their organs and this Positive Energy would flow all over inside their bodies."

She looked to see that Jill was listening. Jill wondered if Corrie might be in some kind of shock from the afternoon. She'd never seen her so intent.

"One hour after you get it started, you're cured, no matter what you're hooked on. We're talking booze, smack, nose spray, anything. Addictions. It also fixes ulcers, arthritis, I think even heart attacks."

"What do you do?"

"You have to find the points, is what he said. He wasn't too clear on where they were, though. That's why I needed the charts."

Corrie unfolded her legs and stretched them out, careful to avoid the pile of things in front of her. She scooted closer to them and looked like a child getting ready to play jacks.

"Look at this, this is great," she said, sorting through and picking up one of the packages she'd taken from Robbie's mother. She read from its cover. "A Needle for Every Need. That's perfect."

"I don't follow any of this."

147

"Which ones do you think I should use? These long fat ones or the skinny sharp ones?"

"I suppose it depends on what you want to make. My mother died before she taught me about sewing. What are those, patterns you got out of the library?"

"Sort of."

Corrie withdrew one of each kind of needle from the packet. Only the Sharps and Betweens seemed fine enough. She measured them and rejected the Betweens as too short. Then she picked up the diagrams, spreading the one labeled "Principal Veins and Arteries" in her lap.

"Here goes," she said.

She grabbed a needle, licked it, closed her eyes, and jabbed it into the center of her left palm.

"Oh shit," she said.

Her hand stiffened like a claw, then relaxed. She looked at the needle protruding from it as if she wondered how the thing had gotten there.

"Nothing."

She picked up another, turned the hand over, and stuck it in the top, right in line with the first needle.

"Maybe if they touch their points together it'll make the Positive Energy come out."

Jill just stared. She looked from Corrie's hand, which showed very little blood, to her eyes, which were quite clear. She was too stunned to cry out.

Corrie watched Jill's reaction. "Don't worry. I know what I'm doing. Robbie explained how it works. It like releases an electrical charge, he said. I just must've missed the point I was supposed to hit, because when you get it right he said it doesn't hurt."

"You can't do this!"

"Keep your voice down. I can do this. And you said you wanted to help me."

"But this is crazy. You have to know what you're doing. You could hurt yourself."

"That's a chance I'll take. Leave if you want to, but stop throwing out these negative vibrations. I told you, the deal is Positive Energy."

"I'm not about to watch you stick pins in yourself."

"Then don't watch." She picked up another needle. "Look away, because here goes."

She jabbed it deep into the tip of her thumb. She leaned back to rest her head against the building. "Maybe I should've warmed it up first."

"They should be sterilized," Jill whispered.

"Shit, I didn't think of that. Threw my lighter out with the crack before."

Jill stared at Corrie's hand. "Do you feel anything?"

"Yeah. It hurts. But I don't feel any charge yet." Corrie's voice became milkier. "There was supposed to be a charge." She leaned forward. "Wait a minute, Robbie did say something about ears, now that I think on it. We'll try the ears next."

She picked up another Sharp. She reached for her earlobe with the hand that had the needles in it, but the pain made her wince.

"I should've done my hand last." She looked at Jill, who was already shaking her head. "You're going to have to do this for me."

"No." Jill put her hands over her mouth.

Corrie's eyes filled with tears. "It's going to work, Jill. I just know it is. It's going to get me clean. Please help me. It won't hurt."

Without a word, Jill pulled Corrie's earlobe down, inserted a needle, and jumped back as if she'd been hit.

The needle was barely inside the flesh. It drooped onto Corrie's hunched shoulder.

She flexed her hand, then reached up and withdrew the needle. "Oh well."

She pulled her lobe tight again, felt around with the needle's tip, and pushed it slowly all the way through until it could hang by its own weight.

Without letting go of her ear, she picked up another and shoved it through just above the first. Then she leaned back to catch her breath.

"Anything now?" Jill asked.

"I know what you can do. Run back to the car and get me a mirror. There was one stuck on the visor, Robbie's always checking his zits. But hurry. I think I'm starting to feel something. I'll try my neck next."

* * *

149

When Jill returned with Robbie's mirror, Corrie had three needles in each earlobe, one just below each cheekbone, and the three in her left hand. There were also needles on each side of her neck, protruding like the screws holding Frankenstein's head in place. She was running her fingertips over her eyelids, trying to figure out how to get the next round of needles into them.

She must have felt trickles of blood on her face and tried to wipe them away. But the thumb was the worst bleeder and it spread blood when she touched her face. The skin was mottled.

"Do you feel it yet?" Jill asked.

"A little." Corrie leaned away from the wall so she could use the mirror in the fading light through the stairs. "I see what's wrong."

"You're bleeding."

"Hardly at all. It's not so bad. But these aren't the right kind of needles, that's the problem. One look and you can see that. While you were gone, I saw those pins in the plastic box, the ones with yellow heads on them like sunflowers, and it hit me. They're quilting pins. Don't you see? That's what I should use, quilting pins to patch myself together again. Chinese things are always like symbols, I just didn't think of it before."

Jill picked up the box of quilting pins. Corrie reached for it, put it on the ground between her legs. She plucked all the needles out of herself and threw them aside.

"I'm going to get this right, Jill. And then I'll be ok. You'll see." Corrie checked her face in the mirror. "It's going to work," she said.

Jill scooted closer to her. She tried to wipe away the dried blood and got most off with her fingernail. It had clotted fairly quickly around each needle.

"One more thing. After I get these pins in, I need to stick one here." Corrie pointed to the thick vein in the crease of her elbow. "That's the other thing I thought of. It should be like I'm mainlining, only this time I'll be shooting up Positive Energy."

After ten minutes, Corrie opened her eyes. She found Jill without turning her head.

"Twang them."

"What?"

"You know. Wiggle the pins around for me."

"I can't, Corrie. We've got to get out of here. Santa might come back. We should get home."

"I don't have any home. Besides, it's ok if Santa comes back. He's on my side. Do the pins."

"I don't like the ones in your arms, Corrie. I'm going for help."

"No help."

Jill started to cry.

"Wait," Corrie said. "Just sit with me for a minute more. No help. I think it's working."

Jill felt that she should go. Corrie seemed weak. She'd lost some blood and Jill wasn't sure how much was too much. Things weren't clean under these stairs.

But it was clear to her that her friend wanted her to stay, still needed something from her. At least Corrie was finished sticking herself with pins.

"Yeah, I'm starting to feel it now." Corrie settled back in Jill's arms. Her eyes closed. "Yeah, I feel something."

Jill sat under Santa's stairway, holding onto Corrie as the evening darkened.

45

"THE FUCK you doin here, Daddy?" Santa said. "Dint you know this was my alley?"

"Where's my daughter?"

"What, I look like the Children's Services?"

Timothy took a step toward him. Santa didn't move. He was smiling.

"Are you Santa?"

Santa folded his arms across his chest, arms tucking under his biceps. Thick veins stood out like the veins on a horse's leg.

"I asked your name," Timothy said.

"You don't fuckin recognize me, that's the problem. I'm Bill Cosby."

"Do you know a Corrine Gable, goes by Corrie? Skinny girl, eighteen nineteen years old, got a drug problem."

"Girls, they got a drug problem it's usually they skinny too. Drugs'll make em lose their hungry."

"Look, I'm not here to play games with you. My daughter is missing. I want to know if you're the pusher named Santa I've been hearing so much about. If it wasn't hard for me to find you, it won't be hard for the cops either."

"Who you hear about Santa from?"

"This guy I know. He's about my age and likes to fuck teenage girls."

"You got some bad friends."

"Says he's been giving Corrie money all summer so she'd get crack downtown, come home and be sweet to him. She mentions the name Santa whenever she gets tight. So I'm asking is that you?"

"Sure, Santa. And this is the North Pole." He pushed himself away from the wall, cocking a finger at Timothy. "You leave or you freeze."

Timothy gestured with the windbreaker that was folded over his arm. "I'm dressed for it. Now where's my daughter?"

Santa shook his head. "I don't know nobody's daughter."

"Guys like you are supposed to be smarter than this. I'm not back here interviewing you for the Sunday newspaper. My daughter knows Corrie. Corrie gets her drugs from you. The two of them are missing. Now I'll ask you one more time where my daughter is."

"You askin me a whole lot of questions for a guy with no badge." He relaxed back against the wall. "No way to behave."

"You don't tell me where my daughter is, I've just got one more question. Tell me about what's hanging on your hip. A ray gun?"

"Why, that's my beeper, Daddy. I'm a businessman, see, not no drug pusher. The kind of businessman that needs a beeper to keep in touch with his clients, be available they need me. Aint you a businessman like me?"

"It's not a gun?"

Santa sighed. He began to walk toward Timothy.

"Guns are dangerous, Daddy. Now you walk while you still can. Hear me?"

"Have it your way."

Timothy pulled out the filet knife he'd hidden under his windbreaker. He dropped the jacket and held the knife up.

Santa sprang. He was on Timothy in an instant. He wheeled around, kicked the knife out of Timothy's hand, and immobilized him with a grip under the chin.

Then, slowly, Santa reached behind him to withdraw the buck knife he had holstered to his belt. He grinned, poking the knife between his thumb and forefinger against Timothy's throat.

"Shit, I look like a fuckin bass to you, Daddy? This here's a knife you wanna do a man with."

"My daughter."

Santa let go of Timothy. He backed up a few steps.

"I aint seen her."

At the park by Grand Traverse Bay, Timothy found a cluster of teenagers at a picnic table. Given what he'd heard from Eliason and Miriam, he was sure they'd be here somewhere.

The benches around the table were full and several kids were lounging on the ground nearby. A fat boy sat on the table beside a portable tape player, his legs dangling off the end.

They stopped talking when Timothy approached. Leon Boyd pressed a button and heavy metal music blared.

"Evening." Timothy was trying to sound relaxed.

"Yes, it is," Leon said.

"Maybe you can help me. I'm looking for somebody."

"We just got here," Brendan said. He stretched languidly, bringing his black Megadeth tee shirt taut across his chest. "Haven't seen a soul, except ourselves of course." A few of them laughed.

So this wasn't going to be easy. "Do you know who I am?" Timothy asked.

"I know that line!" Brendan snapped his fingers. "You're the man from the American Express Card commercial on tv, right?" They all laughed at that one.

"I'm Timothy Packard, Jill Packard's father. Do any of you know her? Has red hair, wears lots of earrings, clothes like yours." He pointed at one of the girls.

No one volunteered to speak.

"We've been here a couple weeks," Timothy continued. "She hangs out with a girl named Corrie, comes down here most days babysitting for two little blonde-haired sisters. I'm sure you've seen them."

"We don't have much to do with out-of-towners, mister."

Timothy could feel anger making his pulse accelerate. He deliberately focused on each teenager's eyes in turn, taking his time, trying to penetrate, to find one who would ease up. He wished they'd turn down the music.

"I think you may know this Corrie. See, there's been some trouble out by the river. She's missing. One of the little kids she babysits for is missing. And my daughter is missing. Now, I think Jill's with this Corrie, I think they're somewhere downtown, and all I'm interested in is finding out where they are."

"Wow," Brendan said. "Missing. That doesn't sound good."

Slowly, leaving a lot of room between each word, Timothy said, "I don't know how Corrie and Jill could have been so foolish as to go to the river alone with those little girls. I hear that this Corrie does a lot of drugs. I sure hope she isn't doing something foolish now, since my daughter's with her."

"Yeah, I know what you mean," Leon said. "Well, you might look around at that comedy club Clippers. Wouldn't know, myself, but I hear there's lots of drugs done there."

"I did."

"Don't know what to tell you, then."

"How about where that sonuvabitch named Santa lives. Someone there might've seen them."

"You say they went out to the river alone, huh? That's really something."

"Leon!" Brendan hissed.

"I'll have to talk to Jill about that," Timothy said. "Make sure she understands it wasn't real smart. Going out there by themselves."

154

"Right, you wouldn't want her to make mistakes like that again." Leon nodded, coming to an agreement with himself. "I think I've heard about this guy Santa you mentioned. Operates above an old office east of town. White door in the front. At school they warned us to stay away from guys like him."

46

AFTER ROBBIE Aswell found his car near The Pit, he thought he knew where Corrie was. But he wasn't certain he wanted to find her.

All that seemed to be missing from the car was his mirror. He took the keys, locked the door, and walked back toward downtown.

It had been dark for about two hours. Everybody would be in the park, as if this were a regular night. Diet Cokes, some beer, maybe a couple of wine coolers. If they had enough cash there'd be a pizza.

After a while, they might improvise Bartles & James commercials, acting them out for each other. They might talk about Robbie, or whoever hadn't shown up yet, explaining that he was soft. There'd be Metallica or Dio on the boom box.

He doubted they'd talk about what happened at the river, though. Probably made a pact that they'd never mention who was really there. Not ever, not even next year at school.

He wondered whether anyone knew if TUSART had found the little girl yet. Robbie could not forget the look on Leon Boyd's face when he realized that Russell was gone. He could still hear that girl Jill screaming while she ran back and forth over the bridge, trying to find Corrie.

Just before the city limits, Robbie saw a man he didn't know running on his side of the street. Robbie backed out of the light to watch what would happen.

Timothy ran easily, his head turning as he checked for movement around the houses. Robbie was impressed by the man's efficient stride. The guy looked like he could run all night. At least he wasn't a cop. Robbie knew all the cops in Traverse City.

Something caught Timothy's eye. He checked behind him without slowing and crossed the street. When he spotted the white door, his stride lengthened. He sprinted toward the staircase, hands forming fists.

Robbie stepped back into the street. He thought he'd just keep going into town. Find his friends in the park and tell them something was going on at Santa's house.

Maybe Corrie had gone to the cops. But he knew she'd never do that, not if what she told him about her past was true. Robbie turned around and followed Timothy.

Timothy charged up the stairs two at a time. He rattled the door, kicked at it, pounded the glass. He lowered his shoulder and tried to ram the door in, then gave up and came stomping down.

The racket woke Jill. Her body was sore from being huddled in one spot and twisted around Corrie. Corrie didn't stir.

Jill couldn't see who was making the noise. But if it was Santa, she didn't want to attract his attention. She sat up, but didn't make any noise.

Then she saw her father's beat-up Nikes and his good luck red and white socks. She recognized the catch in his breathing after he'd been running hard. He was stopped at the bottom of the stairs as if sensing her presence.

"I'm here, Dad. I'm under the stairs. I need your help."

Robbie drove them to the hospital. He left them at the emergency room entrance, saying he had to get home or his mother would kill him.

In the waiting room, while the doctor dealt with Corrie, Jill told Timothy what had happened. A *Tonight Show* rerun flickered on the overhead tv with the sound turned down. They sat side by side looking at the screen while Jill talked.

"I know about Corrie and Eliason," Timothy said when Jill was through. "Margaret Eliason spent the evening at our cabin telling me that it wasn't really his fault. She said that Corrie was a sorceress and she seduced poor Ken for drug money."

"That's not true."

"How do you know?"

"Corrie told me. She said he came on to her the day they got here."

"We don't know very much about her, really."

"Well, I know enough. I believe Corrie. Eliason should go to jail, that's what I think. The court trusted him to help her and look what he did."

"What court?"

"Back home. They placed Corrie with the Eliasons instead of sending her to the Farm."

"According to Margaret, Corrie showed up this spring at the school in Indianapolis where Margaret's a counselor. She said nobody knew her. Corrie claimed she was twenty-two, an orphan, and was trying to track down her 'birth mother.' So they went through the school's records together, but didn't find anything that helped. All Corrie could tell her was that her mother's name was Smith and she would be in her late thirties. Margaret felt sorry and took Corrie home for dinner, the little girls liked her, she was looking for summer work, etcetera etcetera. Now what's that got to do with the courts?"

"I don't know."

The doctor knocked on the window of the waiting room. He beckoned them out into the hall.

He was young, dressed in a plaid cotton shirt and old jeans held over his belly by a pair of striped suspenders. His thick black hair gleamed in the harsh light.

He stuck out his hand. "Doctor Saul. Hugo Saul."

Timothy shook Dr. Saul's hand and introduced Jill. "How is Corrie?"

"Tell me again. You're not relatives of hers?"

"Neighbors, just a couple weeks. Out there at the town-end of Star Lake. Jill's become friends with her."

"Well, the young woman is exhausted and dehydrated," he said.

"Also she suffered a little exposure. But she didn't hurt herself serious-ly. Blood pressure was down, but there's no evidence of shock. I gave her a tetanus shot and saline infusion. Tried talking to her, but she did-n't make much sense."

"So she'll be all right?"

"The wounds will heal. What can you tell me about her?"

"Not much. You could say we've had conflicting reports."

"I have a friend out there in those cabins by Star Lake. Maybe you know Terrence Delannoy?"

Timothy nodded.

"He mentioned this young woman who was staying nearby, an *au pair* that he found delightful. But he was worried about her, something about the family she was working for. Would this be her?"

"Sounds right."

Dr. Saul turned to Jill. "It'd help if you could tell me more about her pattern of drug use."

"I saw her smoke crack one time." She spoke carefully, looking from Dr. Saul to Timothy and back. "I never actually saw anything more than that, but she told me she was hooked again. I think she did it a lot."

"Couple times a day?"

Jill shrugged. "Probably."

"More?"

"All I know is she bought a bunch of it this week. She said it would last all month."

"Ok, one more thing. The puncture wounds. What was she doing to herself?"

"Trying to release her Positive Energy."

"Boy, that's not what she told me. It sure is an odd procedure for an abortion."

Dr. Saul didn't press Jill any further. He decided to admit Corrie for observation. He imagined they might have to get her into detox.

"Let me tell you the thing that bothers me most," Jill said when he left. "It's not what you think."

"I don't think anything, Jilly. I'm too shaken. When you didn't come back for dinner, and when I heard what the Eliasons heard, I went a little crazy." He swallowed hard and stopped walking so that he could face her. "I'm not prepared to lose you."

She put her arm around his waist. They walked toward the exit.

"Here it is: The wrong people are going to get blamed for this. Corrie's going to get blamed, I am, everyone at the river. Probably Miriam too, for leaving Mary alone. It's just the kids who are going to be wrong."

"It doesn't have much to do with right and wrong."

"The hell it doesn't. That's exactly how adults think. But what about him, what he was doing to Corrie? And then he expects her to be responsible, lets her babysit his children? He was just asking for trouble. It's all his fault, but who's going to buy it?"

"Jilly, I don't think that's the way this thing fits together."

"I do. I think Eliason deserves what happened. And I hate him for making me think like this. It bothers me that I do."

He put his arm over Jill's. "Fair trade, I'll tell you what bothers me. None of what happened surprises me. I know about a woman who shot her three kids because her boyfriend didn't like having them around. A guy who put cigars out in his son's eyes. It's common. Razor blades in Girl Scout Cookies. But it did surprise you and most of what happens from now on probably won't. It's like part of your life is over, a part you kept safe from the world. Had to happen sooner or later, but it happened now. I couldn't help you and that bothers me."

"I think I'll write about something else when they ask me what I did on my summer vacation."

As they were leaving the hospital, they overheard that TUSART had located Mary Eliason. The men were bringing her in. There was nothing to be done for her. It was over.

Jill was beyond crying. She walked with Timothy through the nearly empty streets of Traverse City to where he'd parked near the alley behind Clippers. They drove back to Fonzie and Oregano without talking and Jill fell asleep with her head on his arm. When he carried her inside the cabin, Timothy Packard was not beyond crying.

47

TIMOTHY DECIDED to build a fire. It would be their last night in Michigan and they hadn't had a fire yet, though the nights were always cool.

The trouble was, he wasn't good at building fires. Growing up in Long Beach apartments, he'd never had a fireplace. Not that Mrs. Packard would have allowed a fire anyway, with its potential for cinders and soot.

Then, when he was married, Charlene took care of the fires. It was something she'd learned from her father.

So Timothy tried to remember what Charlene used to do. There was definitely a right way to start these things.

He remembered her, one evening before Jill was born, crouching naked at the fireplace, engrossed in her procedures. When the fire had caught, it illuminated her, seeming to set her skin aflame. She'd spun around to face him, shrieking like a banshee, holding out her blackened hands. Along with the memory came a feeling, vague at first but then growing sharper. Timothy realized that he missed Charlene. Despite everything that had happened between them, he missed being with her.

As he crumpled newspaper into wads and placed them among the kindling, Timothy thought of Jill outside by the lake. She'd been so quiet the last few days, since the disaster at the river.

They'd taken the canoe out together, swept and tidied the cabin, talked, but her lassitude didn't fade. He couldn't get her to talk about Mary's death.

He knew, though, that she was having nightmares. He could hear her through the thin walls of their adjoining bedrooms. Last night, she'd gotten out of bed around 3:00 and come into the living room by the fire. Timothy heard her, but kept quiet, thinking she wanted to be alone. She blew her nose a few times.

Soon, Jill came over and stood in his doorway. All he could hear was her breathing. She tip-toed inside and sat in the old caned chair by the dresser, but still tried to avoid waking him. She sat there for at least an hour while he lay facing away from her, breathing as evenly as he could.

Now he wondered if, perhaps, she should be in here with him, learning about making a fire as he tried to learn. He wondered what other things he'd failed to teach her, failed to prepare her for.

He stacked three logs on his pile of paper and twigs, then lit the paper. It burned a while, but the logs didn't catch. He wadded up more paper, added more twigs. He considered splashing on a little gasoline.

Looking out the window, the thought occurred to him that he was making too many mistakes. He was fathering badly. What a word.

Had Jill smoked with Corrie? That, it turned out, was the question that he kept coming back to. And if she had, was it his fault? Would she again? You heard so much lately about how addictive crack was and how cheap.

And what about that boy in Long Beach? Had he raped her? Was she worried about being pregnant. He was always so proud of being close to Jill, but it was becoming clear now there was so much he didn't know about her.

As he watched her and stayed with her these few days, it seemed certain that Jill wasn't addicted to anything. Good God. He wasn't paying enough attention.

He worried that Jill felt she was to blame for Mary Eliason's death. He worried that she didn't ask any questions about Corrie, or seem to want to visit her.

He lit the paper again. He knocked the logs off until there was a legitimate fire in the kindling, then reached in and put a log back on. His hands smelled of ash.

As he walked out to invite his daughter in to see the fire, he faced the questions that had troubled him since Jill's school year began. Was he giving her too much freedom? Was he letting her turn into an adult too fast?

Say it, he told himself. Go ahead. It happens without you.

* * *

Leah Bell followed them out to the airport the next day. She took the keys to the cabin from Timothy and promised to send him anything that might have been left behind.

"We checked twice," Timothy said.

"Everybody leaves something. Never fails. So why don't you give me the address and phone number where you're going to stay in Oregon. I'll let you know what we find."

It was Leah's way of saying she would keep him posted, warn him in case something more was needed from Jill. The police were still trying to piece together the events at the river. They weren't getting much help.

The Eliasons had packed up and left Traverse City within thirty-six hours, taking Mary's body home for burial. Jill spent most of that day taking care of Miriam, who never asked where her sister was and never asked where Corrie was. Eliason told the police he wasn't interested in pressing charges against anybody. He just wanted to get out and never have to come back. People understood that.

The police picked up Santa in Petoskey, at the house of a woman who said they'd lived together ten years. He was playing roly-poly with their baby on the kitchen floor and listening to reggae music when the police arrived. He said he couldn't remember the last time he'd been in Traverse City and never heard of anyone named Corrine Moran. Or Corrie. Or Timothy Packard.

Corrie told the police she had no memory of anything that had happened to her since June. She refused to see any visitors, including Timothy, including Robbie Aswell. None of the names were familiar to her.

Nobody could provide a complete list of the teenagers who were at the river the day Mary Eliason drowned. Of course, Leon and Russell Boyd were there. Little Russell said he knew that his friend Miriam was there because they'd gone on a hike together, but that was all he could be sure of. He hadn't been around the river for long. Leon said the usual crowd was probably there, but one summer day was like another and he wasn't sure if that was the day Robbie skipped, or Ridley, or who.

The police posted the parking lot in front of Grand Traverse

Distillery. City Council would consider paying for a fence behind it, to keep people from using the river there for inner tubing.

It didn't appear that Timothy or Jill would have to be bothered further by the authorities in Michigan. Leah would keep him advised.

She walked with them into the terminal. Jill went on ahead of them to handle check-in and locate their gate.

"Remember me to Jerry Phillips when you get back to Illinois," she said.

"It's Monroe, Leah. Jerry Monroe. And I will."

"Still thinking about getting into commercial property?"

"You were pretty persuasive. I'll stick with residential, maybe develop a couple duplexes. It's a market I understand better."

"Well, good luck."

They embraced, then walked over to Jill, who was waiting with the boarding passes. Leah shook her hand.

"Sorry we didn't get to know each other better while you were here," Leah said. "Maybe next time you visit."

"Next time."

Jill didn't really think so, but she kept quiet about it. Their flight was ready for boarding.

SUMMER BLUE

PART FOUR

Oregon

48

FOR ABOUT an hour, since the pilot had pointed out the Great Salt Lake through the haze below, there had been little to see. Land gradually faded. It was replaced by gleaming sunlight and a skyless field of vapor, then drops on the window.

Timothy dozed, hearing rhythmic sounds from the headphones plugged into Jill's ears since they left O'Hare. Now she was nudging him awake, headphones down like a necklace, and gesturing to the windows.

"Look at that, Dad."

On both sides of the plane, all they could see were tips of mountain peaks jutting through thick clouds. Against the sheer blue sky, they comprised a stark dreamscape. Everything beneath the peaks was obscured, but they claimed their private realm with massive authority.

To the right was the rounded dome of Mt. St. Helens. Timothy remembered when St. Helens erupted, back in 1980. He had been alone at home, although it was a Sunday.

Thirteen hundred feet of the mountain's cone had disappeared in one white hot blast. He remembered there was a feisty old man who refused to leave his lodge on Spirit Lake and was never found. Blizzards of ash on the streets of Yakima and people trudging through the streets wearing surgical masks.

Timothy had taken Jill to Gardner Park a few evenings later, at dusk. They hoped to see the strange glow of light that would mean drifting ash had reached the midwest. Jill kept pointing at the moon, swearing it had been sliced in half by the volcano.

Beyond Mt. St. Helens they could see Mt. Rainier and even Mt. Adams. To the left, closest to the plane, was the carved blade of Mt. Hood. There was something noble about its shape, its harsh thrust, the clarity of its detail despite being ridged and shadowy in the summer sun.

"That's the one where those kids died," Timothy said. "The ones on that school hike. Remember? We watched it for two days on tv."

Lost in their separate thoughts, they watched as Mt. Hood passed from sight. The plane began its descent.

"Yeah. I remember that," Jill said. "Good old Unger announced over the p.a. that we should all turn our thoughts to our fellow students in their time of need. Something like that. I think he meant we were supposed to pray, but he wasn't allowed to say so. It really blew me away when they showed the helicopters bringing the kids to different hospitals all over the city."

"Right, and I kept thinking about the parents lined up near the ski lodge, watching the rescue teams through binoculars. There was that one color shot of the mountain at sunset, I'll never forget it. The commentator was talking about alpenglow, that orange light around the peak at sunrise. And he said the mountain doesn't care."

"Did they ever find out what went wrong?"

"A couple bad decisions, bad weather all of a sudden, bad luck."

"Basically like the man said, huh? The mountain didn't care."

In Oregon, it was always supposed to rain. It was supposed to be overcast and dank, with about fifteen minutes of sunlight even on the best August days.

But the temperature when they landed in Portland was 97. The clouds they had seen socking in Mt. Hood had covered the city a few hours ago, but now the sky was the color of Jill's eyes and clear to the west.

Even though the humidity was lower than in Michigan, Timothy wasn't fooled. It was hot. It was going to be a miserable Friday afternoon trip to the coast.

It took them fifteen minutes to drive the dozen miles from the airport into Portland. Two hours later, they'd managed only five more miles through the city, finally reaching the Sunset Highway. Reporters in helicopters called it typical weekend traffic, not bad unless you were headed for the coast.

"What's the word I'm looking for, Dad?"

"Inauspicious. From the Latin *auspicium*, for bird divination. The finding of omens. Its current meaning, however, is 'this shits.'"

Between Portland and the Coastal Range, Oregon could have been Michigan. There were rolling hills and pear orchards. Fruit stands along the road offered blackberries, boysenberries and raspberries, cheaper if you picked them yourself. They passed wineries with makeshift tasting chalets, filbert farms, dozens of craft galleries and antique shops in refurbished sheds.

It was getting hotter as the afternoon deepened. But when they had crossed the Coastal Range, the temperature dropped twenty degrees. They stopped for coffee and Diet Coke at a cafe in Elsie and Jill put on her Velvet Underground sweatshirt.

Then, as the road crested one last hill and swung them away from a ragged clear-cut, the ocean suddenly flashed in front of them above Tillamook Head. They turned onto Route 101, which could take them all the way to Mexico, and Jill laughed with excitement.

"It's so much rougher than the other ocean," she said.

"I remember that, now."

When he saw her, Timothy couldn't believe the ways in which Natalie had changed. Seeing her made things instantly come together.

It was as though the women in his family had all moved one square ahead in some kind of weird game. Jill had evolved into a woman very much like the younger Natalie while Natalie had evolved into Charlene and Charlene had been removed from the board.

Natalie came out of her house when she heard them pull off 101. Her smile was a little too wide. She shook her arms as if unfurling a Welcome sign, pointed to its imaginary writing, then lost her grip on it and sadly watched it sail away over the house.

She wore a yellow softball shirt with a black lightning bolt across her chest and People's Power on the back. She had on a baseball cap with a small lightning bolt on its crown and her red hair stuck through the adjustable band in the back.

Her black cotton pants were skin tight. They ended in stirrups which disappeared into a pair of spike heeled shoes.

Natalie walked right past Timothy and gathered Jill in her arms.

The last time Timothy had seen Natalie was in the period after Charlene's funeral. She was twenty-six then. She had come to visit a few times while Charlene was in the hospital and, after the funeral, stayed on for six months to help with Jill.

Her willingness to leave the rest of her life in limbo for half a year astounded Timothy so much that he stopped thinking about it. He simply accepted her presence as one might accept a rainbow after a tornado.

She would pick Jill up after school and spend most of each afternoon with her eight-year-old niece in Gardn____, or visiting and revisiting central Illinois' few sights.

They'd seen all the Lincoln memorials—his homes, office, and tomb; the restored site of his 'House Divided' speech; the train depot where his body had arrived from Washington; the gardens where benches were engraved with his famous sayings. They'd seen the place from which the Donner Party departed on its calamitous trek and Natalie talked to Jill about the ferocity needed for human survival. They took steamboat rides on the Illinois and the Mississippi.

Timothy seldom came along. He spent most of the six months on the telephone with lawyers and insurance people, with realty companies and prospective clients, immersed in what he kept calling the real world.

Natalie had made no friends herself, although she encouraged Jill to play with other children and would not leave until she was certain Jill had enough friends. Timothy had lost these memories for years.

"Do you remember Lincoln's Home?" Jill was asking Natalie now. They held hands, smiling.

"Do I ever." They walked around the house to the back porch, where the view of the Pacific was clear. "We went there at least twice a week."

"And that awful film we had to see each time?"

"You know, I still think about that. How there's absolutely no pictures of little Eddie Lincoln. Not one. The dog Fido, yes, but no Eddie. Remember how we'd pretend he was too squirmy to sit still long enough?"

"And I'd always cover my ears when they talked about Tad and Willie dying."

Timothy trailed behind them. He heard the force of the waves and was mesmerized by their action. He hadn't remembered how much more power they had than the waves he knew at the Atlantic coast.

"My God, look at that," Natalie said. "It still gets me. Every time I show this view to somebody new, it's like I'm seeing it the first time myself."

From the back porch, they could see down an overgrown cliff, which plunged two hundred feet to the water. There was a narrow path zigzagging down the cliff, opening onto a crescent of sand that was Natalie's nearly private beach. From Countryman Point at its north edge to Austin Point at its south, the beach at low tide couldn't have been more than a half-mile wide. As the tide came in, the beach vanished.

They went inside the house. The back wall of the living room was mostly window, with an uninterrupted view of the ocean. Natalie had two pairs of binoculars hung on hooks beside the window, a tide chart on the sill, and a powerful telescope in the corner.

"The best," Natalie said, "is watching January storms come in. The winter here's almost as pretty as the summer."

"What's that thing?"

"Haystack Rock. It's farther away than you think, almost to Cannon Beach. We'll walk there maybe tomorrow—about four miles. Sometimes you can see seals, almost always you find starfish and surf-birds when the tide's out. Just past it is a great place to fly kites."

Jill nestled against her aunt's side as they stood by the window. Natalie draped an arm over Jill's shoulder.

"Forgive us, Tim. I meant to say hello ten minutes ago. How are you?"

Timothy finally hugged his sister-in-law. "It's nice to see you."

"You too. And you're in time. I was a little worried you'd get here late. Tonight's the last night of the run for this play I'm in up at Cannon Beach. You'll come?"

"Sure," Jill said immediately.

"Love to. I'd just like to go for a short run first. When do we leave."

"Now, actually."

49

THE PLAY was at the Coaster Theater, a high-ceilinged barn that shared a courtyard with the Wine Seller. Its cedar wood interior strove for intimacy, an effect carried further by a snug auditorium. A packed house was one hundred fifty.

Written by a local woman two years ago, *The Silent Garden* premiered at The Coaster last summer. During the year, there was a production in Portland that attracted a wider audience than expected. It won the Willie Award given by a local weekly for best play of the year. So by popular demand, the play was back home for three weeks, original cast intact.

The playwright, Alison Vintage, had written the lead role with Natalie in mind. Her character could not speak or hear, but she saw powerfully, with vision like a hawk's. She communicated what she knew through mime. And what she knew were the secrets in people's hearts. Members of the community she lived in would come to watch her performances in the same way they came to church on Sunday to hear the pastor speak. Her pulpit was the rose garden behind her home.

That was all Natalie would tell Jill and Timothy before the show. They drove together to Cannon Beach, where she left them at The Lemon Tree to eat. Natalie went ahead to The Coaster to get ready.

She was on stage alone when the curtain lifted, dressed in a white gown with white ribbons in her hair. Natalie's movements above the roses were precise and purposeful. It took Timothy several moments to register that the roses weren't actually there.

For three minutes, Natalie moved in total silence, working her way through the garden. From time to time, she checked beyond the audience for any movement in the town. Crossing from stage left to right only once, she managed to suggest utter possession of the play's world.

The impression she created was so powerful that the audience did not doubt that she was always there, even when she was offstage. As the pairs of lovers interchanged throughout the first two acts, the implications of their actions were seen through Natalie's eyes. They were given life by her performances in the garden, to which more and more townspeople came as the play progressed.

"Can you tell what's going on?" Timothy asked Jill before the last act.

"Why, can't you?"

The play's final minutes were devoted to a last performance by Natalie's character. All the lovers were assembled in her garden for the first time.

It was only in the instant before the curtain fell that Timothy finally did see what was going on. He'd missed it all before, caught up in the agony of Natalie's isolated character.

That all the men loved Natalie's non-speaking, non-hearing woman had escaped him. As she vanished, he grasped that the men sought their private visions of her in the other women. They were obsessed with her ability to see through them. What they loved was having the secrets in their own hearts taken over by another.

"So what do you think it *is* about Natalie?" Alison Vintage asked. She and Timothy were waiting for Natalie outside the dressing room backstage. Jill was inside.

"She's a compelling performer, that's for sure. I'm very impressed."

"She'll be glad to know that. But what do you suppose gives her this force? Where does her strength to so coerce an audience come from?"

"Maybe it's her body. She has such command of it."

"There is that."

"And her concentration. I could feel the intensity even back where we were sitting."

She nodded. Timothy could tell his answers failed to satisfy her.

Alison Vintage was tenaciously plain. But ten seconds with her undercut the impression she worked hard to create. Every choice in creating her exterior had been made in the interests of restraint and modesty—no lipstick or eye shadow, no jewelry, brown hair parted in the middle and hanging to just below her ears, clear plastic frames for her glasses, earth tones for her simple skirt and sweater. She might be nearing sixty, but she might also be thirty. It was as though everything was assembled to repel close attention.

However, her gray eyes were keen with curiosity and her deep voice, though carefully modulated, commanded attention. She spoke with a stillness in her face, hands resolutely clasped behind her and body devoid of the least movement. Nevertheless, Dylan Thomas had no greater sway over an audience than Alison Vintage. She exuded will.

"Those are technical considerations, Mr. Packard. Though accurate, they are not truly germane to the impact she has. If you'll forgive me, I believe she has true magnetism. A field of force."

"Star quality, is that what you mean?"

"Hardly. You said you were trained as an engineer. You must know about superconductivity, Mr. Packard?"

"Well, superconductivity always seemed like a laboratory concept to me, an idea without practical use. I mean, there are other, simpler ways to create a magnetic field. But yet these physicists wanted prizes for achieving two seconds worth of superconductivity."

"Ahh. And you haven't much use for theoretics. Indulge me for a moment, then. When conditions can be made right, as through the use of intense cold, it is possible to alter the actual structure of basic reality. For instance, when liquid nitrogen—which they use now—eliminates all resistance, electricity is suddenly permitted to flow without loss. This is superconductivity. It is an entirely new state of affairs, you see? Now, this is what seems to me to be Natalie's secret. What happens to her on stage is like what happens when certain materials are transformed, by exposure to special conditions. Everything lines up in a new way to permit something to happen which otherwise would not happen. Like them, she can be made to have properties she normally would not have. She becomes a chamber of limitless possibilities. That is what I think."

"Fascinating, Ms. Vintage. You really think Natalie has that kind of talent?"

The dressing room door opened as a cast member left. Timothy glanced up quickly. He caught sight of Jill on a chair beside Natalie, who was removing her makeup by a wall of mirrors.

"Call me Alison, if you will. Or Allie. Perhaps I may call you Timothy?"

He nodded and looked away from the door. "Of course. Tim."

"And the answer to your question, Tim, is no. I don't think she has great talent. She has magnetism. With greater talent, she would be a brilliant actress; now she is merely a riveting performer."

50

"THAT'S ALL you're going to wear?" Timothy asked.

"I'm going sunbathing," Jill said. "People don't wear jeans and sweaters when they sunbathe."

"But it's fifty-two degrees."

"So what?"

"Jill, listen to that wind. And the sun's not even out."

"I don't care. You can get a good tan in the haze too."

"And pneumonia in the cold."

Jill opened the back door. She walked out on the porch and slipped into her sandals.

Timothy followed her partway out. He leaned through the doorway.

"Plus," she said, "I intend to go body surfing after the sunbathing. Then I'm going to lie on a beach towel and let the air dry me off."

"I'm standing here considering earmuffs. What're you trying to prove?"

"Who says I'm trying to prove something? I just want to have one day of the kind of summer I signed up for. Is that all right with you?"

"What're you mad at me for?"

"Who says I'm mad?" She stomped down the porch stairs, blowing into her cupped hands.

Timothy watched her walk down the path until she disappeared. He took down a pair of binoculars and scanned the ocean, watching a few charter boats move across the horizon. When Jill reappeared at the base of the cliff, he followed her awkward movement through the soft sand.

He thought she might walk out of sight, across Countryman Point, to sunbathe where he couldn't watch her. But she spread her blanket directly beneath the house.

Suddenly, she spun around to face the house. She looked up and waved at him.

51

EBB TIDE dictated a late morning run. Timothy took off south, heading past Austin Point toward Short Sands.

Natalie and Jill walked north, rounding Countryman Point and skipping toward Hug Point. Since it was her day off, Natalie was willing to accommodate Timothy's schedule. But she preferred to walk in the evening.

The cliffs along the beach near Hug Point were gouged with caves. Some still had pools of tidewater in them, although they would be dry in another hour. A fleet of sandpipers skirred the water's edge for food. A chocolate Labrador romped nearby, circling a hooded figure walking ankle-deep in the surf.

Natalie and Jill strolled along the line of wet sand at the edge of the waves. Their hands were deep in their pockets and they wore baseball caps backwards against the wind.

"She's probably my closest companion," Natalie said. "Allie was the first friend I made when I got to Oregon."

"I've never met a real writer before."

"Guess what she was before she started writing."

"The way she talks, probably a professor of something. Philosophy, maybe."

"She'd get a yuk out of that one. It's pretty strange, though—she was an investment counselor. Right away, she offered to help me manage the settlement money I got in my divorce. God, I didn't trust her at all."

"But now you must, huh? I mean, you two—what's the word I want here?—aren't you sort of closer than friends?"

Natalie didn't answer. She bent down for a sand dollar, took Jill's hand and turned it over, then put the shell into her palm.

"You almost never find sand dollars intact like this. They're a kind of sea urchin. Usually I find them chipped, or broken in pieces by the gulls. No, Allie and I aren't lovers, Jill. Just very good friends."

"Sorry. I didn't mean to pry."

"Do you believe me?"

"Sure. You're my aunt."

"It's ok. Listen, do you remember Chutes and Ladders? We played it, what, six hundred times that year?"

Jill smiled. "Oh, wow. I haven't thought about Chutes and Ladders forever. That used to be so much fun."

"Well, why don't we play it now?"

"You're kidding me. It's too nice to go back and play games. Anyway, I want to see where you work."

"We'll play right here."

Natalie stopped walking and looked up toward cliffs to the east. She turned back to check the tides. Then she began marking off a huge square in the sand, digging the lines with her shoe.

Jill watched her. "I don't believe this."

"You don't have to believe it. Just play it. Now help me set up the board."

Jill didn't move, but she did begin to smile. Shaking her head slowly, she gave in, toeing perpendicular lines within Natalie's square.

Natalie crisscrossed Jill's with lines of her own until they'd made a hundred uneven boxes within the boundaries. She stood back to survey the work.

"Now you do the chutes," Natalie said. "I'll draw the ladders."

"I don't remember where they go."

"Make it up."

When the gameboard was finished, they found twelve small clamshells to use as dice. Natalie drew a circle beside the board.

"Throw the shells at the circle. However many you get in, that's how many squares you can move."

"What if the tide comes in? It'll ruin the game."

"Sure it will. But we're only playing one game, not a tournament. Winner takes all. Now no more talking, we do the rest in silence."

Natalie picked up the shells and threw them at the circle. She hopped ten squares, gestured toward the circle, and folded her arms across her chest.

Jill threw a two. Natalie turned to watch her hop to the base of a ladder, then scurry up to square number twenty-two.

She frowned enormously, the corners of her mouth turning so far down Jill thought her aunt's face was melting. Then Natalie fetched the shells and got all twelve within the circle. Smiling, she jumped ahead until she reached Jill's square, arriving with a spray of sand.

After the game, they continued walking north toward Haystack Rock. A couple on horseback cantered toward them, emerging from the shadow of the cliffs.

Natalie said, "So this guy asks me, even before we leave for dinner, can he take my picture? Out on the back porch, with the nice view. What am I going to say, you know? It's not like he asked me to pose nude. So about two weeks later, we're back at his cabin after a movie and he's got this photo album on his coffee table. I look and there's maybe fifty, sixty girls in it. And nothing else. I go, What's going on? and he says, 'This is my Book of Love. I got every girl I went out with in the last couple years.' He was real proud of the collection. I'm sitting there thinking this is not a good sign. What do you think?"

"Based on my many years of experience," Jill answered, "I'd have to agree with you."

"Oh, maybe I shouldn't be talking about this so much. You must be just getting started, right? With boys, I mean. I don't want to prejudice you."

"Actually, I've been thinking a whole lot about retiring from boys for a while. Say, till I'm thirty."

Natalie nodded, silent for a few strides. "You want to tell me a little more?"

"I don't think so."

"Fine. We can rent a couple of three-wheel funcycles and pedal around the beach like ten year olds if you want."

"That's not what I meant."

"It was just an offer."

"I meant I want to tell you *a lot* more. Everything." She grabbed Natalie's elbow and they stopped walking.

"I'd like that."

"Even if we had to walk all the way up to Canada?"

52

TIMOTHY SPREAD *David Copperfield* face-down in his lap. He looked out toward Haystack Rock, imagining that it was Mr. Peggoty's home on the Yarmouth coast. An old boat, high and dry on the beach, with an iron funnel sticking out of it for a chimney. The image fit well enough. The one place Copperfield knew a family that functioned.

He looked down at the book and turned it over to see what page he was on. Good Lord, he'd read 293 pages, enough to have finished most novels already. And here he was, what?—he could still do it quickly in his head—only 36% complete. At this rate, he'd be finished in late October. How did people find the time to read 814-page books? Ok, maybe in 1850 there was more time for reading, but Timothy knew people read Charles Dickens now, too. Otherwise why would a company like Bantam publish them?

He stood and stretched, scanning the beach for any sign of Natalie and Jill. Then he went downstairs to the bathroom.

On the way, he stepped into the utility room to check out the condition of the pipes and wiring. He'd been wanting to give the place a realtor's once-over since they'd arrived.

Just as he'd guessed, the pipes were small. Not much water pressure to begin with and you can't wash dishes or flush the toilet while someone's showering. He tapped them. Probably clogged up as well. Natalie had mentioned that everybody around Arch Cape used untreated ground water. No wonder the pipes choke up.

He scanned the walls and ceiling. At least the wiring looked new. There was a gray circuit breaker box beside the utility room door, with its scheme neatly marked inside the cover. Webs of frayed, older wires still dangled from the ceiling, although none were connected with the fuse box underneath the stairs.

He went into the bathroom, which was always damp and cold. Timothy lifted the edge of the carpet, which wasn't tacked down, and pushed at the floorboard. You could practically feel the air coming through. He remembered there was a crawlspace outside, screened by latticework. Obviously, she ought to tighten that up. She ought to put down some kind of lining under the floorboard, maybe a plastic sheeting. He'd have to talk to her about it.

With the newish roof and the storm windows, the house was fairly tight. He'd noticed the fire place floor looked recently built up with a couple layers of brick. Probably had a smoke problem in the house for years. Natalie was taking pretty good care of the place. She must have gotten a nice settlement from her ex.

In the space between the bathroom and stairs there was a large freezer. It didn't seem to be plugged into a socket anywhere. Timothy wondered what she stored inside. Maybe extra blankets or old costumes? Jellies and potatoes?

He opened the freezer. It was filled with grocery bags. Inside the top bag were scripts, all marked up with Natalie's blocking directions and terse character notes. They must have been from plays she'd acted in. He hadn't realized she'd been so serious about it. Another bag had photographs, which Timothy flipped through quickly. A loose scrapbook, nobody and no place he recognized.

The third bag had the letters. As soon as he pulled them out,

Timothy recognized Charlene's sharply slanted handwriting and the lavender ink she'd used during those last weeks in the hospital.

He didn't want to read them.

Timothy turned the packet over, fanned through them like a deck of cards, held them to his nose. Nothing. Tucking the letters back into the bag, he shut the freezer and bolted upstairs.

In the kitchen, he made a fresh pot of coffee. While it worked through, he stood by the window and used binoculars to see if Natalie and Jill were in sight.

Before the coffee was even ready, he headed back down to the freezer. The letters were held together loosely by a cloth belt, the kind that might come with a matching pair of men's slacks.

They were in inverse order of composition, the top one post-marked five days before Charlene's death. Timothy saw that the letters spanned only four months. At first, given the size of the stack, he'd thought they might have covered all the years of their marriage.

He started in the middle, working his way back toward the first letter. It must have followed Charlene's first phone call to Natalie, telling her that she was going to die.

Within an hour, he was done. He folded the last letter and put the belt around the stack. He carefully placed the grocery bag back where it belonged among the others, then went to his bedroom to lie down.

"Just don't let me fall asleep," he said aloud. He folded his arms across his chest.

At the end, it was clear, Charlene was not afraid to die. She was welcoming death for several reasons, most of which he'd guessed at the time.

There was one that stunned him. It was something he'd never thought of. It was clear that Charlene had tired of waiting for Timothy to forgive her.

In an early letter, she forgave herself—and Timothy—for the mistakes in their marriage. She knew she was responsible for much of his pain and had accepted it. Before, she'd thought his ideals were his own problem. If he were a more flexible man, nothing she'd done would have mattered so much. After all, she was never in love with someone else.

But she understood that her affair (not affairs?) had stripped him of his belief in marriage. She also understood that he had nothing, and she'd given him nothing, to use in its place. *He abandoned marriage and clung to paternity.*

He withdrew from her after that. Charlene understood and forgave him, but he could not do the same with her.

And it parched us, Nat. I look at it as if the sun had finally defeated the life-giving rain. The fertile field of our life together turned into a desert. I couldn't walk away from it entirely, but there was too little nourishment left to support us.

53

THE NEXT Saturday was Sandcastle Day on Cannon Beach. Jill and Natalie wanted to go.

They got up early enough to watch the sun rise over the Coastal Range. From the hill opposite Natalie's house, the smell of fir and cedar was mixed sharply with the salt mist. By 7:00, they had cooked French toast and brought a plate down to Timothy, who slept through his alarm.

"Chow down, Dad. We don't want to be late."

He sat up in bed, hair mussed. "Go ahead without me. I want to sleep in."

"Look at him, Aunt Nat, " Jill said over her shoulder, keeping an eye on Timothy. "Doesn't his head look like one of those sea anemones we saw yesterday?"

He flopped back down and pulled the sheet over himself. "Who wants to watch a bunch of grown people making sand castles? Sounds dumb to me."

"Timothy Packard, now you've insulted my friends and neighbors," Natalie said from the hall. "Sandcastle Day's been a Cannon Beach tradition since 1964. Give it a chance and you'll get into it, I promise. Now come on, we've got to get there before the hoards arrive."

They walked up together along the beach. Timothy straggled into the surf without seeming to realize he was doing it, then skipped back to them with a sweet smile, suggesting they race to the next wayside table. When they refused, he darted off as stiff-legged as a sandpiper, calling *krip krip* and holding his arms motionless at his side.

By the time they reached Cannon Beach, the contest had already begun. Natalie led them through the crowd until they reached the rope that separated spectators from sculptors. She said there was supposed to be more than a hundred sandsculptors this year, the most ever.

"It's a bigger draw than a Seattle Mariners game," said a young man standing beside them.

The sculptors were competing for the Art in Sand awards. There were categories for both adults and children. The jurors sat on lifeguard towers at the far end of the building area. Alison Vintage was one of them. She waved when Timothy looked up.

"How long does this thing last?" Timothy asked.

"Till high tide," Natalie said. "We're talking perishable art, here."

"You mean we're staying here till the afternoon?"

Natalie dismissed his question with a wave. She leaned toward Jill and whispered something that made her laugh.

They watched the sandsculptors scurry around their huge figures, working with rakes, shovels and buckets. Some had brought feather dusters, funnels and melon ball scoops in retooled tackle boxes. Others used trowels and toothbrushes for detail work—making creases in the pockets of a sand man trying to crawl inside his sand igloo, making whiskers on the face of a sand catfish buried from the gills down in sand waters. Several sculptors brought tank sprayers to keep the delicate parts of their pieces from crumbling.

After an hour, Timothy wandered off. "I need some coffee."

He left the beach and walked the mile along Hemlock Street from downtown to midtown. He felt too jittery for coffee. There was no reason for him to be hungry, but he was hungry anyway. He read menus in the windows, but nothing he saw looked good to him. He turned back to the north. Seashore Pizza was just opening for the day, so he went inside to buy a slice and took it to the park with a Coke.

"I liked the octopus best," Jill said.

"Maybe the dragon next. How could they give it to the snakes?"

"Politics," Natalie said. "The Portland crowd must have intimidated the judges. I hope Allie held out."

"First prize to a vacuum cleaner? It wasn't even a nice vacuum cleaner."

"Yes it was. An old electrolux. I liked what happened when the waves got to it."

They were walking down Hemlock trying to locate Timothy. With its shops clustered in a dozen blocks, Cannon Beach wasn't a difficult place to track someone down. But they had no luck.

"I know what you're thinking, Aunt Nat. But he's not like this."

Natalie chuckled. "Ok. What is he like, then?"

"Something's bothering him, that's all. Maybe it's what happened in Michigan. Whenever I look at him, I see that scab on his throat and think of him in the alley with that guy I told you about. Santa. He could've been killed."

"Sure, he's a good father, I know that. Don't get me wrong, Jill. Tim's a good man, too. But good men can be boring for some women to live with. And they're awfully easy to hurt. That's what I think he is now. But I'm not sure why."

"Maybe because of me."

"Maybe because of me."

"What did you ever do to hurt him?"

"Be your mother's sister."

Timothy wasn't anywhere in town. Figuring he'd headed for Natalie's house alone, they went back to the beach and started for home.

They found him standing in the rising tidepool at Haystack Rock. He was turning a live starfish over in his hand. One of its legs was missing. He probed the stump with a finger, lost in thought, and didn't hear Jill and Natalie until they were at his side.

54

"IT'S FOR you, Tim. A woman. Sounds like long distance."

He wiped his hands, which were a little greasy from the chicken, and took his glass of Chardonnay with him to the phone. Jill got up to help Natalie clear the table.

"Hello?"

"Hi, Tim. Hope this isn't a bad time to call."

"Jane? Jill and I were just talking about you today. How funny that you should call."

"Listen, this isn't a call I wanted to make. It's not good news."

"What's the matter? You fall in love?"

Jill stuck her head around the kitchen door, hearing the change in his tone. Timothy's eyes were closed.

"It's your mother, Tim. I'm afraid she's been in an accident. She's badly hurt. I think you should be here."

After he'd hung up, Timothy sat in the small rocker Natalie used for a desk chair. By then, Jill was at his side.

"What happened?"

"Jane said they didn't know much. The cops are still investigating. A van from the meat market hit her broadside and they had to use torches to get her out."

"Is she," Jill stopped, trying not to cry.

"The car's a total loss."

"How is Grandma?"

"I know the corner where it happened. One of those boulevards with cars parked all around it. You can't see what's coming from the corner."

Natalie came into the room. "Tim, did she survive the crash?"

Timothy looked at Natalie as though he didn't recognize her. Then he looked back at Jill.

185

"Intensive care. Internal injuries, broken legs, they don't think her head's hurt. I didn't ask too much, I guess."

"That's good," Natalie said. "About her head, I mean."

"Jane thinks I'd better get there as soon as possible."

"Should I come too?" Jill asked.

Timothy stood. "Nat, could you open another wine? I'd like a little more."

She left them only for a moment, bringing the new bottle and the corkscrew back into the living room. She worked on it in the corner by the window, keeping her eyes on Jill.

"What do you think?" Timothy asked.

"I should go. Keep you company, help out, maybe make Grandma feel better."

"This is your vacation, Jilly. I don't know." He looked toward Natalie. "Maybe she could stay here? It might be a while."

Natalie nodded.

"Dad, shouldn't I be with you?"

Timothy put his arms around Jill and rested his cheek against her head.

"This is very strange, everything at once. I don't know what's best."

"Can I say something?" Natalie asked.

"Go ahead."

"Let Jill stay with me. If you get there and think she should join you, I'll put her on a plane right away. Meanwhile, she can have a break. I hope you don't mind my saying this, but it sounds like this has been a doozy of a summer for her. Why not spare her any more stress if we can?"

Timothy could feel that Jill had begun to cry. He looked away from Natalie, out the window at the fading light.

55

HE DROVE back to Portland early the next morning. There was a flight at 6:30 that would get him to LaGuardia by 4:00 pm, without having to change planes. Jane would meet his flight and bring him to Long Beach.

Timothy tried to imagine his mother now. He'd never seen her injured, never seen her further from consciousness than in sleep. There would be tubes everywhere, he was prepared for that, masses of white bandages and bedclothes, her legs splinted and splayed. She would be bruised, unable to speak, perhaps unable to open her eyes and see him.

He could hear her thick voice during their last phone conversation from Michigan. It was as if her vital capacity had been halved by fifty years of smoking Chesterfields.

No matter how hard he tried to avoid it, his mind kept producing images of the impact. The van bulged with meat. There was a bull's head on its hood, with razory horns gleaming in sunlight, long as lances. His mother, tilted way back in her seat, chin raised so she could see over the wheel, barely paused at the stop sign before accelerating across the boulevard. Out of the corner of her eye, she saw the van charge toward her. There was no time to react.

He stopped for coffee at the first open restaurant, just past Sunset Summit. There was little traffic and he reached Portland by 5:00.

Alpenglow tinged the peak of Mt. Hood orange as he approached the airport. He knew it was a trick of light, a matter of reflection. Still, for a few moments, the carnelian tinge of the morning sky was very beautiful.

Timothy set his watch to eastern time. He skipped breakfast and slept until Denver.

During the layover, he didn't get off the plane to stretch his legs or buy the local paper. He didn't try to read and knew he couldn't sleep.

Instead, he curled in his seat to watch the baggage being loaded off and loaded on.

Between Denver and New York there was a movie. Timothy refused the earphones, but stared at the screen. Two buddies, undercover cops, were in trouble with everybody. The black one had a girlfriend and the white one had an ex-wife. Timothy recognized that most of the film was shot in Chicago, places he'd seen with Charlene. Suddenly there was a coast, maybe Florida.

Deplaning in a light rain, Timothy shouldered his bag and headed for the terminal. He walked past Jane without seeing her until she grabbed his arm.

56

MRS. PACKARD's feet were smeared with orange germicide. There were plaster of Paris specks on her toenails. She won't like that, Timothy thought.

He walked away from her bed, thinking about colors. So much blue and green, as though these two fishbowl rooms of the ICU were awash, a subaqueous zone. The screens and scopes flickered green on black, peeping constantly. Everything that was hard was blue, even the monitor leads planted on his mother's body and the plastic tubes that twisted across her chest.

He had been prepared for white, for the starkness of critical care, the alabaster of multiple trauma. Maybe that was why he felt so unsteady and tight, as though he'd run too fast too early in a long race.

The ICU reminded Timothy of Control Center at the power company where he used to work. It had the same steely hush, the same intensity, a faint aura that exuded from the borders of exhaustion.

One wall was a bank of monitors, their digital readouts constantly shifting. Clocks were everywhere. Like dispatchers, nurses seemed to ignore the apparatus, moving purposefully between the large blue beds. But Timothy studied the numbers, trying to block out the eerie sound of respirators that filled his ears.

He left the room and sat on a gurney in the hall. She knows I'm here, he thought. When he whispered to her, Mrs. Packard's eyes seemed to clench, then fluttered open. She made a sound deep in her throat, blinked, then shut her eyes.

"Do you want to stay with me?"

"Later on, I think I might. Tonight I'd rather stay at her apartment."

"It's no trouble for me."

"The apartment's closer."

"Is that good or bad?"

It took four keys to get into his mother's apartment. One key opened the main door, another was for the lobby, and two were for the apartment itself. Out of habit, Timothy clopped his shoes together in the hallway to remove any sand.

He put his bags in the den and unpacked quickly. Then he ferreted out the Dewars. This was one of his rare hard liquor nights.

The apartment was oppressive, torrid from the heat his mother had left on. Timothy slipped the cover off the radiator and shut it down.

He opened the windows, unfolded the bed, and sat listening to the jets roar overhead toward Kennedy. He knew he should call Jill and Natalie. He should call a few of his elderly relatives, people he hadn't spoken to since his voice had changed, and let them know what had happened to his mother.

Instead, he set his alarm for 5:30 and slept.

Timothy ran in the morning. As he left his mother's apartment, keys looped through his shoelaces, his plan was to run on the boardwalk to its end and back again. But the wind was from the west, the boardwalk was only two miles long, and he felt like running for hours.

He headed north and crossed the Long Beach Bridge, setting Mack's Clam Bar as his turnaround point. That would be about five miles out, five miles back. Just right.

As soon as he crossed the bridge, he saw his mother's car. It was parked beside the fence at Cobb's Auto Body, the first building on the Island Park side.

He should have remembered Cobb's was where it had been towed. Jane mentioned it when they were driving in from LaGuardia.

Timothy ran past, looking the other way. He needed more miles before he was ready. On the way back an hour later, he stopped at Cobb's.

He'd gone to high school with Marco Cobb. Marco set the county javelin record and was notorious for his savage bellow that accompanied every throw. His father, who owned the body shop, had once been a stock-car driver. The old man was sipping coffee from a 7-11 cup when Timothy came in.

He looked at Timothy, then back into his coffee. "I'm not open, pal. Come back at 9:00, hey?"

"You don't remember me."

"Before 9:00, I only remember cars. After 9:00, I remember people. Provided they're over fifty."

"I went to school with your son."

"Yeah? Well now I've seen you more in the last ten years than I seen him."

Timothy explained what he wanted. Jane would drive him back after his shower to get his mother's stuff from the car.

"The brown Toyota?" Cobb asked.

"Honda. How bad is it?" He still hadn't examined the car close-up, hadn't seen the driver's side.

"You say she's still alive?"

Cobb helped them move Mrs. Packard's suitcases from the Honda to Jane's Audi. Mrs. Packard had been headed for her annual week in the Poconos. There was also a shopping bag in the trunk, filled with wrapped gifts for the old friends who would always meet her there.

"She's gone to the Poconos every year since I was fifteen," Timothy told him. "It was the only time she ever wore pants."

"Where at?"

"Lake Wallenpaupack. You ever been there?"

"What're you, kidding me? I go to a place like that, the regular people stop coming. Nah, I did some racing at Long Pond once. That's about it for me and Pennsylvania."

Cobb reached through the space where Mrs. Packard's window had been. He emptied the contents of the glove compartment into a shoe box and handed it to Jane. The dashboard was covered by a crust of glass.

"Why didn't she fly someplace instead of drive alone, a woman her age? Maybe Canada, it's nice up there in the summertime."

"She's afraid to fly." Timothy stopped moving and looked at Cobb. He felt as if he were about to cry. "She's afraid of a crash."

"Well, could have been worse," Cobb said. "Could have happened on a mountainside, you know?"

Timothy nodded, then bent into the back seat where his mother's white shawl was heaped. He lifted it out of the car. In its center was a large circle of blood. When he held it up, the shawl looked like a tattered flag of Japan.

Cobb invited them into his office. Jane and Timothy stood with their backs against the window, looking away from the lot. A boy was fishing in the channel just beyond the back fence.

"You ask me, I'd say get the insurance guy out pretty quick. It's seven-fifty a day, storage."

"Thanks," Timothy mumbled.

"You know what happened?"

"Not yet," Jane answered. "She got hit by a van, looks to me like he was going a tad faster than the ten miles an hour he told the cops. They're investigating, but so far no tickets."

"It's a no-fault state, right lady? You'll want to move fast, though. These things take a long time, what with lawyers involved."

"We'll remember that," Jane said. She led Timothy out of the office.

The scan confirmed there was no head injury. But Mrs. Packard was still asleep and hadn't been alert for more than a few seconds. The doctor thought she should have longer periods of consciousness soon.

"Why isn't she awake?"

"We don't always know, Mr. Packard. Your mother's not young. There's been a shock, surgery. There was internal bleeding, which we have under control. The woman's been through something significant, if you see what I mean. We're easing up on the medication. But it takes time."

"Does she know anything? She know I'm here?"

"That's very difficult to say."

"She must be in pain."

"We've helped her with that."

"Look, can you tell me if she'll live? At least what the odds are."

"This isn't Las Vegas. I will say we're fairly sure she'll survive these particular injuries. But whether she walks again, whether she can care for herself by herself? That will be up to her. We have to get her up as soon as we can. Our goal is to get her moving."

57

"THEY'RE NOT toys."

"Sure they are. Who flies kites except kids?"

"You've got some of the strangest ideas, Jill. We've got to do something about you."

They stopped on the sidewalk to pass a blueberry danish between them. The morning was cool enough for sweaters.

"You're trying to tell me kites aren't toys?"

"They're not *just* toys. They're many things."

"You know what my dad would say? He'd say 'Natalie, you can't see the forest for the trees.'"

"Well, I'll bet you dinner on it. I'm right, you cook; you're right, I cook. A good 75% of the people I sell kites to are adults."

"No deal." Jill popped the last of the danish into her mouth and licked her fingertips. "Maybe adults buy the kites, but their kids fly them."

Natalie dug into her paper bag. She drew out a roll shaped like Haystack Rock, which collapsed into itself when she took the first bite.

"Ok, I'll bet you 75% of the people we see flying kites on the beach today are adults. Count them, I trust you."

They reached Wayward Winds. Natalie unlocked the store and led Jill in. She pointed to a broom against the back wall.

Wayward Winds was only a block from The Coaster Theater, where Natalie taught mime class twice a week. Jill volunteered to work at the store alone during the two hours Natalie would be gone, sparing her the need to lock up during a busy time.

"You've got to change your attitude if you're going to work here," Natalie said, sorting through the cash register. "Kites are art. People hang them on their walls. Kites are sport. Without kites there might not be airplanes. And did you know they were used in the war to snag buzzbombs? This is serious stuff, here."

Jill swept the front rooms of the store. "Ok, ok," she called. "What's a buzzbomb?"

"Forget about it. Just sell kites."

"But it's not windy enough to fly a kite."

"Wrong again, poor child. It doesn't take a lot of wind, just a kite to match the wind you fly it in. Sell them Deltas on a day like this."

"What's a Delta?"

Natalie came into the room where Jill was sweeping. "The ones that look like triangles, silly. And remember to tell them this." She handed Jill a card that said 'Leave Only Your Footprints On The Beach.'

Jill read the card. Then she put her arms around Natalie and hugged her.

"One more thing," Natalie whispered. "Advise them to look around out there. If the branches of a tree sway a little, it's kite weather. If papers rustle on the pavement, kite weather. If your hat blows off, we're talking box kites."

"What are these?" Jill let go and pointed to a display above the front window.

"High tech. The pros add extra wings. They put those wind socks on the string, the ones that look like dragons or squids. I once saw a guy using full balloons for kite wings and he was skating along the sand behind them like he was water-skiing."

58

WHEN HIS relatives heard from Timothy, when he identified himself as Norma Packard's son, they thought she must have died. They were relieved to hear it was only an accident, then shocked at the extent of her injuries.

"I've seen the car," he told Aunt Dixie. She was his grandmother's youngest sister, now eighty-four. "She's lucky."

"Don't you repeat this, but the way Norma drives, I'm surprised it didn't happen years ago."

"I've seen the car," he told Uncle Ried, his mother's older brother. "She's pretty lucky."

"Imports," he grumbled. "I told her ten times to buy General Motors."

"I've seen the car," he told Paige Hammerford, the widow of his mother's younger brother. "Lucky to have pulled through at all."

"That's how my Edward went. Car. Your mother's first boyfriend, way back before your father (Vernon should rest in peace), was killed in an automobile wreck himself. Someplace in Arkansas, did you know about that? I don't think I'd drive anymore if I were you."

By the eighth call, Timothy felt like an actor during Wednesday's matinee. He recited the litany of his mother's broken bones, her bruised spleen, the hemorrhaging when she was first brought in. He tried not to seem remote, but the story sounded blunt instead of overwhelming.

"We almost lost her," was how he brought the conversations to an end.

The Police Station was located behind City Hall in a two-story structure that had been temporary since Timothy was in the seventh grade. He could walk there from the hospital in fifteen minutes.

He was supposed to wait for Jane to go with him. But after another hour at his mother's bedside, he felt compelled to accomplish something. Anything.

"Where's the Traffic Division?" he asked the first officer he saw.

"Same place as the Narcotics Division, the Canine Unit, Vice and the Crime Lab. Tenth floor, rear, take the elevator up. Whaddya, joking?"

"I want to know about an accident."

The officer nodded. "It's usually that there's a report, pal. You give us your client's name, we send you the report, is how it's done."

"This is about my mother. A couple days ago and she hasn't woken up yet. So come on, just tell me where there's someone I can talk to, find out what happened."

"All right, sorry. Third door on your left. The guy you want's Tomas Sierra, I think he's there if he's not in the can."

Sierra sat in the far corner of the room under the only window. Squeezed in between a row of gray filing cabinets and a massive photocopy machine, he was talking on the phone.

He waved as Timothy entered, motioning him to come around the counter and have a seat. The phone was tucked under his jowls. He held an unlit cigar, chewed till it drooped, between his middle and index fingers. As he spoke, he kept tapping a stack of red, green, blue, and beige manila folders arrayed on his desk.

"Ok, ok. I understand. Top priority." He emptied the contents of a green file as he spoke, reinserting them into a red file and switching labels. "Tuesday. Fine."

When he hung up, he didn't look around. He removed the contents of a blue file and exchanged them with the contents of a beige file, again switching labels. Then he took a deep breath and swiveled around to face Timothy.

"I know you from somewhere," Sierra said.

"It's possible. I went to high school here. But I don't remember seeing you before."

"When?"

"When what?"

"Were you in school."

"Early sixties."

"Ever in trouble, I seen your picture in a file?"

"No."

"You got a brother looks like you, lives here?"

"No. Just my mother. Who doesn't look like me at all."

"It'll come to me." He put the cigar in his mouth and looked at Timothy closely.

"Mr. Sierra, I don't want to take up your time. All I'm after is what you know about this car accident my mother was in a couple of days ago. No one seems to know what happened."

"She ok?"

"Alive. Not much more, yet."

"So this is, potentially, a legal matter?"

"I suppose. That's not why I'm here, though."

"You got a lawyer?" When Timothy nodded, Sierra went on. "He ought to be the one we deal with."

"She's been in touch. It's just that you haven't told us much."

"She? That Brock girl? Excellent choice, my friend. You said your name was? Wait a minute, you're Packard, right? Here we go. The miler, I seen your picture in the school, the trophy case. Anchor leg, the relay team. Here we go. And you're the guy was back in town this summer, saw a lot of little JD Brock, everybody was talking about that. Which is how come we knew who to call, they got your mother to the hospital. Here we go."

Timothy was getting angry. He had no idea his activities had been so closely followed. He stood.

"If you're Sherlock Holmes, what're you doing in traffic work?"

"Easy, Mr. Packard. This is a small town. Sit down." Timothy didn't move. "Ok, have it your way. What do you want to know?"

"What happened."

Sierra reached for a green file. He scanned its contents.

196

"No citations, if that's what you're after. And it doesn't look like there will be."

"But what happened? How did she get hurt?"

"Guy in the van, Ike Zwindel just bought it two weeks ago, a new Dodge, he says your mother ran the stop sign at Laurel and Beech. Says he was going ten miles an hour but he couldn't stop in time. Didn't see her till she was right there because of the high bushes on the corner."

"That's bullshit and you know it. I saw the car, he must've been going forty."

"He may not have been going ten, but we have no witnesses. Not much in the way of skid marks. Those little cars, you hit them with a van it always looks like that. There's not much we can do."

"Right. And it's a no-fault state."

"Right. Maybe your mother can tell us something."

Timothy frowned and looked up through the little window. "This wasn't much help."

"What did you expect, the guy in handcuffs?" Sierra turned back to his desk, picked up the phone, and began dialing. "I hope she's all right, your mother."

59

ALLIE CAME for dinner the night Jill had to cook. At least Natalie didn't make Jill pay for the food.

The bet hadn't even been close. She had counted thirty-one kiters during the day. Only five were children, and two of those were almost old enough to vote.

"You shouldn't take advantage of children," Allie said to Natalie. "You were dealing with inside information."

"You call Jill a child? For a playwright, you're not very perspicacious." Natalie turned to Jill and smiled. "How's that for a fancy word?"

After the table was cleared, and Allie left to write, Natalie said she had a surprise for Jill.

"No more bets, I hope." Jill said.

"Did you bring along a fancy dress?"

"Dad insisted. I haven't worn it once."

"Well put it on and let me see how you look. The program is, tonight you're twenty-two. Maybe I can help with your makeup."

"What's going on?"

"There's this man I want you to meet, Casey Kindred. I think we're ready for this. He's playing over at The Orca and you've got to be twenty-one to get in."

"All right!" Jill darted into her room, already lifting her sweater over her head. "What's he play?"

"The autoharp."

Jill walked back into the living room, dressed only in her bra and panties. "The what?"

"Traditional folk music, Jill. It won't hurt you."

"Auto parts?"

"Autoharp. It's like a cross between a zither and an accordion."

"Maybe I ought to put on jeans and cowboy boots."

"Jill Packard, what am I going to do about you? I offer to expose you to one of the few instruments truly native to America, I offer to let you meet the man of my dreams, I offer to sneak you into a real live tavern, and you stand there in your underwear sassing me."

Jill came out to model the dress. Black suede and backless, it was billowy at the shoulders and tapered to become form-fitting at the midriff and waist. Its skirt was long and slit to behind the knee.

"Saints preserve us," Natalie whispered.

Jill had removed her feathered earring, which reminded Natalie of a fishing lure, and replaced it with a pearl that matched the one in her right lobe. She also removed her woven bracelets and anklets, substituting two silver circlets of Natalie's.

"All you need is a pair of heels. I don't think those Birkenstocks will do."

"I forgot to bring them."

Natalie loaned her a pair. They were a half-size too large, but fit well enough so Jill could walk without tottering. Natalie observed her carefully, then marched her into the bathroom.

"Now let's tamper," Natalie said. Jill sat in front of the vanity. "Maybe a little eyeliner and a touch of gloss. You've got great color."

There was no trouble bringing Jill into The Orca. She smiled at everyone and spoke in a throaty whisper. They took a table near the edge of the smoky room and were mostly silent during Kindred's forty-minute sets. Natalie nursed a glass of beer while Jill drank Diet Cokes.

She tried to see what her aunt might see in this Casey Kindred. He was thin and scraggly, with graying hair that tangled to his shoulders. He had a sparse beard and wore granny glasses. Because he sat slouched, Jill didn't appreciate how tall Kindred was until she saw him on the stage. His hands were enormous. His long, bowed legs seemed to end above his waist and his jeans sagged around the slim, compressed hips. But what Jill noticed most clearly was the sweetness in his hazel eyes.

Kindred would begin his sets with "The Battle Hymn of the Republic," which he used to demonstrate how the autoharp worked. He wore picks on the tips of each finger, making his right hand look like a robot's claw. Each finger pursued its own task—rhythm with the thumb, melody with the middle finger, low line with the index finger, and high lines with the ring and little fingers.

"It's all about getting your hand to the right place at the right time," he said. "Like a lot of other things."

Natalie leaned over and whispered to Jill, smiling, "He knows what he's talking about there."

Kindred's singing voice was much higher than Jill would have guessed because of his size. But few of the songs were familiar and by the end of each set she was watching her aunt more than Kindred.

Natalie gazed at him raptly, clasped hands supporting her chin. Jill hadn't seen her guard down like this before. She smiled throughout his performance, applauding after each number with her hands above her head.

Afterwards, he went with them to the beach, holding Natalie around the shoulders while Jill walked a little to the side. He was relaxed, not keyed up like Natalie was after her shows.

Casually, Natalie's hand slipped down inside the back of Kindred's belt while they walked. Her other arm reached across to keep in contact with his chest. He towered above her.

For a long time, no one spoke. Jill was not uncomfortable, though she wanted very much to watch what happened between them.

"I'd like to come back to your place, if that's all right."

"Jill's a big girl, Case. It'd be fine."

"Would that be a problem for you?" he asked Jill. "If I was to be with Natalie tonight?"

"Actually, I think that would be very nice," Jill said.

60

"SHE CAME out of intensive care this morning."

"That's wonderful news, Tim. How is she?"

"Improving. Still in a lot of pain. They're starting her on Demerol today, see if that's any better."

"You sound like you're holding up all right."

"It's been five days. I feel pretty disoriented, like it's still Monday." He checked his watch, surprised to find it was before noon, but he didn't say anything about that. "Let me speak to Jill."

"She's out on the beach with a friend." Natalie didn't say the friend was Casey Kindred. "I could have her call your mother's apartment tonight, if you'd like."

"Don't know if or when I'll be there. I can talk to her next time."

A trapeze dangled over Mrs. Packard's chest like a ghostly triangle. She continued to doze between hallucinations from the Demerol.

"Where did you put the paprika? You're old enough now to put the paprika back where it belongs."

Timothy sat beside her, murmuring "that's all right, mother."

She opened her eyes, looking harried. The motion of her hands in front of her suggested precise folding. "Of course it's all right. Here, take these drapes and put them in the closet." Then she shut her eyes.

When the nurse came in to check her, Mrs. Packard was running her hands above her hair. "I can't get all the glass out. Pick out the glass from my hair, Darling, be careful you don't cut yourself."

"Mother?" he said. "It's me. I'm with you."

"Of course it's you. What do you think, I'm crazy too?"

"I'm not sure we should," Jane whispered.

"Please. I want to," Timothy answered. "Need to."

At least he was talking. It seemed like days since he'd put together a string of three sentences.

Jane took his hand and silently led him to the bedroom. "Me too." She put her arms around him, stepping closer. "Have, all week."

Timothy held her. But he didn't kiss her, didn't caress her, didn't even seem to breathe. His skin felt very cold.

"Are you there?" Jane asked.

He responded by tightening his grip on her. A shiver overcame him.

"Tim, there's plenty of time."

"Time?"

"We can tomorrow."

"Oh." He began to unbutton her blouse, struggling with the material. Jane didn't help him until he tried to slip it off and snagged the still buttoned cuffs on her wrists.

She backed from his grasp, turning to the bed, and removed her blouse. Timothy came up behind her, fumbling for her bra snap.

"It opens in front," she said, releasing it and turning back to face him. "This is awfully strange, Tim. Let's wait."

He shook his head. "Maybe if you closed the window. I'm not warm enough."

"Why don't you lie down. I'll put on some music, close the window, maybe we can just cuddle for a while. That sounds good to me."

When she lay beside him, Timothy reached for her, drawing Jane on top of him. His hand stroked her buttocks once, then fell to his side. They kissed, but he seemed to lose focus and she thought he might even have fallen asleep.

"This is just too grim." She sat up. "Let me get you a drink."

He let go of her and pulled the sheet to his chin. At first Jane thought he was going to weep. She looked down and noticed that the sheet over his penis was as flat as it was over his chest. He wasn't weeping at all—in fact, his eyes were wide and clear where they stared at the ceiling fan still above her bed.

Although visiting hours in the semi-private rooms started at 2:00, they let Timothy go up when he arrived at noon. Mrs. Packard was lucid, arguing with her nurse about the food.

"You need to eat."

"*You* need to eat. *I* need to lose weight."

"Mrs. Packard, please, you need nutrition now so you can heal."

"Nonsense. I have enough fat on me to heal a dozen broken legs. What I need is to weigh what you weigh. Then, when I stand up next, my bones won't snap."

"That's not how it works."

"Aha!" Mrs. Packard barked, seeing Timothy. "Here's my son. Where have you been all day?"

"I'm two hours early."

"Timothy Packard, this is Leah my nurse."

"Leila, Mrs. Packard. Leila Millette. It's a pleasure to meet you, Mr. Packard."

"Timothy. Please Leila, call him Timothy."

He sat at the end of his mother's bed while Leila worked. Mrs. Packard struggled to lift her head so she could see him clearly.

"Just remember what you're here for, young man," she teased. She could not conceal her delight, although Timothy was not sure if it was over playing Matchmaker between her nurse and son, or over feeling so much better since Percodan had replaced the Demerol.

Timothy stepped forward and ran into a stiff-arm from Leila. His mother's face contorted in pain.

Seeing this, Timothy backed into the corridor as Leila whooshed the curtain around Mrs. Packard's bed. He turned toward the nurses' station, hearing his mother sob like someone bereaved.

* * *

"Do Jews have last rites?" Mrs. Packard asked.

Lunch sat uneaten on the tray across her chest. Viscid gravy, bite-size chunks of stringy beef, mounds in pastel shades, and milk to drink. The room smelled like a grade-school cafeteria. Timothy knew she would sooner drink lye than milk.

"That's a sacrament. I don't think we have those."

"What do you mean 'we?' You haven't been a Jew since your father died."

"That's not very fair, Mother. I went to services for him every night for a year, you know that."

"And how many times since?"

"We've been through this before."

"Well, you never should have left. It was something you were very good at."

Timothy took a deep breath, closing his eyes. "What's this about last rites? You don't have to be worrying about last rites."

"I like to worry. You said we don't have sacraments, but what about your Bar Mitzvah?"

"That's a ceremony. It's different from a sacrament."

"You see? What did I tell you, a fine head for religion. You're good at it."

Their eschatological discussions always did sound like Abbott and Costello routines. He sat silently while she dozed again, hoping she would forget this topic when she woke.

"Ceremony, sacrament," she mumbled. "There should be something like last rites."

"The *Talmud* is silent about the soul leaving the body after death. I think that's it. So there'd be no point to last rites."

"A scholar, a rabbi." Her eyes were still shut. "Keep talking, I love the sound of your voice."

"I remember Rabbi Rakov haranguing us about superstition. That was what he thought of the Christians and their sacraments. But maybe I could have used some superstition when father died."

"You know he came to see me last night?"

"Who?" Timothy thought she meant his father, dead now longer than they had been married. Maybe she was still hallucinating.

"Rabbi Rakov." She opened one eye to stare at him. "Who did you think, Paul Newman?"

"He must have been making his rounds. That's all."

"He was standing right where you are, like a ghost. I woke up and he was holding my hand. Chanting. I thought he was giving me last rites."

"He was probably giving thanks that you're doing so well."

"It didn't bother me at all, Timmy. It made me comfortable. In Hebrew yet. The man refuses to learn Yiddish." She shook her head in pity. "And he's all skin and bones. He looked worse off than me."

"I saw him downstairs this morning, myself. He didn't recognize me."

"Why should he? You're a little bit older than the last time he saw you."

"You don't have to remind me."

Suddenly, Mrs. Packard struggled as if to sit. She batted at the trapeze, lapsed back against the pillows, then fixed Timothy with a watery gaze.

"And what about Heaven?" Her eyes opened wide. "Can't we at least have Heaven?"

In an instant, she was asleep, her eyes coming down like curtains. She seemed more comfortable than at any time since coming out of the ICU.

Timothy knew she'd sleep as long as the telephone was silent. She insisted on having the phone near her head, insisted on talking with everyone who called to wish her well. He unplugged the jack and sat in the chair by the window.

The sound of his mother's breathing, as it shifted toward snore, seemed as familiar as old dreams. Timothy thought of a bungalow beside a lake in New Hampshire where he and his mother had spent many summers while his father worked in the city. He could hear her snoring through the thin bungalow walls. That was before she started going to Lake Wallenpaupack on her own.

He looked at the heels of her thigh-to-toe casts, the sock over her toes, the sheet he should pull down to cover them. It comes down to this again, he thought. By the bed of someone dying, or someone close to dying, and it is time for grace.

He had failed before. Now he was afraid that he was failing again, unable to find it in himself to offer right comfort.

Timothy walked to her side. He took her hand. She opened her eyes and, seeing him, smiled.

"You can," he said, bending to kiss her. "You can have Heaven, if you want it."

Mrs. Packard swallowed. Her throat was dry and Timothy offered her the glass of milk, tilting it so she could reach the straw.

The milk clung to her lips when she lay back down. It connected them like a spider's web when she spoke. "You think so?"

61

"CAN I ask you something?" Jill said.

They were sitting on the rocks at Hug Point, watching the tide recede. Casey Kindred had on his *Radio Free Utah* tee shirt and one of Natalie's People's Power hats. Jill was wrapped in his battered windbreaker.

"Uh oh."

"Come on, I won't be rude."

"First I should warn you there's only three subjects I know anything about. And I don't think you're going to ask me about playing the autoharp or basketball. So I may not be much use to you."

"Is Casey Kindred your real name?"

"That's it?"

"Not really. But you made me back off with your little speech."

Kindred smiled at her. "Didn't mean to. Let me make it up to you with a deep dark secret: my name is Charles. Charles Buckhannon Kindherd. Charles after my granddaddy on my mother's side, Buckhannon after the town in West Virginia where I was born, and Kindherd after the guy Momma said was my daddy. He wasn't from our part of the world."

"How'd you get to Casey Kindred from Charles Buckhannon Kindherd?"

"Figured music names have to sound right. Chuck and Charlie might have been fine if I played the guitar, but I needed something rarer for the autoharp. You look at my station wagon, all you see is stacks of autoharp cases. So Casey. Then I strummed Kindherd around a little till it sounded more folksy, Kindred."

"I wish I could change my name too."

"You can if you want to. Just do it and it's done."

"Gillian, I used to think. But now I want my name to be a whole lot different from Jill. Erika, maybe, with a 'k.' Or Penelope."

"But nobody would call you that. Penelope. You'd probably get stuck being Penny Packard. Which isn't you, that much I know already."

"Then I should get rid of the Packard too. Junk it like a dead old car. It's a fake name anyway, my grandfather picked it when he went into business. It sounded rich."

"What was it before?"

"I don't remember, some long name with a lot of c's and z's in it. I'll have to ask my dad again. But he's not going to like the idea of me changing it. He'll think I'm rejecting him or something."

"This isn't what you started out to ask me about, is it?"

"Sort of."

Kindred waited, looking at the waves. "Sort of," he said.

"Lots of the songs you sing, people know them and they sing along. They're pretty happy songs, some of them are funny and all. Then the songs you wrote yourself, everybody gets quiet and listens to them, they're always the sad ones. How come?"

"I hadn't thought of that."

"I was going to ask which one was you? But now, I guess maybe the happy songs are Casey Kindred and the sad ones are Charles Buckhannon Kindherd. How about that?"

"You and your aunt," he said, still looking at the waves.

"This is the third time you guys were out when your father called," Natalie said. "He's going to think I don't take care of you."

"Seems like weeks since I spoke to him."

"Not quite weeks, but it's been too long for him. He said he'd call back exactly at 7:00, after visiting hours are over. He wants to talk to you about going home."

"Home!" Jill put her hands on her hips. "It's not time yet."

"Well, I don't think he wants to travel out to Oregon again."

"He doesn't have to. I'm doing fine here by myself."

Natalie didn't respond. She went to the kitchen and brought out the pitcher of mint tea and a Diet Coke for Jill.

"I know you are," she said. "I told him. But you still ought to stick around and talk to him when he calls back. Case and I can go to The Orca by ourselves tonight."

"But I want to come too. It's only two more nights before he goes to Seattle."

Natalie nodded. "I know. I was thinking of going up there with him."

"Oh," Jill's eyes widened. "I see." She put the can down and walked to the window. "You want me to go home too, is that it?"

"No, that's not it. If you don't know you're welcome here as long as you want to stay, you haven't been paying very good attention. The issue is your father, Jill. If he wants you to come home, you have to work that out with him."

After they left, Jill settled by the fireplace. The afternoons were getting chillier.

She sat in the rocker with her feet folded and tucked up under her bottom. She had put one of Casey Kindred's tapes on Natalie's stereo. The music, which days ago would have bored her, now was soothing. She rocked gently, eyes closed, imagining how Kindred looked when he sang them. She had most of the lyrics memorized.

At 7:00, when the phone rang, Jill considered not answering it. When she did, Timothy's voice filled her with sadness.

"You sound so far away," she said. "And tired."

"There's a reason for that. But it's very nice to hear you."

"How's Grandma?"

"Much better. She sends her love."

Jill remembered sitting beside Mrs. Packard, listening to her sing *can't help lovin' that man of mine*. The Melody Girl of the Air. "Tell her me too."

There was a pause as Timothy gathered himself to change the subject. Jill carried the phone toward the window.

"Did Nat mention about coming home?"

"She did. I don't know why you can't come back here for a couple of weeks. School doesn't start till after Labor Day."

"I'm not up to it, Jilly. This has been a crazy couple of weeks. Besides, I should be closer to my mother, in case I have to come back here."

"You could stay with Jane, couldn't you? Stay in Long Beach for a couple weeks instead of going home."

"That wouldn't work."

Before she could stop herself, Jill said, "Why not? Her house is big enough."

"The size of the house isn't the issue."

"Oh. What, did you have a fight?" She had a flash of anger. Just because he broke up with another girlfriend didn't mean he had to ruin *her* fun.

"Let's just leave it at 'that wouldn't work,' ok?" Jill could hear the effort at calm in his voice. He was trying to remain steady.

"Just asking."

"I want to leave here and I don't want to come all the way to Oregon. It's as simple as that."

"But what about me?"

"I'd like you to be with me."

"Dad, I'm having such a wonderful time with Aunt Nat. It's really been good for me out here."

"What are you saying?"

"Just that."

Looking at the ocean, Jill thought of her midwest home—all flatland, every August day hot and humid. She thought of Gardner Park, of which she'd covered every inch twenty times over. She thought of going to school again. It would be so nice to start over somewhere, to not have to go back. She thought it would probably help her at school if she lived in a place where she could never exhaust the land-scape. Then she heard her father's breathing, sensed his terror as he waited for her to speak again.

"Couldn't I stay here? You don't really need me with you. You've got Lauren there. And your work, there would be a lot to catch up on. I could just go on living with Aunt Nat for a while."

"You mean for good?"

"I don't know. For a while, anyway."

Again, there was silence.

"Did Natalie put you up to this? Is this her idea? Let me talk to her."

"No, Dad. Don't get angry. She doesn't know I'm thinking about this at all. And she isn't even here now. It was just an idea, the words came out before I thought about it."

"So you didn't mean it?"

"No, I think I did. I just didn't know that's what I was going to say."

"I've got to hang up, Jill. I've got to think about what you're saying. This isn't what I had in mind at all."

"I know. I didn't mean to upset you any more than you are already."

"I'm not upset. Well, maybe I'm a little upset."

"Sorry. Really, I am."

"I'm going to take a shower, get some sleep. Tomorrow night, same time, I'll call again and we'll talk some more. See if your aunt can be around too. All right?"

"All right."

"Good night, Jilly."

"Dad? I love you. It's not that."

"Good night."

62

TIMOTHY COULDN'T believe how calm the ocean was at night. Or how warm.

He waded out waist deep, keeping his eyes on the sliver of moon that told him where the sky must be. Drifting seaweed brushed against his thighs as he moved.

He had thought the landward energy of the waves would be greater. But the waves seemed spent, rocking gently as though catching their breath for tomorrow's efforts. He could feel more strongly the longshore current as it moved across his body.

He turned to face the land. Lights from the hotels and apartments replaced the stars as he gazed at the place he once considered home.

Half a life ago, he'd been elated to leave. He couldn't wait to begin his adult life, separate from his mother, live a continent away from here. Long Beach was a failing resort town, the boardwalk rotting, the old hotels becoming nursing homes, young people moving away. He belonged gone.

Now the engineer in him saw the beach profile for what it was—how the season shaped the sand, building the beach up in summer, flattening it with winter storms, rebuilding it with fair-weather waves in the spring.

The realtor in him saw how unrestrained development had buried marsh, dune, and beach beneath layers of concrete and brick. He thought of the new condos he'd walked through this week at the west end of town. The swimming pools had no water in them yet. Tarnished supports were perched above the pools' azure surface to hold diving boards that weren't there yet.

So now, he thought, I believe I understand this place. I understand my place in it and its place in me. He turned away, walking further out.

Soon his mother would die. Maybe not as a direct result of this accident, but she would not be able to get around easily anymore and he knew she would decline quickly. She refused to consider living with them in Illinois. She refused to discuss a nursing home. When she got out of the hospital, she was going to live in her apartment. Period, end of discussion. If she needed help, she would hire help.

Soon he would have no reason to come back except for memories. Jane would not be enough to bring him here, they both understood that. He was up to his chest in the water.

Count them. His wife, dead. His mother, soon to be gone. Now his daughter wanted to leave him. He could hear that in her voice. She loved him, of course she loved him, but if she could choose her life it would be different than the life he was giving her. She wanted to leave him and live with Natalie. She, they, were so much like Charlene— what could he expect, in the end, but betrayal?

No.

Out here beyond the breakers, he could believe it might be different than that after all. Apparently, if the letters were to be believed, Charlene came back to him at the end, although he had been unable to see it. Why would she lie to Natalie? So it was possible that the issue wasn't whether to forgive betrayal but whether to accept autonomy. She had offered back his life, but for years he refused to close the deal, insisting that he harbor her betrayal. His love was off the market.

The way it looked from here, realizing what he was a part of, and realizing what he was apart from, at last put Timothy's life in his own hands. He lay on his back and floated. To the east, a buoy winked red at land's end.

63

"Do you think I should call him?" Jill asked. "It's past midnight there."

"No. He's probably tied up," Natalie said. "Besides, you don't know where he might be."

"But this isn't like him. He said he'd call tonight, same time as last night."

"Give him time."

"I could call Grandma's apartment. Maybe he just fell asleep. You wouldn't believe how tired he sounded."

The night before, Jill had waited up until Natalie and Casey Kindred got back from The Orca. She certainly couldn't sleep after talking with Timothy.

"I told him I wanted to stay here."

"Did he flip out?"

"Wait. I said—before I really thought about it—that I wanted to stay here like for school, not just the rest of the summer. I want to live here."

Natalie sat at the foot of Jill's rocker. She reached for Jill's hands. "That must have been hard."

"I probably shouldn't have, you know. With all he's been going through. I mean, I'm not even sure that is what I want."

"Now what do you think?"

Jill looked over toward the window, where Kindred was standing with a can of beer almost hidden in his huge hand. He smiled, lifting the hand in a kind of salute.

"That I'm happy," Jill said.

"So am I," Natalie said.

"What I really want is to be with all of you. You guys and Dad."

"That's not in the cards."

Jill laughed. "I can dream, can't I?"

"There's no answer."

"So he's not home, that's all it means. Hang in there."

"I could try him at Jane's. No, wait. He said something funny about her, I think maybe they're not seeing each other anymore."

"Just wait. It'll keep."

Jill refused to go for a walk the morning after Timothy was supposed to have called. It was the first time since she'd arrived that she didn't spend time on the beach.

Shortly after noon, she was drowsing on the couch, binoculars in her lap, when the phone rang. She leaped up, sending the binoculars crashing to the floor, and got to the phone before the second ring.

"Dad?"

"Hi, Jilly. Sorry I didn't call last night. Just wasn't ready yet."

"You scared me."

"Let me get all the way through this before you say anything, ok?"

"Ok."

"First, I want to have you with me. I want that more than I want anything in the world. But I realized something after we talked—and I don't know exactly how to put it. You're fifteen, that may be young, but this year you've changed so much. So much happened. I guess you've got a right to choose your life, is what I'm saying. So even though I want you with me, I want the decision to be yours."

"Dad."

"Wait. There's one more thing, something else that's part of the deal, I have to say this. Aunt Nat is family. She's my family, yours. I accept that and I know you'd be all right with her. But Jilly, you can't think for a minute that my saying this means I don't want you here." He took a deep breath. "There, I'm done."

"Now is it my turn?"

"Yes. But you don't have to decide now. You can call me later."

"You would really do that?"

"Do what?"

"Let me decide where I live?"

213

"I would really do it. If nothing else, this summer taught me that. It's your life."

Jill couldn't speak, but she was smiling. She turned to face Natalie, who had come in from the kitchen, and handed her aunt the receiver.

"Tim?" Natalie said. "When do you want me to send her home?"

64

A BELL sounded in the corridor. Over the intercom, a stern voice announced that visiting hours had ended.

Mrs. Packard woke and squeezed Timothy's hand. Leila looked in, looked back down the hall, and held up one finger. He'd have to leave in a minute.

"So?" Mrs. Packard said.

"So you have to exercise," Timothy warned her. "You have to move around, get up as soon as you can, start walking."

"*You* exercise. I'm going to lie here and let my bones heal."

He bent to kiss her, singing the old song they used to sing together when he was a boy. "Dem bones, dem bones, dem dry bones."

"Nevermind."

"And another thing: Eat right, like Leila keeps telling you."

"What does she know? If the young always know so much, how come they end up old?"

"I give up. Promise you'll come see us."

"Sure. I'll dance at Jilly's graduation." She pointed to the end of the bed and Timothy cranked it up so she could see him more comfortably. "Now you listen to me. Take care of that granddaughter of mine. You see that she does well in school and keep the boys away from her."

"You don't have to worry."

"Of course I do. It keeps me alive."

Leila came back to the doorway. "I'm sorry, Mr. Packard, you really have to leave now."

"Timothy," his mother said to Leila. "When you call him Mr. Packard, I get very confused."

65

TIMOTHY COULD see the lights of the plane for miles before it landed. He finished his drink and walked to the gate.

Capitol Airport was carved out of the prairie and its control tower was the tallest structure for miles around. He imagined you could see all the way to Kansas from inside.

The prop jet stopped twenty yards away. Jill was the first person to get off, clomping down the narrow steps in her Birkenstocks. Timothy took a step toward her, then held himself in check. Jill dropped her carry-on bag and ran to him.

Inside the terminal, waiting for her luggage, they looked at photographs Jill had brought back in her purse. Timothy was glad she had. Otherwise, he might not have been able to talk at all.

"This is Aunt Nat's boyfriend. Casey Kindred. Tomorrow, I want to see if we can find his tapes out at the mall. Too bad you didn't get to meet him. I think they're going to get married."

"The musician and the mime."

"You'd like him."

"Maybe I'll get to meet him. Christmas, Nat and I already promised we'll all meet in San Francisco for a week."

Jill hugged him. "I can't wait."

On the drive home, Jill wanted to get caught up on all his news.

Timothy went through Mrs. Packard's recovery stage by stage, ending with her pledge to dance at Jill's graduation.

"Do you think she will?"

"No, Jilly, I don't. I'll be surprised if she can ever get around without a walker again. But I hope so."

"What about Lauren?"

"What about Lauren?"

"Are you still seeing her? You were separated for the whole summer, I thought maybe things could change."

"Things sure could. She won her race at the county fair while we were in Michigan. From what I hear, the guy she took to St. Louis with her for the free weekend has a promising future in the investment business. Sounds like a match made in heaven."

"I see."

"It's ok. I'm ready for a fresh start."

"Here," Timothy said after Jill had unpacked. "Read this."

He handed her an article clipped from the Traverse City newspaper. Leah Bell had sent it, the headline circled in red.

Petosky Man Slain In Alley Here.

TRAVERSE CITY—A 33 year old Petosky man, Eddy Rodney, also known as "Santa," was found murdered this morning in an alley behind Clippers Comedy Club, 301 State Street. Police arrested Corrine Moran, 19, also known as Corrie Gable and Corrine Smith, at the scene.

According to police spokesman Dale Harrison, Rodney was killed by several gunshot wounds to the chest and neck. A small caliber pistol, recently discharged, was found in Miss Moran's possession.

Police would not speculate about a motive for the slaying. Rodney had been arrested several times since 1984 for possession and sale of controlled substances. He was never convicted of these charges. Police are not ruling out drug-related activities as the motive.

Outside the Grand Traverse County Courthouse, sources indicate that Miss Moran had been distraught in recent weeks. She had been discharged from Traverse City Hospital six days previously.

Hospital spokesman Ralph Beverly refused to comment about

the circumstances surrounding Miss Moran's admittance there. Sources familiar with the young woman told reporters Miss Moran had attempted suicide after learning that she was pregnant earlier this summer. According to one source, Miss Moran told him repeatedly that Rodney was responsible for her pregnancy.

Miss Moran is scheduled to be arraigned before Judge Howard Barney tomorrow.

Jill handed the article back to Timothy. They looked at each other for a moment without speaking, then reached out to embrace.